Whatever Happened

to Billy Parks?

Also by Gareth R Roberts

That Immortal Jukebox Sensation

Whatever Happened to Billy Parks?

GARETH R ROBERTS

The Friday Project
An imprint of HarperCollins*Publishers*
77–85 Fulham Palace Road
Hammersmith, London W6 8JB
www.harpercollins.co.uk

First published by The Friday Project as an ebook in 2013
Paperback edition first published 2014

1

Gareth R Roberts asserts the moral right to be identified as the author of this
work

A catalogue record for this book
is available from the British Library

ISBN 978-0-00-753151-6

Set in minion by FMG using Atomik ePublisher from Easypress
Printed and bound in Great Britain by Clays Ltd, St Ives plc

MIX
Paper from
responsible sources
FSC™ C007454
www.fsc.org

FSC™ is a non-profit international organisation established to promote
the responsible management of the world's forests. Products carrying the
FSC label are independently certified to assure consumers that they come
from forests that are managed to meet the social, economic and
ecological needs of present and future generations,
and other controlled sources.

Find out more about HarperCollins and the environment at
www.harpercollins.co.uk/green

For my mother, Eirlys Ann Roberts

'Some people believe football is a matter of life and death.
I'm very disappointed with that attitude.
I can assure you it is much more important than that.'

Bill Shankly

Prologue

The Unbearable Weight of Failure

They had to win. That was all.

If they won, everything would be alright. If they won, there would be happiness; the rest of the English autumn would be mellow and misty, then the winter would be brilliant white with snow, and Christmas would be merry, then the spring would prosper giving rise to a World Cup in the summer in West Germany.

They just had to win. That was all. Against Poland. That's all.

We all remember it; even if you weren't born, even if you hate football, even if you don't remember it, you remember it because everything changed that night. That night, all they had to do was win. They didn't win. They drew.

Mr Clough had said their goalie was a clown. And Mr Clough was always right. The BBC showed the game live so that we could

1

all revel in the joyous tension that would precede the campaign to reclaim the World Cup, England's World Cup.

Sir Alf picked three strikers: Channon, Chivers and Clarke. They would score, because the Polish goalie was a clown.

And Billy Parks was on the bench.

Billy Parks: the best of all of them; the most natural, the most beautiful, the most easily distracted, as he carried the immense weight of his talent on his slender shoulders.

The Polish Clown saved from Chivers.

The Polish Clown saved from Currie.

The Polish Clown saved from Clarke, then Channon, then Channon again.

Then. Then. Then. Norman Hunter didn't tackle Lato, the Polish midfielder. Norman Hunter, who normally took bites out of human legs, who never let anyone past him, missed the tackle and Lato played it through to Domarski who sent it tamely past Shilton. They weren't winning. They were losing.

Attack.

The Polish Clown saved from Chivers and Channon and Clarke and Hunter and Bell.

Then Clarke scored a penalty. But that wouldn't be enough. They had to win.

And Billy Parks sat on the bench. In between Kevin Keegan and Bobby Moore. His knees drawn into him against the cold, his mind wandering to the two hundred and fifty quid he'd bet on an England win.

A win that would make everything alright. A win would bring colour to the grey beige of the seventies. A win would change everything.

But the Clown saved every shot that came his way.

So Sir Alf looked to his bench. Destiny called for someone. Sir Alf looked at his bench and thought about which valiant hero would bring forth triumph. Who would forge their name in the fires of destiny. Score a bloody goal.

Billy Parks sat, cold. He avoided Sir Alf's gaze, his mind on the barmaid from the Golden Swan whom he would pick up later in his inferno-red TR6.

Eventually, because he knew he had to, he looked up. Five minutes to go. He looked towards Sir Alf and Sir Alf looked away from him and called upon Kevin Hector. Kevin Hector would deliver the goal. Kevin Hector would make everything alright. He had scored over 100 goals for Derby County. He was reliable. We would be alright – wouldn't we?

England got a corner. Tony Currie swung it in. For once, the Clown was nowhere, he was beaten by the flight of the ball. The ball fell on to the head of Kevin Hector. This was his chance. This was *his* chance. This was his destiny. He headed it towards the goal. The Clown was beaten.

Kevin Keegan and Bobby Moore rose up from the bench. Billy Parks didn't move.

The ball went towards the goal. Just a ball heading through time and space. It means nothing. It means absolutely everything. All England has to do is win. One goal would do it.

The ball left Kevin Hector's head and went towards the goal-line. Everyone stood up, everyone waited for the goal, everyone waited for the triumph, for the tension to be broken, for everything to be alright. But it wasn't a goal. The net didn't bulge. A Polish defender kicked it off the line.

Keegan and Moore sat down again. Sir Alf sat down again. Parksy looked towards the crowd. The mass of grey faces. Kevin Hector's destiny was fulfilled. The man who missed the chance.

If only things had been different.

Perhaps they could have been.

Perhaps they could be.

(*Taken, in part, from the little known, but highly acclaimed, 1977 biography of Billy Parks*, Parksy: The Lost Genius of Upton Park, *by veteran* Sunday Times *football journalist, Philip Clarence.*)

3

1

There are two bar stools on the small makeshift stage.

One for me, and one for my whisky tumbler. The crowd like that. A little visual joke, just to break the ice, just to make them relaxed. I've been doing that for years.

I'm sixty-odd now. I still tell people I'm fifty-eight, but with the bloody internet and Wiki-whatsit, every bastard knows that I was born in 1948, which makes me, well, sixty-odd.

Christ, *sixty*-odd? How did that happen? How did the years crumble away so bloody quickly? Sixty-odd, but still in good nick I reckon; like a well-preserved Dodo, rendered ageless in a glass cage by the blurred images of my youth that I know the crowd prefer to keep in their memories: Sunday afternoons with Brian Moore; Saturday nights with Jimmy Hill after Parkinson with a cup of tea; Peter Jones's dulcet Welsh tones; Harold Wilson: Ford Capris; the Yorkshire bloody Ripper. It's all up there in flock wallpaper purple with me somewhere in the midst of it making my way down the wing at Upton Park or the Lane.

Sixty-odd now. Still got all my hair though – well most of it – even if the happy blond is rudely interrupted by the odd bit of dirty grey. I'll admit that, but, hey, I am sixty-odd.

I smile at the crowd. There are about twelve of them here. A few more are by the bar getting a round in before I start. I don't blame them. This is a drinking afternoon. Drink's part of it, of course it is.

They look at me and I know that they don't care about the deep black ridges under my eyes, or this suspicious purple brown spot that has recently appeared on my cheek. I smile again, with my eyes twinkling just as they remember and my teeth glistening like a Hollywood starlet (courtesy of a bit of work I had done a couple of years ago using the last of my testimonial money). I am still capable of lighting up a room, still capable of sending a full-back the wrong way.

I am Billy Parks.

I lift the cheap whisky tumbler, neat, of course, and drink it. That's for them. They expect it. It's part of the legend.

The last of the drinkers take their seats and I notice the poster on the wall above the bar, handwritten in black marker pen proclaiming:

SPORTSMAN'S LUNCH AT THE ANCHOR,
This Tuesday, 14th March, 1pm
Former West Ham, Spurs and England Legend, BILLY 'PARKSY' PARKS.
Ticket £5 (includes free pint of Foster's)
(Samantha and her Boa will be back next week)

Bless 'em.

They had cheered when I came on to the stage, 'Parksy, Parksy, Parksy,' they had chanted. Drink helps all of us.

I wave in a quiet understated way and they smile and sit back in expectation of an hour's drinking and a good laugh. I wonder how many of them have actually seen me play? But that doesn't matter; they all know the stories, and that is what they're here for – the stories and the brief journey into a world they all feel they know and belong to.

I like to think that I don't disappoint; hell, I've been telling the same stories for twenty-odd years.

'Good afternoon, gentlemen. Good to see that so many of you have used your day release from Parkhurst to be with me today.'

They laugh. I knew they would.

I go into my spiel and ignore the two fat City-boy types who are standing at the bar, talking loudly, probably about money; I even ignore the bloody fruit machine by the exit that, for some reason known only to the evil misguided bleeder who designed it, lights up like tracer fire every ten minutes and plays the opening bars from *Coronation Street* at top volume. I've told Alan, I don't know how many times, to turn the bloody thing off when I'm on stage.

I tell them football stories, because that is what they've come to hear. I tell them about the characters of my era – proper characters, true lions of another better time, long passed over into the realm of myths and legends with the telling and retelling of tales. I tell them of their drunken exploits, their sexual exploits, the fights, the put-downs, the fast cars, the funny stories that made them godlike and mortal at the same time. I tell them of the managers who were hard bastards, and lunatic chairmen. I tell them about magical footballers, old friends, whose very names conjure up colours and tastes and sounds and sensations and people long gone: Georgie Best, Rodney Marsh, Chopper Harris, Norman Hunter, Alan Hudson, Charlie George, Frankie Worthington – legends each and every one of them.

I tell them about a tot of rum before kick off and a sneaky fag at half-time, fish and chips on the bus on the way back from Newcastle and the time Terry Neill got so angry at Loftus Road that he put his foot through the changing room door and missed the second half as a couple of stewards and our kit man tried to pull his leg out. I tell them that they were good honest pros, though. Good. Honest. Pros. And the crowd fills itself with lager and scampi and smiles and feels, for a few minutes, closer to that time, closer to the legends, and that feeling that if there had been any justice it would have been them. I know that they all think that. I've always known it. It's the way they look at you. *You were one of the lucky ones, Parksy.* Luck: it's got nothing to do with luck, son.

I've emptied the glass on the other bar stool, so I turn towards the bar and wordlessly call for another. And another. Fair play, Alan treats me well at The Anchor.

Any questions?

The same questions I've been asked a thousand times. I don't mind.

Who was the best player you ever played against?

I sip my drink as the question's asked, then I answer as the alcohol surges down my throat and loosens the connection between my tongue and my mind and my memory. They expect it.

'The best player – that's easy,' I tell them. 'Georgie Best.' Hushed respectful tones and thin lips when talking about Georgie; the best player ever to grace a football pitch, bar none. God rest his mad Irish soul.

Who was the hardest opponent?

'Paul Reaney – Reaney the Meanie of Dirty Leeds. The others would try to kick you, but he was the only one who was fast enough to catch you –' I pause '– then he'd kick you.' They laugh. Oh, yes, Paul Reaney, dirty, hard, fast bastard. I smile at the thought of being kicked by a good honest pro. 'Good bloke,' I add quietly, because I mean that. And that's what good honest pros did – a kick, then a handshake and a few beers in the players' lounge bar after the match. None of the nonsense you get with footballers these days, with their fancy cars and their fancy agents and their one hundred and ten fucking grand a week.

Not that I blame them.

I've answered these questions thousands of times. I've emptied a thousand glasses. I've smiled on thousands of fans. This is easy money, money for my memories and a few minutes of adulation to remind me that I'm still alive.

I'm getting warmed up now. The crowd is a good one, suitably boisterously pissed and attentive to all my best stories. I've become good at this.

My eyes wander towards the back of the pub, and there, standing close to the blessed *Coronation Street* fruit machine, stands a man in a tan sheepskin coat and trilby. There's something familiar about him, something about the thick furious grey eyebrows that explode across a forehead that's creased and serious. I know I've seen those eyebrows before, but where?

I catch him watching me intently, his face a humourless shade of thunderbolt grey. For a second I meet his stare, just a second. Where the bloody hell have I seen him before?

I turn away just as the man's voice cuts through the muggy atmosphere of the pub to ask a question.

'What would you give to turn the clock back and put a few things right?' he asks.

God, not that old chestnut. I try to stifle the furrowing of my brow. There's something about the way in which he asks the question though; it lacks the smiling compassion that usually accompanies my inquisitors. There's a cold, understated masculine aggression to it. Perhaps he is one of the nutters that I sometimes get. Sad, bitter, twisted old bastards – back in the day, they'd want to fight me; now, occasionally, they want to humiliate me.

I pour more of the cheap neat whisky into my mouth. I can deal with it – I've heard this type of question a thousand times before:

If you could change anything, what would it be?

Do you have any regrets?

Where did it all go wrong?

I know exactly how I will answer it. I know that my mouth will form itself into a quick smile before opening and allowing meaningless soft words to tumble out like little balls of cotton wool harmlessly falling on to a bouncy mattress. Puff.

I put on my most sincere voice and answer, as the man in the sheepskin coat stares: 'Football has given me a very lovely life and great memories,' I tell him. 'I wouldn't change a second of anything. I've been very lucky.' I pause, then smile. 'And so have hundreds of birds and everyone in north and east London that was lucky enough to see me play.'

I grin, some of the audience chuckle, but the man's expression doesn't change, which gives me a sharp pang of discomfort, as though I was being chastised by an old and respected uncle. Well, sod that. I glance towards the bar, where the barmaid, Leanne, a rather hefty girl who obviously likes a bit of artificial tanning, stands bored, cradling her chin in her hands. Thirty years ago we might have been up for a bit of fun later – but not now.

It's time to finish.

I turn again to the audience and ignore the bloke in the sheep-skin coat.

'Right, gentlemen, thank you very much, you've been lovely.'

The crowd applaud. Not Anfield, not Stamford Bridge, not Wembley Stadium or the San Siro, not the deep, pure, momentary masculine love of an adulating crowd roaring after the ball has ripped into the net, but smiling faces and clapping hands and a muted sincere cheer.

'Thank you very much, fellas,' I repeat. 'I'll tell you what, if any of you want to ask any more questions, I'm happy to oblige over by the bar.'

I always do this. I know that a little coterie of drinkers will surround me, try to get closer to me, close enough to breathe my air and buy me drinks and talk to me as if I'm one of the lads, one of them: 'So, what do you think about the Hammers, eh? It's a fucking disgrace.'

I'm not one of the lads. But I will be for a drink. They expect it.

'You havin' a drink with us, Parksy?'

'Thank you very much, mate – I'll have the same again. Yes, the Hammers – fucking terrible, I've not been down there for a while.'

After about an hour the crowd leaves: happy, drunk sportsmen. I'm alone. Alan, the landlord, a large man who wears brown short-sleeved shirts and steel-rimmed glasses, comes over.

'You alright to get home, Billy?'

'Don't worry about me.'

'You sure?'

He looks carefully at me. 'Did you know that your pupils have gone yellow? You should watch that.'

Yellow? What does he mean yellow? The daft bastard.

'It must be something you're putting in your scotch to water it down with,' I say, and he grins at me with concerned eyes.

'Here you go, son,' he says, handing me a brown envelope. 'Forty quid, I've taken out the twenty you owe for your tab, alright?'

I nod. I'm not going to quibble over a few quid.

I leave the safety of The Anchor, stepping out into the late afternoon. The pub door shuts behind me and the south London air stings my eyes. I hate that, I hate that moment when the pub door shuts and the moroseness hits you. The devastating lonely feeling of insignificance. My past means nothing under the massive spitting sky. Cars whip by creating movement and noise in the gloom. They ignore me. They don't know who I am. But if they did, if they had seen me …

I stumble, then grab hold of the railings by the side of the road. Better take myself to The Marquis close to the park. Yes, there would be friendly faces there, friendly faces and the same conversations and the same drink: people to tell me how worthwhile my life has been, people to love me. Perhaps Maureen, the landlady, will be there and I might find solace in her comfortable body.

I start to walk; my knees hurt, the result of Paul bloody Reaney no doubt, him and the hundreds of others without an ounce of talent who'd been told to kick me as hard as they fucking-well could. I feel tired. I rub my eyes and start to cross the road.

'You didn't answer my question, Billy?'

I turn around abruptly, drunkenly, to see the man in the sheep-skin coat and trilby walking towards me. My eyes narrow as I try to focus on the man's face. Where the bloody hell do I know him from? There *was* something familiar about him.

'I know you, don't I?'

'I should hope so,' he says, and he smiles slowly and mechanically at me.

I stagger slightly and move my head back trying to get a better look at him, to picture him, put a name to the face, put an age to the face.

'I'm sorry, mate,' I say. 'I can't remember. You'll have to remind me.'

'Come on,' says the man ignoring the request. 'Let's take a walk through the park.'

We walk through Southwark Park. Some kids kick a ball on a strip of concrete. We stop and watch them: it's what old football men do.

'You see that?' asks the man in the sheepskin coat.

And I turn to face him. I'd seen nothing of worth in the boys' kick-about and am starting to feel a bit weird, light headed, there is something about this man that confuses me, weakens me, makes me feel ill.

'The grass, Billy,' the man continues. 'Those boys are playing on the concrete because the grass on the park is useless. It's just mud.'

I look at the empty field, heavy and rutted with green and brown, then back to the boys.

'Not many people know this, but the grass on that park is Bahia grass which comes from South America. Did you know that, Billy?'

I shake my head. I've no idea what he's going on about. Suddenly I want another drink like I've never wanted one before.

'Some clot decided that if the boys of south London were going to play like South Americans, then they should have South American grass.'

'Oh,' I say. But I don't want to stand still talking about grass; the open space of the park is starting to hurt my eyes.

The man in the trilby gives a throaty laugh. 'Of course, they didn't realise that Bahia grass would struggle in our climes – it doesn't grip the soil in the same way, you see. It's rubbish.'

12

The man smiles and looks over towards me as I start to feel a warm sensation in my temples.

'That's where you know me from,' he says, warming slightly. 'Brisbane Road. Gerry Higgs. I was head groundsman and coach at the Orient when you went there as a boy.'

Gerry Higgs, of course, Gerry Higgs. I nod my head slowly then rub my temples. There is sweat rushing down the side of my face. Why am I sweating?

'Gerry Higgs,' I mumble. 'Yes, I remember.' I look at him, my eyes narrowing and clouding as I examine him more closely – Gerry Higgs. Bloody hell. But that doesn't make sense. 'Mr Higgs,' I say, confused, 'you were old then – you haven't changed. Why haven't you changed?'

'Ah,' he says, 'there's a reason for that, Billy.'

'What's that then?' I try to muster a clever joke, despite the pounding in my head. 'Porridge every morning? Cod liver oil before you go to bed?'

'No son,' he says. 'I went into the Service a few years ago.'

Service. Service? What is that? What does he mean, Service? I rub my eyes again – my body becomes heavy. Why? What's happening?

The man's eyes train on me. I need a drink. I turn away from him.

'How's your daughter, Billy?' I hear him say, as though he's talking from another room. I note the slightly sinister tone to his voice. I want to answer but I can't. I want to ask him why he's mentioned my daughter, Rebecca. But I can't. I can't muster an answer. I hear more words, this time from even further away, 'And your grandson – what's his name? Liam isn't it?'

I'm reeling now. What did Gerry Higgs know about my daughter and the boy?

'I dunno.' I'm stuttering, trying to shout. 'How do you know about them?'

The man smiles. 'I know everything, son. As I told you, I'm in the Service. And now I want to help you, Billy. I want to help you to put everything right. You do want that don't you? We can do that in the Service.'

There was that word again: Service. What does he mean? My eyes blur and I feel something loosen in my mind. I don't understand. Gerry Higgs. What does he mean – how can he help me? What is the Service? I look around for something to hold on to, and as I do an image forms in my mind of Becky and Liam – my daughter and my grandson. I'm not with them. I haven't been with them for bloody ages, years. The image is one of longing and spiky, prickly, guilt. Why has Gerry Higgs mentioned them? Gerry Higgs, the groundsman at the Orient who coached the kids and drove the youth team bus on a Saturday. What did it have to do with him?

Was it really him?

I feel a little explosion in my mind then a cloying lightness that spreads throughout my body, starting with my eyes then rippling downwards, jumping from my torso to my knees that suddenly veer in spastic directions.

No balance, no control.

I fall. What's happening? What the bloody hell is going on?

Is this it? Is this the end? Is this death?

For a few seconds everything is quiet. Nothing. Not a sound. There's just me, Billy Parks, Parksy, bloody Billy Parks of West Ham United and England, legend, lying, alone, on the ground, crumpled and small and breathing with a violence that makes my body shudder.

I can hear anxious voices in the distance. 'See that, that old geezer's fallen over,' they say and the boys who'd been playing football start to run towards me.

I'm not old, I think.

And my lips move, silently.

I'm Billy Parks.

2

I was six and I'd cried when I had to leave my cousins' house. I'd gone on the bus with my mother all the way to Dagenham. All the way, just the two of us – her in a pretty cotton dress with red flowers on it, me in my Sunday bib and tucker. It had been the best day of my life. And when it was time to go I'd felt my head go down and sticky silent tears force their way into my eyes: proper painful tears brought on by the awful, heavy, horrible dread that I was going to have to go back home. I wiped them away furiously because you get nothing for crying, Billy.

My cousins' house had a back garden. My Uncle Eric had ruffled my hair and Aunty Peggy, gorgeous Aunty Peggy, who always smelled of the promise of something exciting that I didn't yet understand, had smiled this lovely smile at me and my cousins, twins, Bobby and Keith and their sister Alice, as we ran around, laughing out loud, big carefree childish pointless laughs, and shouted and pretended to be Cowboys and Indians. It *was* the best day of my life and it had made the whispered tick-tock silence of home seem unbearable. I hadn't wanted to leave. I wouldn't leave. I would stay – why couldn't I stay? Even Mother had seemed happy here in her dress with red flowers on it, sitting in the kitchen drinking only tea, smiling at me as I played.

Smiling at me.

God she was beautiful that day.

We'd left, me with my head down and my mother's hand in between my shoulder blades. I'd sulked all the way to my home where my father, Billy Senior, never ruffled my hair.

Oh my poor, poor father. The poor, poor bastard.

That day, as I played and my mother laughed, he had sat in his usual place in our house, in the open back doorway of our kitchen, looking out at the back yard and up into the east London sky at the clouds that passed on their heavenly journey, waiting for the day when his own celestial cloud would arrive and mercifully take him away. Every day. Every single silent, wasted, disappearing, bloody day.

Sometimes I would stand in the kitchen with a little ball in my hand and look at the back of his head. Other dads played games, I knew this, I'd heard this, so I would shuffle my feet against the lino and make a noise before Mother would arrive and tell me to be quiet and go and do something else on my own.

Home was sad silence. Home was doing things on my own. Home was listening to the footsteps of my sister Carol, who was ten years older than me, clip-clopping across the stone hallway on her way out of the house to wherever it was *she* went to seek solace. Home was the slow monotone sobs of our mother and my own breathing as I lay on my tummy and played with little toy cars and little wooden animals that I liked to line up in a quiet row.

I had known nothing else, but then I went to my cousins' house in Dagenham and I discovered a wonderful truth: not all homes were like mine. I was six. I was six and I'd had my hair ruffled and smelled the feminine smell of my lovely smiling aunty. And now, like an addict, I wanted more of that, that wonderful life.

I feel guilty admitting that. I mean, my poor, poor bastard dad. It wasn't his fault. He'd not always sat mute in the back kitchen. Once upon a time he and Mother had smiled and laughed too,

16

once upon a bloody time he had held her and told her not to worry because he was only going there to 'mend broken tanks, not to fight'. And she kissed him and pressed her breast against his chest and he had pulled his face away from hers so that he could see her and remember her, and as he looked at her he'd promised, 'I'll be fine, it'll be just like being in Mile End', and then he'd smiled his lovely smile with his twinkling blue eyes and joked, 'Only hotter.'

That, I discovered, was 1941 as he left for Burma.

He was taken prisoner the next year and it was another five years until she saw him again. She saw him and she held him, but he never really returned to her. The poor bastard – the poor pair of bastards.

He had tried. Or so I'm told. He had gone back to the garage on Woodgate Road and a pint down The Albion and West Ham on a Saturday afternoon. He had bounced Carol on his knee and smiled because she adored him, and he'd got on with the task of blotting out the images of Burma and the camp at Thanbyuzayat and the corrugated iron shack with the waist-high ceiling that had been his jail and the rats and snakes and scorpions and the slow death brought on by malnutrition and the exhaustion of working day after day on that bloody railway, or the faster, better, death brought on by dysentery and malaria and typhoid.

He got on with the job of blotting out the images of his dead friends and of the camp guards with their sticks and their swords and the 'Hellship' home when the Americans accidentally torpedoed them, and the awful, overwhelming gut-wrenching feeling of guilt when he eventually reached home in 1946 and walked down what was left of our street, Scotland Street, in Stratford.

It was the guilt that did it.

At first he could block out the images. He could deal with the pain of loss. His body recovered, he put the weight back on, he was always an athletic man – but the guilt never left him. The guilt grew like a creeping winter shadow, placing everything into cold darkness. And once the guilt had gnawed at everything, stripped him bare, the images couldn't be blotted out any more.

Even me, little Billy, born in December 1948 and loving him from the moment I first formed a memory, even I couldn't stop the images that came to him each day: of his mate Eddie Hastings from Romford, who had been a postman – a postman, from Romford, he shouldn't have been in bloody Burma building railways, he shouldn't have died in my dad's arms, incoherent with disease and weakness and thirst; and the big Colour Sergeant, Harry Green, who was executed, and how he had shouted out for his wife and his sons just before they decapitated him; and all the others, all the bloody others, who came to him every day and did their spectral dance around his poor suffering head.

I couldn't take away those images. Not even when I held my little ball and looked up at him with the same twinkling blue eyes that he had once had.

'Why are you sitting by the back door, Dad?' I asked, and I curse myself now, because I know now that my presence, my question, my little bloody ball, would have just added to his guilt.

'Will you play with me, Dad?'

'I'm sorry, son, I'm tired. I'm so tired. Maybe tomorrow.'

My poor scared broken dad.

I would nod, disappointed. I wanted him to hold me and I know now, I'm sure now, that he *wanted* to hold me, but it wouldn't happen. Ever. He would never play with me.

And as my father sat quietly and neatly waiting for the turmoil in his head to go away, the life was sapped from my mother.

During the war, she'd worked as a clerk for the London General Omnibus Company keeping tidy ledgers to try to stop herself from worrying. She *had* worried though, of course she had, every day for five years. Worrying and fantasising and yearning for his twinkling blue eyes and his sandy hair and his lean athleticism and an end to the crushing weight of loneliness.

The man she yearned for never came home.

So she stayed lonely.

And the local women gathered around, because that was what they did round our way. And they helped her when she fell with me after one of the few times Billy Senior had come to her as a man, and they helped her when he stopped going to work, and they helped her when he woke every night crying. They told her that it was alright to have a couple of snifters of Mrs Ingle's home-made gin from time to time.

But from time to time became every day, so they stopped gathering around.

I would be sent in the morning round to Mrs Ingle's (*always go round the back, Billy*) with a coin in my trouser pocket and a note. And Mrs Ingle would ask me how me ma was and how me old man was and give me a flask and send me on my way. *Your mother's tonic, don't drop it, don't break it, get home straight away.*

I broke it once. Only once. And that was on the day that I discovered football.

I always took the same route to Mrs Ingle's: up our road, past the corner shop and the Nissen huts, through the lane that ran between Eric Road and Vernon Street and across the waste ground that had, until the Luftwaffe had bombed it into oblivion four years before I was born, been Singleton Street and Sharples Street. Now it was just a derelict piece of ground about the size of, well, the size of a football pitch.

On the day that I discovered football I crossed it on my way to Mrs Ingle's just like I did most days. Then I went round the back of her house, just as I was told, knocked on the door and was met by Mr Ingle in his vest and braces chewing on a mouthful of thick brown bread. He looked at me witheringly and motioned for me to stay where I was. A little while later Mrs Ingle came to the back door – funny, recently our transactions had become more businesslike. She had stopped asking me about my parents; instead I would silently hand over the money and she would silently hand over the flask, we would exchange a knowing look and off I'd go.

This particular morning was no different. I took the flask and put it into the little brown paper bag, just as I was ordered, and started to walk back home. When I reached the waste ground at Singleton Street there was a football match going on. I knew a bit about football, not much, just bits and pieces I'd picked up from my cousins. What I did know though was that if the bigger boys were playing I would have to walk around the pitch or risk a cuff around the ear from some twelve-year-old psychopath.

Wisely, I started to walk around the makeshift pitch, skipping over the puddles that formed in the blast craters to make sure that I didn't get my shoes wet. It was the last childish thing I would do because halfway around the pitch my life changed for ever.

'Oi you, kid.'

I turned around to see an enormous nine-year-old shouting at me. Chris Cockle, his name was, a boy with thick arms and legs and a head of dark wavy hair. He wore his grey V-neck jumper taut across his chest like chainmail. I knew Chris Cockle, everyone knew Chris Cockle. He was a fearless slayer of any beast that crossed his path.

'What?' I said, trying to sound somehow more confident than I actually was – a trait that has got me out of countless good hidings over the years.

'Come on,' said Cockle, 'we're a man short. Put your bag down by the goal, you can play for my team. You can play right-back. You can be Alf Ramsey.'

'He can't be Alf Ramsey. He's just a kid, he's rubbish.' The dissenting voice was that of Charlie Scott, who was ten and had a dozen brothers and sisters who would hang around outside their house like cats. Chris Cockle wasn't having that.

'If he's going to play right-back, he's got to be Alf Ramsey.'

I had no idea whatsoever what they were going on about. I had no idea what right-back meant, never mind the name of Tottenham and England's Alf Ramsey. I assumed that Alf Ramsey was one of the other lads on his team. All I knew was that if Chris Cockle wanted me to play, then I had no choice – Mother would have to wait for her tonic. I put the bag down by the goalposts, which were made up of a mound of rocks on one side and a stick stuffed into a hole on the other, and strutted cautiously on to the pitch, which was marked by a series of jumpers and coats.

This was serious. This was football and football is more serious than anything else.

'Come on,' said another gigantic boy. 'Go and stand over there, we're playing the lads from Manor Park. Don't go near the ball unless I tell you, and if the ball comes to you just kick it to me. Alright? I'm Billy Wright, you're Alf Ramsey.'

Billy Wright! This was even more confusing, surely the lad who'd introduced himself as Billy Wright was, in fact, Ginger Henderson who lived behind the corner shop and whose dad had been killed in the war. I decided against saying anything.

The game kicked off with the lads from Manor Park attempting to play a long diagonal ball out towards where I had been told to stand. Ginger Henderson (or Billy Wright) went to head it, I moved out of the way, Ginger missed the ball completely and the Manor Park left-wing was left with only the goalie, Lanky Johnson, to beat: thankfully, he put the ball wide of the pile of rocks.

Ginger picked himself up, Lanky Johnson, or Bert Williams as he had taken to calling himself, gave him a bollocking, so Ginger gave me a similar bollocking and the game continued.

This was football.

There were goals and movement and swear words and arguments and kicks and shoves and I loved it all. Lads became spitting, snarling men imbued with a sense of purpose. I started to relax. I started to watch the ball and work out, instinctively, where it would go. I started to watch the movement of my teammates; I worked out that Chris Cockle was good because he was big and fast, but little Archie Stevenson who was sat in the middle of the park, just in front of the enormous water-filled bomb crater (*If the ball goes in there, we restart with a drop ball, OK?*), was by far the best player, as he could spray passes out to the right and left. On the right, was a little fat boy called Stanley Matthews who was quite good, but the tall gangly boy, called Tom Finney, on the left-hand side, was rubbish because the ball would just bounce off his legs.

Impulsively, like a salmon lured upstream by invisible forces, I wandered from my given position at right-back and made the diametric move to the left-wing. It just seemed the most natural thing for me to do, as though it was where I belonged; I wanted the ball, I wanted to play football, I wanted to kick it, I wanted to be part of this, to feel the rush of scoring a goal, a prospect that caused a pounding of excitement that I had never felt before. Now, playing football, I was alive.

And then it happened. I scored my first goal.

Stanley Matthews, who I would later come to know and adore as Johnny Smith (oh poor, lost Johnny, Johnny Smith), cut in from the right and tried to swing over a cross for Chris Cockle: Chris jumped marginally early and the ball glanced off his bouncy brown hair across the face of the goal towards me. It dropped perfectly. I controlled it – alright, not particularly elegantly with my knee (my beautiful close control would come later) – and then instinctively, without considering anything, without a conscious thought in my little mind, found that my body had naturally formed itself into a position to shoot at the goal.

'Shoot!'

I shot. With all my tiny six-year-old frame behind it, I shot and the ball headed towards the piece of rusty iron railing that was the near post of the Manor Park goal. Then, with the assistance of the uneven pitch the ball bounced over the goalkeeper's leg (if he had dived with his hands he would have prevented my first ever goal, but such are the vagaries of sport) and inside the near post.

Goal. Goal. My first goal. My first bloody goal.

I felt my body and mind surge with the glorious fresh air of life. My face beamed triumphantly for the first time. Chris Cockle came over and ruffled my hair. 'Well done, son,' he said. 'What's your name again?'

'Billy Parks,' I said and Chris Cockle smiled at me: 'Well done, Parksy,' he said, then turned to the opposition with a bellowing, captain's roar: 'That's eight all. Next goal the winner.'

Next goal the winner. Next goal was a cause of problems and strife.

As I chased everything on the pitch, and some of the lads started to feel a bit tired, our team became vulnerable to a break-away attack. The Manor Park centre-half, Lennie Hansen, kicked long, Ginger didn't deal with it and the Manor Park striker, a talented little lad called Spider, who was later destined to drown in an accident involving an old well, nipped in and steered the ball past Lanky Johnson. The ball clipped the piece of wood knocking it over on to the paper bag that contained Mother's tonic.

All hell broke loose. As Spider reeled off in celebration, Chris Cockle, Ginger Henderson and Charlie Scott declared that it wasn't a goal as it had hit the post. Lennie Hansen wasn't having this and he and a couple of the other Manor Park lads squared up to them.

As Chris and Lennie, now reinforced by most of the other players, exchanged blows, I ran over to my brown paper bag and surveyed the damage: the flask had smashed and the tonic had seeped out emitting a pungent oily smell. I put my hands up to my head. This was bad.

I walked home. I knew that the broken flask was a tragedy. I knew I had to think of a good lie, a good story, but all I could think about was my goal. How the ball had left my foot and how the other boys had shouted 'Shoot!' and I had smashed it into the near post, and how everyone had smiled at me, and how Chris Cockle had ruffled my hair and asked my name and christened me Parksy. This was what life was about. This was an elevation above and beyond the mere existence of my usual days. This was living.

But the flask was still smashed. The goal couldn't mend that.

Back at home Carol was waiting for me. Her face swollen with tears and rage.

'Where have you been, you idiot? Mum's been waiting for you

all morning. You know you're supposed to come straight back from Mrs Ingle's. Where have you been?'

'I've been playing football,' was all that I could muster.

She screamed at me, 'Football? Football? Who cares about bloody football?' She paused, then seethed through gritted teeth, 'Just give me the bottle.'

She held her hand out and my head dropped.

'It got broken. It was an accident. I didn't mean for it to happen,' I was mumbling.

Carol started screaming at me again.

My mother appeared at the bottom of the stairs: her face was lined and taut and anxious. 'Where's the bottle from Mrs Ingle's, Billy?'

'He's broken it, Mum,' my sister squealed. 'He's been playing football.'

I saw my mother's face break into a desperate ugly rage, and she advanced on me and rained down blows on my head and back in syncopated rhythm as she scolded me.

'You silly, silly boy. I-only-asked-you-to-do-one-thing. You silly, silly boy.'

As the force of the blows diminished, I looked up, my own face now a mass of rushing tears, and I could see through the kitchen the back of Father's head tilted upwards, looking, as ever, towards the heavens.

'Dad,' I shouted through sobs. 'Dad, I scored a goal. You should have seen my goal. Stanley Matthews crossed it and I smashed it into the net.'

Father didn't turn around.

A few weeks later they fished him out of the canal.

Details: Match 1, March 1955
Venue: The Waste Ground by Singleton Street
Chris Cockle's XI 8 v. Lads from Manor Park 8
(Match abandoned after brawl erupts following Eddie 'Spider'
Linton's controversial disputed winner)

24

Line up: Lanky Johnson (Bert Williams), Billy Parks (Alf Ramsey), Tommy Weston (Bill Eckersley), Ginger Henderson (Billy Wright), Topper Winters (Jimmy Dickinson), *An Other* (some lad with glasses who was never seen again), Archie Stevenson (Alfredo Di Stefano), Peter Scott (Wilf Mannion), Johnny Smith (Stanley Matthews), Chris Cockle (Ferenc Puskas though changed to Nat Lofthouse shortly after half-time), Brownie Brown (Tom Finney)

Sadly, other than Lenny Hansen and Eddie 'Spider' Linton, the Manor Park line up has been lost in time.

Attendance: 6 (including Charlie Scott's little sisters and a policeman who arrived to break up the fight)

3

The first thing I see is the drip. I know it's a drip and that must mean that I'm in a hospital. But I can't for the life of me think why? The last thing I remember is looking at the grass on Southwark Park. What was it about the grass?

I look at the drip and see a little blurry bubble – which may be a droplet of my blood – make its way down the drip-line towards the needle that leads, via a vein in my hand, to me.

I'm uncomfortable: I've been sleeping at a weird angle with my neck turned sideways in a different direction to the rest of me.

I turn my neck – that's better, that's comfy. My eyes close again and I give a warm welcome to the wondrous feeling of sleep without giving any more thought to where I am or why, or the drip that's happily filling me with some kind of liquid.

Funny how sleep can do that.

The next time I wake up there's a doctor staring down at me; a smiling Asian fella, who's close enough for me to taste the cheese-and-onion butty he's had from the canteen. Behind him are two nurses; one of them is looking at a clipboard and nodding at something the doctor is saying, the other one is smiling at me like I'm some kind of half-wit.

'Ah, hello, Mr Parks,' says the doctor. 'Nice to have you back in the land of the living. How are you feeling?'

'I'm fine,' I say, and instantly try to get up on my elbow. One of the nurses intervenes, plumping up my pillow and easing me slightly forward – she's got nice breath; she must have had the salad.

'I am Dr Aranthraman,' says the doctor. 'They tell me that you are a famous footballer?'

I am. I am Billy Parks.

He doesn't wait for any response, instead he starts to say things to me in a doctor-type of way, talking quickly in heavily accented English. I can't understand him. What's he going on about? He tells me something about some tests. Then something about my liver and only 15% of it working or perhaps he said 50%, I'm not sure. But they were going to clean it or something by giving me some medication.

And how often do I drink?

'Now and again,' I say, then I try to smile at one of the nurses. 'The crowd expects it,' I add. But the nurse doesn't appear to understand.

Dr Aranthraman gives me a lecture about not drinking. I've heard it before.

'Your liver is in a bad way,' he tells me, 'just one more drink could kill you.' Then he tells me that he's placed me on the waiting list for a transplant, but I won't have one if I continue to drink alcohol. As he speaks I start to feel very tired: perhaps it's his halitosis?

'Do you have any questions?' he asks me.

'Has anyone been in to see me?' I ask. The doctor's lips thin and I see a nurse shake her head.

When I wake up the third time, I am startled by the sight of Gerry Higgs sitting quietly in the corner seat of my room. What's he doing here? I stare at him. He appears to be asleep, his hat on his knee and his head bowed. What the fuck is he doing in my room?

I remember now, his question, and the park, and what was it

he told me he was part of? The Institute or something, no, not the Institute, what was it? The Service. Yes that's right, the Service.

As I look at him, one of his manic eyes jerks open and stares at me, before the other one joins it. He smiles, like he's played a really good joke.

'Mr Higgs,' I say. 'I didn't expect you to be here.'

'All part of my work,' he says, then quickly changes the subject before I can ask him what in the name of God he's going on about. 'So, what have the doctors said then?' he asks.

I shrug. 'Oh it's nothing, something about me liver not being too good,' I say and I mutter something about a transplant, which gets me thinking that surely I should have some say about whether I actually want a transplant: I mean they just can't haul out bits of you. Can they?

'You don't want to worry too much about what these doctors say, Billy,' says Gerry Higgs, 'half the time they're more interested in their statistics: it looks good if they perform so-many operations and procedures and transplants.'

He's probably right.

'You see, Billy,' says Gerry Higgs, who's now pulled his chair closer to my bed, 'I need you fit and well.'

What? I find myself smirking at the incredulity of this. 'Why's that, Mr Higgs, does that Russian bloke want to sign me for Chelsea?'

I watch Gerry Higgs's face crease up scornfully as I mention Roman Whatshisname from Chelsea. 'Don't talk to me about that gangster,' he says. 'No, Billy, I'm talking about proper footballing men, geniuses.'

Now, for the first time, it crosses my mind that Gerry Higgs might actually be a few players short of a full team.

'Gerry,' I say. 'Mr Higgs, I've no idea what you're talking about.'

He leans in towards me, his face close to mine. I can see the hairs that explode from his veined nostrils and the blood pumping to the pupils in his eyes.

'The Council of Football Immortals, Billy,' he whispers, giving each of the words the heavy weighty air of importance.

'Who?'

'The Council of Football Immortals,' he repeats putting his face even closer to mine. 'The greatest footballing minds that ever lived.'

His lips wobbled as he spoke and spit flew out indiscriminately. He is definitely mad, and if it is his intention to scare me, then he has succeeded, because I'm shitting myself. I consider pushing the red 'help' button by the side of the bed.

'That's why I asked you the question I did, Billy,' he says, and he asks it again, though this time in a rather sinister rasping whisper. 'What would you give to have the chance to turn the clock back and put a few things right?'

No words come to me, instead I move myself as far away from him as I can. Our eyes meet and we stare at each other. Then he breaks off and turns his face away from me.

'That's why I asked about your daughter, Billy. You see I know that you and her have,' he paused now, searching for the right words, 'got a few issues to settle.'

My daughter. He's right. My little girl. As soon as he says it, the image of her and her boy, my grandson, Liam, forms in my mind. He's right. But I don't want him to be right. I want to tell him that he's talking bollocks and that everything between us is tickety-fucking-boo, but before I can say a word in response, he's waving his craggy finger at me: 'Don't worry about it, Billy, I understand, old son, it's not just your fault. But we can help you to sort it all out.'

'We?'

'The Service.'

Oh, Christ, there it is again, that word 'Service'. Just the mention of it makes me swoon and slip down my pillows. He watches me, and I wonder what he's going to do next. To my surprise, he taps me gently on the hand.

'I'll tell you what,' he says, still tapping, 'I'll leave you now to get some rest; the Council haven't formally called you up yet, so we've got a few days, but I'll be in touch when I know a bit more. Who knows, they might let you sit in on one of their sessions before you go before them.'

With that he stood up and was gone.

4

Billy Parks's mum, smells of bubble-gum,
Billy Parks's mum, smells of bubble-gum.

The three bastards had been keeping their chant up all the way home. Bastards: Eddie Haydon, grinning and gurning like a melon; Pete Langton, shouting at the top of his newly developed, but still squeaky voice; and Larry McNeil, the biggest bastard of the lot, defying me to turn around and confront them so that they could give me a right good pasting.

I'd been in secondary school for a week: St Agnes School for ruffians, rogues and arseholes. Each day, for some reason, these three had decided to follow me home goading me with their chant. I knew that their words had nothing to do with bubble-gum; this was their assertion that my mother had cavorted with a Yank during the war: it was a suggestion that I was the illegitimate child of an American soldier. A suggestion made solely on the basis that I didn't have a dad. The morons – I mean I wasn't even a war baby, I was born in 1948, three years after the Yanks had either gone home or been blown to high heaven in Normandy. Historical detail, though, meant nothing to Larry

33

McNeil and his cronies. I was small, with no dad and that made me an easy target.

'Hey, Parksy,' one of them shouted, 'was your dad Frank Sinatra?' They laughed as though this is the funniest thing any of them have ever heard. 'Or was he John Wayne?' said another joining in a thread of mindless abuse that could have gone on for some time had they actually known the names of any more Americans. 'Perhaps he was a nigger,' said one of them. I turned to confront them, my teeth clasped together and my fists tight like rocks by my side. Straight away their laughing stopped and they hardened their own stance. 'Come on then, Billy,' said McNeil. 'Come on if you're going to fight us.'

I was outnumbered. I was not a fighter. I wanted to protect the honour of my unhappy mother and poor bastard father who went to Burma to mend tanks for these little arseholes and who ended up in the canal – but I couldn't. I turned away from them and they jeered and howled and made chicken noises and continued with their chant about my mother smelling like bloody bubble-gum.

I got home and closed the door behind me; the still silence of our house put its arm around me like an old mate, I was safe. I put my foot on the stairs with the intention of going up to my bedroom, but my mother's voice stopped me: 'Billy, is that you?'

'Yes, Mum,' I said. I didn't want to talk to her. I didn't want to see her. I knew that she'd be sitting in the front room, perched on the edge of the armchair. Fidgeting. Nervous. I knew that. What I didn't know though is how she would be with me. I didn't know if I was going to be the *waste of space and accident that she wished had never happened,* or her *lovely son, her little sunshine, the light of her otherwise dark bloody life.*

'Billy,' she said again. 'Yes, Mum,' I answered and wandered into the front room.

There was no trace of her drinking, not a clue, there never was then. She'd stopped going to Mrs Ingle's years earlier. I didn't link her mood swings with drink. It would be a debate I would avoid having all my life.

'Come and sit down,' she said, 'have a chat with your old mum.' She looked pathetic, holding one shaking hand in the other; did I nearly lose my temper for this? Did I nearly get my arse kicked in a fight to protect this? Nearly.

'How's school going?' she asked.

And I shrugged. 'Alright,' I said unhelpfully and she looked at me as though she was trying to gauge if I was telling her the truth.

'Good,' she said and I looked down, knowing that she was staring at me, hoping that I'd say something that would make everything somehow better, even for a second, but I couldn't. I bloody couldn't.

After an age, she continued. 'Listen,' she said, 'I tell you what, why don't we go to the pictures on Friday, *The Alamo* is showing down the Roxy, my treat.' She smiled doubtfully at me, and I hated her weakness but I hated myself even more, because deep down I knew it wasn't her fault.

'It's got John Wayne in it,' she continued, 'you like him', and I grimaced at the ironic mention of John Wayne. 'Well?' she said, and I nodded and her face broke out into a smile. 'Good, that's a date then.'

I knew that by Friday, she'd have forgotten.

'Come and give your old mum a hug.'

I tentatively got up and slowly walked towards her, my body hardening against the thought of hugging her. And she knew it, and it just made everything bloody worse.

I went outside to the back yard and kicked my football against the target I had drawn on the gate. I kicked it alternately with my right then left foot, 200 times, it had to be 200 times and if I missed the target just once, I had to go back and start again. I kept missing because I was angry.

The next day Larry McNeil and his mates were waiting for me again. This time we were in the changing room before PE. It was my first PE lesson at St Agnes. Pete Langton spotted me: 'Hey look fellas, here he is, the Yankee Doodle Dandy.' McNeil joined him and scowled at me as the changing room went quiet. 'Billy Parks's mum had it off with a nigger,' he declared and I had no choice, I rose up and went for him – immediately the whole year of boys closed around us chanting, 'fight, fight, fight,' as they did. I put my head down and swung a few hopeful punches in McNeil's direction, but, as I said, I was no fighter.

Mercifully, the fight was broken up by the muscular grasp of the teacher, Taffy Watkins. He pulled us apart and stared at us. 'Right,' he bellowed, 'what on earth is all this about, I've never seen such a woeful fight in all my life: like two squirrels squabbling in a hessian sack.'

It was the first time I'd heard a Welsh accent. 'Well?' he repeated, but neither of us responded. 'Right,' he said, 'you two shall come to me after the lesson and I will cane your rotten backsides.'

Then he turned to the rest of the class. 'Now,' he said, 'on to the pitch so that I can laugh at your desperate attempts to play Association Football. The only thing of any worth invented by the English.'

At the mention of football, I felt my insides warm.

Outside on the school pitch, we were put into two teams. To my delight, Larry McNeil and his two mates, Langton and Haydon, were put on the opposing side to me. I knew what was about to happen. The gods of football had meant for this.

I got the ball pretty much from the kick off and set off down the pitch. I knew what I was going to do without even thinking. I could see the space on the pitch, I could feel the desperate lunges by the opposing team as they tried to take the ball from me. I was in complete control, my body responded instinctively – one boy, two boys, three boys, they couldn't get near the ball as I feinted and shimmied and burst past them. Eventually there was only one player left between me and the penalty area, Larry McNeil. His face contorted with pathetic rage as he rushed towards me; silly arse, never play the man, always play the ball. He tried to kick me and I prodded the ball with my left foot past him and skipped over his trailing leg. Then, as Little Jimmy Cleary, a lad with callipers, who'd been put in goal, stood rooted to the spot, I put the ball in the back of the net.

On the touchline Taffy Watkins watched with his hands on his hips and the flicker of a smile across his chops.

I repeated the exercise seven more times and each time I made a total cunt out of Larry McNeil: this was for my unhappy mother and my unhappy tragic father and for me, Billy Parks, growing a little bit happier with every goal.

At the end, I traipsed off with the rest of the boys. I knew that in the oh-so-important pecking order of eleven-year-old lads, I had risen like a meteor – I knew it, and so did Larry McNeil.

Taffy Watkins held us back. We sat outside the room off the gym reserved for PE teachers; Watkins's own personal fiefdom where he would reward and nurture the few boys he felt possessed sporting talent, and brutalise the rest. Larry didn't look at me. He was called into Watkins's room first and I heard the thwack of the cane as he delivered six of his Welsh best on to Larry McNeil's arse. McNeil ignored me as he emerged, red faced and gritting his teeth against the tears he knew he couldn't show.

I braced myself.

'Right,' said Watkins and I followed his beckoning finger into the tiny room. It smelled of liniment, dubbin, old leather, dry mud and scared boys. He looked at me: 'The other lad started it did he?' I said nothing. 'I thought so,' said Watkins, 'now I'm going to give you one chance – you're to train with the under-fifteens this Thursday, and if your performance out there was a fluke and you're rubbish, you shall have ten of what McNeil had – you hear me?'

'Yes, Sir.'

'Good.'

'Right, off you go.'

'Thank you, Sir.'

He nodded as I got up to leave.

'Oh, and what is your name again?'

'I am Billy Parks, Sir.'

Details: Match 2, September 1960
Venue: St Agnes Third XI football pitch (knocked down and redeveloped into a Sainsbury's in 1991)
Class 1e 10 v. Class 1f 1
Parks (8)   Eccles (2)
Gillway

Line Ups (formations a bit fluid)
Class 1e: Charlie Hugheson, Tommy Rigby, Alan Hattersley, Brian Collins, Peter Hirst, Johnny Smith, Paul 'Donkey' Edwards, Ed 'Clarkey' Clarke, Billy Hindles, George Gillway, Billy Parks
Class 1f: Little Jimmy 'Four Legs' Cleary, Unknown boy, described as having a cleft palate, Larry McNeil, Sam Smith, Paul Carrington, Pete Langton, Eddie Haydon, Maurice 'Spud' Eccles, Keith Ringer, Richard 'Paddy' Murphy, Dave 'Shorty' Hopkinson

Attendance: 1 (Taffy Watkins)

5

I know it's there. I know it is sitting on the table in my kitchen, at least half-full. It has been growing in my mind over the last few days as I have waited for my release from hospital and is now the size of one of those giant bottles that you see on advertising hoardings: a giant bottle of vodka.

'No more drinking now,' Dr Aranthraman says, 'remember, just one more drink could kill you,' and he smiles, because he's a nice fella, and I smile, because I am the twinkling, dazzling Billy Parks. And then Maureen, who has come to pick me up and take me home, bless her, smiles, but she does so with thin lips, because she knows the weakness in me.

'You look after him now,' says Dr Aranthraman, 'he is a famous footballer.'

'Oh I'll do my best,' she says, looking at me like I am a naughty boy. I smile up at them both, but in my mind, I am being chased by a six-foot bottle of fucking Smirnoff vodka. I know that it is there, on my kitchen table. It is there and it has grown and now fills all the space in my brain with its wondrous evil presence.

We get into Maureen's car. As ever she is immaculately turned out; all teeth and hairdo and posh knickers, that's Maureen. I catch a glimpse of stockinged thigh as she changes gear. I know that underneath her clothes there will be a complicated and exotic system of underwear that is designed to deflect attention from the signs of wear and tear on her fifty-five-year-old body. It works too. Usually. But not today. After two weeks in hospital, even I, Billy Parks, can't think about getting me leg over. All I can think about is the vodka bottle on the kitchen table.

'So,' she says, 'how are you feeling?'

'I feel fantastic,' I say, 'like I've got a new zest for life.' The words float easily from my mouth, they're not weighed down by truth.

'That's great. I kept a couple of clippings from the newspapers for you.'

She's good like that, Maureen, she's been doing it for the entire time we've known each other; she's already told me that there was a paragraph in the *Sunday People*, saying '*Former West Ham favourite, Billy Parks collapsed while out watching a park game*', which is a load of cobblers, I was on my way to the pub; while the *Mirror* ran a story about '*Billy's Booze Battle*'. I don't mind. They've got their job to do. They've got to sell their newspapers. And, for me, I can't lie: it's nice to be talked about.

We drive down round the Elephant and Castle and I look out of the window at the light of the day. After ten days in the hospital, the world seems huge, a bloody frightening, fast moving chaos; the cars are giant metal beasts, careering around corners and across junctions, carrying life and normal, ordinary people. And as I watch them the vodka bottle grows bigger and more powerful.

I try to take my mind off it. I've got to. Dr Aranthraman told me: booze, no new liver, bad end; no booze, new liver, life. It sounds easy.

I try to chase the vodka bottle away by changing the subject.

'Funny thing happened,' I say, 'in hospital, a very funny thing; this old geezer, Gerry Higgs his name is, he used to be like a coach and groundsman at the Orient when I was a kid.'

She pouts and her eyes narrow a bit as she's taking in what

I'm telling her. 'He was there when I fell over in Southwark Park and he comes to visit me.' I stop, because it still doesn't make any sense to me. 'He must be well into his eighties, because he was old back in the day.' I pause and the image of Gerry Higgs back in 1965 shouting and bawling at the apprentices drifts into my mind. 'Well anyway, he tells me that I've been selected to appear before some kind of committee of footballing legends.'

'Footballing legends?' she says. 'What's that?'

I shrug, then sigh, 'I dunno.' Because I don't know, I have no clue what Gerry Higgs meant. 'Perhaps it's some programme on ESPN or Sky Sports or summat, anyway, it was nice of him to visit me.'

Maureen turns to me now. 'Visit you?' she says. 'Those nurses told me that the only person to visit was me.'

'No,' I say. 'Gerry Higgs was definitely there.'

She drives on. She's not interested in the Council of Football Immortals. Instead she tells me that in the back of the car she's got something for me: a jigsaw. A jigsaw. I'm confused. A jigsaw? Me, Billy bloody Parks. I once scored a hat-trick inside twenty minutes at Maine Road, pulled Mickey Doyle all over the place I did – God love him.

What do I want a jigsaw for?

'It's a competition I'm running at the pub,' she tells me. 'There's a prize for the person who can complete the jigsaw in the quickest time. You text me when you're about to start and then text me when you've finished, and I put the times up in the bar. Little Brian Staplehurst, you know that bloke who works at Lloyds Bank, he's already posted a time of seventeen hours. And anyway – it'll keep your mind off drinking and going to the pub – you heard what the doctor said.'

The vodka bottle grows a little bit more and casts me in its magnificent, vicious shadow.

'Seventeen hours,' I say. 'Is he blind or something?'

'No.'

She laughs.

41

She has a nice laugh does Maureen, that's what I first liked about her; she has a light laugh, flirty, but not quite accessible, yes, that is Maureen. It's why we're not an item, never have been, not properly – she's a landlady with a nice laugh and great underwear who has been let down by better blokes than me and knows how to enjoy a bottle of wine and listen to all the bullshit and be seductive without allowing you to get too close. I've known her for years. I like her. If we'd met when we were younger, before the bad blokes, before everything, then, who knows?

We park up. And make our way up the stone piss-smelling staircase to my second floor flat.

It's not there.

It's not bloody there. The vodka bottle is missing from the kitchen table. It's not bloody there. It's not there and its absence has blasted a hole through my very being. How can it not be there? I don't want to drink it, of course not, one more drink might kill me, but I want it to be there, more than anything. I want the chance to drink it.

I turn to Maureen. 'The vodka bottle,' I say, 'the bottle that was on the table – where is it? Where the fuck is it, it was sitting on the table, half finished?'

She looks at me, her face crumbling with incredulity at what I am saying, and I know that's the right reaction, but I just want the fucking massive bottle of vodka, the fucking beautiful massive bottle of vodka which has been chasing me and has caught me and dragged me closer to its open mouth.

'Billy,' she says. 'Billy, are you mad? You can't drink vodka, I chucked it down the sink when I came to get your clothes for you.'

'You silly cow. You silly fucking bitch.' The words just shoot out of my mouth. I'm not thinking; I'm like a cobra, a thirsty horrible black cobra crawling on my belly; I just want it to be there. Is it too much to ask? What has it got to do with her, what does she care if I have a quick vodka now I've been released from hospital? I mean, she's just a friend; we haven't fucked each other for months.

42

'You silly, stupid bitch,' I say, and I've gritted my teeth and I'm so, so wrong. And I've clenched my fists and for a second I am so angry that I want to punch her, but instead I slam my hand against the empty kitchen table.

Maureen puts her hand up, she's dealt with much worse than me. 'Billy,' she says, ice cold, colder than the North Pole, colder than the surface of Neptune, she sighs, and shakes her head. 'Just fuck off and kill yourself.' And with that she's gone, out the door.

I'm left alone. For about an hour I frantically go through the bins and the cupboards and drawers, looking for a drink. I throw things on the floor and rip out stuff from the back of my wardrobe. I search through boxes crammed with my life history, yellow newspaper clippings, old programmes, photos of me, young and beautiful with my arms around the shoulders of missing friends. I ignore them, I discard them in my search for drink. But there isn't any. I know there isn't any. I know that there is no drink in my home. But looking for it has at least made me feel alive.

Alive.

Then tired.

I sit down on my own. I sit down on my bed in my one-bedroom Housing Association flat, panting, and put my head in my hands. Me, Billy Parks, crying like a right twat. I *could* go out to get more drink. Replace the vodka. I could. I want to. But I can't do it. Instead I lie on my bed and try to think about something meaningful. I try to picture my daughter and her son. I want to make plans to see them, take the boy somewhere, perhaps I could take him down West Ham, get in the Directors box, see the players, but I can't make those plans, I can't form the images in my head, images of happy me and happy daughter and happy boy. It's too difficult. I can't even work out how I'll find her.

I get up and pace around. The dark clouds of self-loathing gather. Then I notice the jigsaw that Maureen's left on the table, thousands of fucking pieces depicting a detail from the start of the London Marathon – thousands of heads and bodies in running vests with little numbers on them. I sigh. Seventeen hours she said. I sigh again but before I know it I've taken the pieces out and I'm turning them over the right way.

I have an idea.

I text Maureen telling her that I'm sorry and that I'm a complete twat, and that I'm starting the jigsaw. Then I telephone Tony Singh, a bookie I know from the pub. 'Tony,' I say, 'Billy Parks here. I'm fine mate, never felt better. Listen, you heard about this jigsaw competition Maureen's running at the pub? That bloke who works at Lloyds has posted seventeen hours. Yeah. Yeah. What odds you going to give me?'

Fucking four to one: the tight-fisted bastard.

Still – I have two hundred and fifty quid on Billy Parks.

6

Two days later I find Gerry Higgs waiting by the lift at the bottom of my building. He's got a rather odd, pleased expression across his face. I'm wary, but, I have to admit, intrigued by the old duffer.

'Hello, Billy,' he says.

'Mr Higgs,' I say, 'what brings you to these salubrious parts?'

His face breaks out into his most sinister smile. 'You, of course, Billy,' he says.

Of course.

'It's good news,' he adds, 'the Council of Football Immortals have said that you can watch one of their plenary sessions.'

'Oh,' I say, 'that is good news.' Though in reality I haven't got the faintest idea what he's talking about; what the fuck is a plenary session?

'Actually, I was just off to the bookie's,' I tell him and he smiles at me again.

'Plenty of time for that, old son,' he says. 'Come on.'

I follow him like a kitten, and we get into a cab on the High Street.

'Where are we going?' I ask him.

'Lancaster Gate, of course,' he says.

Of course.

I tell the cab driver. He doesn't recognise me.

Lancaster Gate, once home of the Football Association. We get out of the cab and I follow Gerry Higgs around to the back of a massive Georgian town house; one of those ones that doesn't look that big from the outside, but inside is like a fucking Tardis with ballrooms and banqueting suites and all that. We go through a black back door that leads to a well-lit corridor. On the wall are pictures of the greats: Steve Bloomer, the original football superstar, standing upright and handsome with his hair parted like the Dead Sea. Then Dixie Dean, rising to power in a header. Dixie, what a man, bless him, I met him once at a charity do at Goodison Park just before he died. He'd had his legs amputated, the poor bastard; I mean, how cruel is that, taking away the legs and feet of the man who once scored sixty goals in a single season? Then there's Duncan Edwards, who died in Munich, running on to the pitch all muscle and power knowing that no fucker was going to get the better of him, and Frank Swift, back arched and diving to tip a volley over the crossbar, come to think of it he died in Munich as well, and others, all captured in their prime, beautiful men, athletes, captured before those most horrible devious rotters of all, time and fate, got each and every one of them. Bang, bang, bang, bang.

There are no pictures of me.

At the end of the corridor, Gerry Higgs turns and puts his finger to his lips. 'Come on,' he whispers, and he opens a door that leads to a small room with a window in it; through the window I can see another room in which sit a collection of men around three tables that are arranged in a U-shape: I look closer.

Fuck me.

I feel my whole body move towards the men, my eyes wide, bursting out of my skull. I turn to Gerry Higgs, mouth open in wide-eyed-child-like-cor-blimey astonishment.

'Who are they?' I ask. But I know.

'You know who they are,' says Gerry, grinning like a man who's just given someone the best Christmas present they'll ever have and knows it.

'It can't be,' I say and Gerry Higgs just nods at me, the grin remaining on his slobbering lips.

I turn to look at the three tables again. At the top table sits Sir Alf Ramsey. Then at the table to his right is Sir Matt Busby and next to him Bill Shankly, and across from them, scowling at each other are Don Revie and Brian Clough.

'That's the Council of Football Immortals, Billy,' says Gerry Higgs. 'I told you, didn't I – the greatest geniuses known to the game of football.'

'But, Gerry,' I say, 'they're all dead. I mean, I even went to Sir Alf's funeral.'

Gerry Higgs looks at me like I'm a silly little boy. 'Billy,' he says, 'Billy, Billy, Billy, these men aren't dead. Men like this never die, they live on and on, way beyond the lifespan of mere mortals. That's why they're legends, old son. Proper legends. Not the five-minute wonders you get today.'

I stutter: 'Gerry, I don't understand.' And Gerry Higgs looks at me: 'Don't worry,' he says, 'for now, just listen. You see, Billy, if you play your cards right, they're going to make you immortal too.'

I try to listen. But I can't hear them. I can see that Brian Clough is talking, he is animated and Brylcreemed in a green sports jacket; I see Sir Alf, just as I remember him, quiet and controlled, neat and tidy in his England blazer; I see Shanks in his red shirt and matching tie and Don Revie, looking glum with his thick shredded-wheat sideburns; and Sir Matt, blimey Sir Matt Busby, nonplussed and immaculate. I see them all, and I wonder what on earth is going on. Why are they here? Why am I here?

Gerry Higgs reads my mind. 'Just listen, Billy,' he whispers quietly but firmly. So I do. And now, suddenly I can hear them as well as see them. Cloughie is in full swing.

'No, Don,' he says in that piercing nasal voice, 'the game of football is not simply about winning, it's about winning properly, it's about playing the game how it was supposed to be played. And kicking and cheating is not how the game is supposed to be played.'

Don Revie blusters a response: 'Brian, I'm not rising to that, and the reason I'm not rising to that is two league titles, the FA Cup, a Cup Winners' Cup, two Inter-Cities Fairs Cups and the League bloody Cup, that's why.'

The other three groan. 'Mr Revie,' says Sir Alf, 'Mr Clough. Please, this isn't getting us any further. You both know the issue that we are here to discuss today.'

'Well, we know exactly where you stand, Alf,' says Brian Clough, curtly.

'Thank you, Brian,' says Sir Alf with a school teacher's sarcasm before adding, 'Sir Matt, I believe we haven't heard from you on the question before us – what takes precedence: winning or entertaining, style or results.'

Sir Matt thinks for a second, his lips turning over. 'Well,' he says in his quiet, Glaswegian drawl, 'no one ever remembers the losers do they? But if you can manage both to entertain and win, then you're not far off.'

Shanks joins in, in his more abrasive Glaswegian drawl: 'The question isn't about winning or entertaining, I mean we're not clowns or circus horses; it's about making the working man who pays his money on a Saturday afternoon happy and proud, so that when he goes back to the factory or the shop floor on the Monday, he feels valuable, vindicated.'

'Aye,' says Sir Matt, 'but in that pursuit we can't allow football to lose its charm can we?'

I turn to Gerry Higgs. 'What are they talking about?' I say. But what I really want to know is what it all has to do with me.

'They're asking themselves the fundamental question, Billy,' says Gerry Higgs. 'Why are we here? Who should we aspire to be?

The poor bastard who lives his life according to the rules, makes sure he gets by, pays his taxes, works nine to five and remembers everyone's birthdays, or should we aim to be a little bit different to that, live according to our aspirations in one great big nihilistic fantasy? Because after all, we're not here for very long are we?'

'Well,' I say nervously, 'I suppose we all want to be a bit different, don't we?'

'Yes, Billy, old son.' And he looks at me, and I know that he's wondering how much of this I understand.

He looks back at the Council of Football Immortals.

'It sounds so easy when you hear Mr Clough talk, doesn't it?' he continues, 'but sometimes if you're a bit different, a bit cavalier, you end up hurting the people who love you most. Isn't that right?'

I shrug. I think I know what he's trying to say, and I'm not sure I like it. He stares and his eyes shine like cold steel and I realise that he isn't a mad old duffer after all, he's actually some kind of genius. I avert my eyes and he continues: 'Perhaps Mr Shankly's right,' he says. 'You've got to make people proud, you've got to achieve something worthwhile.'

I feel my face scrunch up in confusion.

'But what's all that got to do with me, Gerry?'

'Well, Billy, you see, Sir Alf has been given a chance to put something right.'

'What?' I glance back through the window again at the five men.

'Poland, Wembley, October 1973.'

'What?'

'You must remember that night, Billy?'

'Of course,' I say. 'I was sat freezing my bollocks off watching the Polish keeper put us out of the World Cup.'

'That's right, Billy, Jan Tomaszewski. The Clown who broke our hearts.'

I nod. Though, if I'm being honest, I don't remember that much about the game, only Norman Hunter's grim face and Sir Alf's desperation in the changing room afterwards.

'Well,' continues Gerry. 'It shouldn't have happened like that: the Polish keeper kept one or two out that night that he shouldn't, that he wasn't meant to, and Sir Alf's going to have the chance to change things.'

I was now utterly, utterly confused and starting to stutter like an imbecile. 'What? How? How will that work? That was forty years ago.'

'The Service has given him a chance to revisit ten minutes of that night and make one change.' He tells me, and again, the word Service causes a quick pain to my temple.

'What will he change?' I ask.

Gerry puts his arm gently around my shoulders and ushers me back towards the window through which we could see the five legends arguing about life and football.

'He brought on Kevin Hector,' he says quietly.

I look up at him.

'And as everyone knows, Billy, Kevin Hector missed the chance to score the winner.'

I stare incredulously as Gerry Higgs ruefully shakes his head: 'It was a bloody sitter.'

He draws his breath in through his teeth, before continuing: 'Well, now, thanks to the Service, Sir Alf's got the chance to put that right.'

Suddenly, like a lovely spring morning, the fog of confusion lifts, the penny drops into the slot and I start to understand. 'He could have brought me on,' I say. '*Me*. I was in the squad for that game. I was on the bench. I was sat by Bobby Moore, he could have brought *me* on, not Kevin Hector.'

Gerry Higgs smiles. 'That's right,' he says, 'he *could* have brought you on; but would you have put it away, Billy?'

I nod, my mouth open, 'Oh yeah, every time, every bloody time, Gerry, you know that. You remember, Gerry? Don't you?'

He smiles again. 'Well, you might get that chance, son.'

'What do you mean?' I am racing with excitement now; what

does he mean I might have the chance? How could that happen? How could I have the chance? I feel my heart beating against my chest.

'How Gerry?' I turn to him. 'How?' I repeat, forcefully, and the five men in the other room all turn as one and look in still silence.

'The Service can grant you that,' he says, then pauses, 'just as long as Sir Alf picks you, that is.'

'Sir Alf,' I state. This isn't good, Sir Alf hates me: he once called me a lazy useless showboating pony. 'Sir Alf won't pick me,' I say.

'Probably not,' says Gerry, 'but, lucky for you, it's not just up to him; he's got Mr Clough, Mr Revie, Mr Shankly and Sir Matt Busby to help him.'

Actually, this isn't much better.

'Don't look so glum,' says Gerry, 'look on the bright side, you've made the last two.'

'Two?'

'Yes,' says Gerry, then he pauses, 'not sure I'm supposed to tell you this, Billy. The Council of Football Immortals has decided that Sir Alf can bring on you or Kevin Keegan. So that's what they've got to decide: you or Kevin.'

I take a slow intake of breath, and then sigh.

'Alright,' I say, 'so what happens next?'

'You just sit and wait until you're called.'

'Called?'

'Yes, Billy, it's a big thing this; changing history can't be done lightly: the Council will want to meet you.'

'What? Like an interview? Or a trial? Bloody hell! I haven't kicked a ball in years.'

'Steady on, Billy, I wouldn't call it an interview, more a little chat. You won't have to bring your boots. And anyway, you've no need to worry, you're Billy Parks, aren't you?'

I am not so sure. My cheeks puff out breath at the thought of it all. 'And what happens then?' I ask. 'What happens if the Council picks me?'

Gerry's face breaks into a big smile revealing yellow chipped teeth. He claps me on the shoulder. 'Then, old son, everything changes, you get the chance to put everything right. You get the chance to make everything bad that's happened in the last thirty-odd years disappear.' He pauses again, adding slowly, 'If, of course, you manage to put the ball in the back of the Polish net.'

7

I don't sleep that night.

Of course I don't.

I mean, this was the biggest thing, the best thing ever. For an hour I lie there. I can just see their faces, the Council of Football Immortals – funny, none of them had aged, they all looked just the same as they used to. I imagine presenting myself before them – answering their questions, but I have to stop myself thinking about that – as the image grows in my mind, a fierce thirst for a fiery drink grows with it.

So I think about something else. I think about what Gerry Higgs had said. *'The chance to put everything right,'* he'd said, *'the chance to make everything bad disappear.'*

I think about this and a smile breaks out across my mouth. Gerry was right: if I was picked, I would be able to live it all again, have a second chance. The idea gathers momentum in my mind; it doesn't seem at all strange, in fact, as I lie there, with the noise of the south London train to Lewisham creaking behind my flat and the footsteps of smashed-out kids running along the landing outside I assume that most people have the chance to go back and right a few wrongs: it seems quite normal. It seems absolutely right.

And what wrongs I would put right, oh God, everything would be so much better; Rebecca and her mother, they would be first on my list, well, maybe not her mother, that was complicated, but definitely Rebecca, yes, I would make sure that this time she had everything, that she would be happy. That would be the first thing.

And her boy, my grandson, Liam, there would be no more mistakes there either: he would know me for a hero.

And, of course, Johnny Smith – oh poor Johnny Smith – I would somehow help him, stop him from doing what he did, find him, be there for him: he would know me for the friend I had failed to be.

And so would everyone else; there would be no trying to run rubbish backstreet boozers or drink driving bans or those pictures in the *News of the World* with that young girl from Gateshead; no begging talentless managers to give me one last chance and being ignored by dishonest chairmen who didn't know the first thing about the game; no, all that would go. No getting kicked to high heaven by some kid who knows that I'm no longer fast enough to get away before being hauled off at half-time at Brentford, bloody Brentford.

None of this. None of this. None of this. All of this would disappear, Gerry Higgs told me.

Just as long as I score the goal.

I sit and consider it all.

And then my smile disappears.

I want a drink. I want a drink so bad. I can taste it. I can feel the glass in my hand, rounded, beautiful, fitting perfectly in the fleshy arc between my thumb and finger, as the malted liquid glints and sparkles like a midnight lake. Christ. Would one drink be so bad?

I sit up. I wipe the sweat off my forehead. I put the light on and everything evaporates in the yellow of the sixty-watt bulb.

I sigh then I make another start on the bloody London Marathon jigsaw. And as I try desperately to try to find the head of a bloke dressed up as some kind of giant Yorkshire pudding,

I vow that tomorrow I'll make a start on finding Rebecca. Yes, that's what I'll do. I'll find her, because everything bad will be about to disappear for her too. I'll find her and make it better, because, if I'm picked, there's no way on God's green earth that I'll not score that goal.

I am Billy Parks and this will be my chance to make everything better.

8

'This is your chance, Billy. This is your opportunity to prove to everyone that you are the best young footballer in the country. Do you understand?'

I nodded.

Taffy Watkins had cornered me in the toilets at White Hart Lane. I was about to play for London Boys against Manchester Boys and I'd snuck off for a piss. Bless him, old Taffy probably thought I was nervous, but I wasn't. Perhaps he thought that my confidence needed boosting – but it didn't. He was more nervous than me: there was a lot riding on the game. There was a crowd of about 5,000 and scouts from every club in England. Or that's what we were told.

'You see, Billy,' he continued, looking down at me, his hands on my shoulders and his neck arched in my direction, searching for my eyes which I had cast downwards, 'there is nothing greater than football, it's what we've been left with, as men. Do you understand?'

I nodded, but I wasn't really sure that I understood him. Not then.

'And you, boy, have a God-given talent.'

57

He paused and I nodded, dutifully, again.

'You could be a person who makes grown men cry or sing. You could be the person they think about last thing at night and the first thing in the morning. You could be the man they worry about when they're doing their shift in the factory or down the mine, or on the docks; you could be the man they want to be. Do you understand?'

'Yes, Sir,' I said, still averting my gaze from the intensity of his glare.

'Good,' he said, then repeated softly, 'Good. Now, there are scouts from all over the country watching this game, watching you, my boy. Remember, the ball is your ball, the pitch is your pitch, there is no other boy on that field who can do what you can do – it's your stage – do you hear me?'

'Yes, Sir.'

'Good, now go and prove yourself.'

Finally I looked up at him, my lips sucked into my mouth and nodded, mute, before taking myself off on to the pitch.

'Oh, and Billy,' he called after me and I turned around, 'pull your socks up and tuck your shirt in, man!'

I smiled my sparkling smile and took myself out and into my position on the left-hand side of the pitch.

It was raining that night; great bucketfuls of splodgy cold rain that seemed to cascade like a dirty waterfall through the dingy yellow of the floodlights. Not really the conditions for a mercurial, sparkling forward like me. I could feel my boots squelch against the cold turf and knew the ball would sting against my thighs.

Opposite me the Manchester right-back scowled. He was a horrible, ugly, bow-legged, northern monkey called Feeney – he probably knew nothing other than bloody rain. He pointed at me, said something I didn't understand, then tried to laugh. I sighed, intimidation was lost on me: I was more worried about the bloody cold.

58

They kicked off; Brian Kidd passing to Stan Bowles, who had his shirt-sleeves pulled over his hands and wore the expression of a kid who wanted nothing better than to get back on the team bus.

They had a good team did Manchester, plenty of their lads went on to forge decent careers in the game, but we had a brilliant one – Trevor Brooking, Dave Clement, Frank Lampard (senior not junior, obviously) and Harry Redknapp – true greats, all of them. We were just kids then: all with hopeful faces and bandy legs. Apart from Trevor Brooking, of course; he seemed older by miles than all of us. Good old Trev, I met him for the first time that evening; he wasn't quite so posh back then, still immaculate though, still brainy and good with words. 'I'm Trevor,' he said. 'You keep making runs inside their full-back and I'll try and play you through.'

I nodded. I just wanted him to pass me the ball. I didn't care where he put it.

The first half was difficult; the ball kept getting stuck in pools of standing water and even Trevor Brooking couldn't get it to go where he wanted. I hardly got a look in and was getting a bit bored with the northern monkey Feeney telling me how he was going to kick me all the way '*oop the Thames*' if ever I got the ball. So I drifted infield and out of position; if the coach of the London Boys, an old pro called Barry Hickman, shouted at me, I didn't hear him, because I was stood in the centre circle, with my back to goal, when the ball finally came to me.

It was another one of those moments – moments that you can't predict, moments that change your life. Fate. As the ball slowly made its way across the quaggy turf to my feet, big Tommy Booth, the Manchester centre-half, a great oaf of a boy, tried to clatter into me from behind; as fortune would have it, though, rather than knock me over, he just managed to put himself off balance and force the ball to wriggle away from us to my right, which also happened to be where the ground was driest; in a flash I was on to it and turned towards the goal.

Ahead of me was a mass of open field. Instinctively, I knew that if I hoofed it forward the wet pitch would stop it carrying through to their keeper. I knew this without a moment's conscious thought. I knew it and I did it: I hoofed it towards the edge of the penalty area where it stuck fast in the mud. Now, there was just a foot race to the ball between me, northern monkey Feeney, who was charging from my left, the Manc goalie Joe Corrigan and Big Tommy Booth. But I was away, my feet gliding along the glistening grass, water sputtering upwards as I went. Out of the corner of my eye I could see Feeney coming towards me, while straight ahead was the massive frame of Joe Corrigan. If Joe had been more decisive, he'd have got there first, but he held off just a second, just long enough for me to reach the ball a moment before he did, a tiny weeny insignificant moment, nothing in the great encyclopaedia of time, but long enough for me to clip the ball over him, hurdle him, and steer the ball into the empty net as Feeney crashed into his own goalkeeper.

I trotted past the mud-splattered defender, grinned at him then shook the hand of Trevor Brooking. 'Well done, Barry,' he said, and I grinned at him as well. 'It's Billy,' I said. 'Billy Parks.'

It was the winning goal.

Afterwards I sat in the changing room, listening to Stevie Kember, Harry and Frankie Lampard; they seemed so confident, so aware, so much bigger and older than me with their skinny ties and winkle picker boots. They were all going to play for Crystal Palace or Chelsea or West Ham. They were all going to be footballers. I thought about my dad. The Hammers were his team. Perhaps I could play for West Ham.

Taffy Watkins stood by the door. 'Parks,' he bellowed, and I looked up as he beckoned me.

'There's someone who wants to meet you, boy,' he said and turned, so I followed him up the corridor, up some stairs and into a lounge bar, which smelled of cigar smoke and booze.

Two men were standing by the bar; by the welcoming looks on their faces I could tell that they were waiting for us to join them.

Taffy led me over. 'This, Billy,' he said proudly, 'is Mr Matt Busby. Mr Busby, this is Billy Parks.'

Matt Busby smiled at me; thinning hair and squint-eyes smiling a lovely warm straight-to-your-soul smile, like the uncle we all wished we'd had.

'Good goal out there, Billy,' he said, or at least that's what I thought he said; to my ear, untrained in Glaswegian, it sounded more like a collection of 'grrs' followed by my name. I nodded, though, and smiled, and muttered something about it being difficult conditions as I sensed that Taffy wanted me to sound vaguely intelligent and interested.

'Billy,' he continued, 'we'd like you to come up to Manchester for a week's trial at our football club, Manchester United, next week. Would you like that?'

Taffy answered for me. 'Of course you would, wouldn't you, boy?' he said. And I smiled again.

Of course I would.

Manchester United.

Manchester bloody United. Of course I wanted to go there. Sod West Ham. Man United – Busby Babes, Bobby Charlton, Denis Law, plane crashes, FA Cups – I would have crawled there. This was going to be brilliant. Taffy beamed down at me, Matt Busby beamed down at me; I beamed at me, all the gods in their heavens beamed down at me. It was all going to be brilliant. I was going to be a Busby Babe. I was going to play for Manchester United and win the FA Cup.

I got the tube and the bus back to Stratford. I wanted to tell my mother. I wanted to tell her more than anything. This would surely make her happy. I rushed through the front door. Exhilarated. The house was dark, still, lifeless. 'Mum,' I yelled, there was no answer. 'Mum,' I yelled again, 'I'm going to play for Manchester United.' Again, no answer. I screamed up the dark and silent stairs. 'I've just met Matt Busby and I'm going to play for Manchester United.'

Silence.

I went up to her bedroom and stood by her closed door. I wanted to turn the handle. To rush in and tell her my news: I was going to be a professional footballer. I knew I was, and with Man United. But the door was closed and I'd never disturbed my mother in her room, and I never would, it just wasn't right. I decided to save my news for the next morning.

At breakfast, I told her; not in the euphoric way I'd wanted, but in a quiet, brooding, matter-of-fact way. She stood with her back to me by the sink. 'I've been asked to go to Manchester next week for a trial with United,' I told her. But she didn't turn towards me. The only reaction was the sudden stillness of her arms as she stopped drying the plate she was holding.

'Matt Busby was at the game last night,' I added. 'I scored a goal.'

She turned towards me now, her eyes dark-red and lined, her mouth trembling.

'Manchester?' she said.

'Yes,' I gushed, trying to express the brilliance of my news in that single word. 'Manchester United.'

'But, Billy,' she said, her voice fragile and tiny, 'Manchester's so far away. I mean, couldn't you play with one of the local clubs? Your cousin has been playing at Barking.'

'Barking!' I said. 'But this is *Manchester United*.'

'Yes, but Manchester is in the north,' she said, tears pricking her eyes. 'It's so far away. It's not for you, Billy.'

She started to cry.

Why? Why was she crying? Why wasn't she happy for me? For us? I didn't bloody understand.

'I thought you'd be pleased,' I said. 'I mean, they're a really big club, they're Manchester United, and if I got an apprenticeship, I'd be on good money and everything. I've heard the apprentices get four pound a week.'

My words vanished in the air between us. Still she said nothing, she just stood silently by the sink holding a plate and a faded blue and white tea-towel.

'I'd be back all the time,' I said. 'Manchester's not far away.'

She turned away from me and went back to the washing up.

I sighed.

I got up and walked out of the kitchen. I had injured her. We had injured each other. But I was undeterred. As far as I was concerned, I was going to Manchester.

I trained all day, I trained all night; down my park kicking my football against trees, joining in any games I could find then returning home to my back yard where I'd kick 200 times with my right foot, 200 times with my left against the target on the back gate. Now, I never missed.

My mate Johnny Smith, the best of boys, helped me. He got the ball when I kicked it into the rough; he ran with me when I was getting tired; crossed it in to help my heading and my control – listened to my dreams and matched them with his own smiling excitement.

'Will you meet Bobby Charlton?' he asked.

'Oh yeah,' I said, though I had no idea. 'I'll meet them all won't I, Bobby Charlton, Denis Law, John Connelly, Nobby Stiles.'

'What will you say to Bobby Charlton?'

'I'll say, Bobby, have you ever thought about a wig?'

In school Taffy Watkins told me that everything was organised: I would get the train from St Pancras at 7pm on the Sunday; I would stay at a boarding house owned by a Mrs Fullaway, in Stretford, with some other lads, one of whom Taffy told me was called George Best who apparently I could learn a lot from. I didn't know who George Best was, but I was excited. It was all arranged. I got called into the headmaster's room for a pep talk: 'Remember, you're representing the school,' he told me. 'Yes, Sir,' I replied brightly but dishonestly: because I knew, even then, that really, I was doing everything for me, Billy Parks.

On the Saturday morning I packed my stuff in a little tartan suit-case: my best suit, my school uniform, my polished and dubbined boots, shorts and top; everything I thought I'd need.

My mother wasn't talking to me, and Taffy had warned me against playing that Saturday, just in case I got injured before my trial. 'Go and do something else,' he'd said.

'Like what?' I asked.

'Use your imagination,' he replied, 'fishing or something, anything where you can't break a leg.'

I didn't fancy fishing. I wanted to do something exciting. I wanted adventure. So, I left our house and took a ride up West. Why? I never did that. Why that day?

I arrived before lunch then hung around, wandering about Leicester Square and Carnaby Street. Why? I'd never shown any interest in those places before? Why that day? Why that bloody day?

If. If. If.

If I had stayed at home, if I hadn't stayed out so long watching the Mods and Teddy Boys on the King's Road, if I hadn't been smiling at the girls in their tiny skirts, if I hadn't been looking at the fancy restaurants and bars and imagining how I'd soon be there, me, Billy Parks a professional footballer with Manchester United, if I hadn't done any of this, I might have been able to stop her; things might have been different. It's a shit word 'if'. You never get a bloody straight answer from a question that starts with 'if'.

I didn't get back until late.

And that's when I found her slumped in the bathroom, damp with her own piss and blood.

Lucky you came home when you did, they told me at the hospital. *She must have fallen and banged her head*, they told me. *If it wasn't for you*, they said, *she would have bled to death. She's a very lucky lady.*

It wasn't lucky for me.

It wasn't lucky for me at all. It was bloody tragic for me.

My train left St Pancras for Mrs Fullaway's and Manchester United as I sat by my mother's bed, cursing my sister who'd run away, cursing my father who'd gone to Burma to mend tanks and been captured and ended up in the bloody pissing canal, and cursing my poor bloody mother who lay there shaking and dribbling.

I couldn't bring myself to tell Taffy the truth, so, instead, I just didn't go back to school for two weeks. And when I did, Taffy Watkins ignored me and the Headmaster gave me six of his bloody best. I was banned from playing football for the school team again.

Details: Match 3, 15 October 1964
Venue: White Hart Lane, Tottenham
London Boys 1 v. Manchester Boys 0
Parks

Line Ups
London Boys: Walton, Clement, Went, Kitchener, Lampard, Redknapp, Fisher, Brooking(c), Parks, Kember, Carmichael
Manchester Boys: Corrigan, Feeney, Singleton, Williams, Booth(c), Wilkie, Johnson, Towers, Paddon, Bowles, Kidd

Attendance: 3,475

9

Christ it is a cold morning. My breath plumes out before me as I walk down to the bus stop and wait with a couple of old ladies and a surly-looking black boy who, despite wearing a massive padded coat, is shivering against the cold.

I take the bus to Lewisham, then the train to Beckenham, then a cab to the road where I hope she still lives; Brompton Street, a collection of neat former council houses, the type of houses where some of the owners put fake plastic butterflies on the outside walls and mock wooden shutters over the windows: you could be happy here.

I stand for a few seconds at the top of the road. How long had it been – four, five years? I'm not sure. I can still remember the stinging way in which she had told me to sling my hook, though: get out of her life and the life of her son she'd said, and that still hurt. But, it would be different now; now, I was going to have a second chance.

I look around and notice a pub on the corner of the road – The Tollington Perspective – I don't remember a pub by that name. I look away, then find myself drawn to it again: dark windows and a double door, inside I know there would be brass taps and full, still optics, and a barmaid with a low-cut vest top and blokes who were hiding in the gloom who would know me and understand.

The Tollington Perspective: odd name for a boozer. It wasn't for me though, it couldn't be. Dr Aranthraman had said *one more drink could kill you, Billy*. And anyway, I had more important things to do.

Maybe later.

I steady myself, take a deep breath and walk up to the door of number 16 Brompton Street: this was the address, but there are four flats. I try to remember which one was hers. Bollocks. I have no idea. Bloody hell. All I can remember are the tears and Rebecca shouting, 'Just. Go. Dad.' I chase that image out of my mind. That was years ago; now things are going to be different: Gerry Higgs had said so.

Was it Flat B or C?

I press B.

There is no answer. I press C. Again, nothing. I press A and D together. I need a drink, I need a bloody drink: I can taste drink.

A voice answers: foreign, definitely not Rebecca.

'Hello?'

'Er, hello, I'm looking for my daughter …'

'She doesn't live here.'

'Yes, I realise that; I think that she lives in one of these flats, her name's Rebecca, Rebecca Parks, or perhaps, Rebecca Leadbetter, that's her mother's name. I was wondering … She's got a little boy; he'd be about twelve now.'

The voice comes back, 'She doesn't live here.'

'Yes, I realise …'

My voice trails off and I stop talking as the intercom crackles for a second then dies.

I walk back to the road, the pain in my legs suddenly becoming un-bloody-bearable. There is a bench by some swings so I stagger across the road and sit down.

Perhaps if I wait here I will eventually see her.

I wait.

Mums come with kids and play on the park swings. Little kids run around in their little multi-coloured clothes, falling off the roundabout and squealing, then laughing, then crying. I watch a couple of small boys, about eight years old, kicking a football to one another. They stab at the ball with the front of their feet; first lesson of football, learn to kick with your instep, that way you get your weight properly over the ball, that way you can keep control of it, that way you make it yours. I'm half tempted to go over and tell them.

I scan the playground searching for Rebecca; as I do, I notice that some of the mums have gathered together and are talking. They keep looking over to me. I wonder if they know me, recognise me from the paper. Or perhaps some of them recognise me as Rebecca's dad. Yes, that must be it; that must be why they keep looking over: they know Becky and had seen the family resemblance.

I decide to go over to them and make some enquiries. As I rise to my feet, I feel a searing pain in my right knee: bloody Paul Reaney! I feel my face grimace, then I limp towards the group of women. As I do so two of them break off from the group and walk a few steps towards me; one is a large, fiercesome-warrior lady with her hair swept back in a ponytail and massive ham joints for calves that are encased in black leggings. She speaks with a rasping and aggressive voice that takes me by surprise.

'I don't know who you are, but this is a kiddies' playground and unless you've got kids here, you should go somewhere else.'

Instinctively I turn around, assuming that she must be talking to someone else, someone behind me, but she isn't, she is talking to me.

'I'm just waiting for my daughter,' I say. I can hear my voice, weak and feeble.

'Who's your daughter?' says the other lady, who is wearing a red cagoule and glasses that give her a startled look.

'Becky,' I say. 'Becky Parks, I'm her father, Billy Parks, you might have heard …'

'Where does she live?' asks warrior lady abruptly and I can't answer. I can only point pathetically towards the row of houses up the street. Where is she? Why isn't she walking up here now?

'I know everyone in this street,' continues warrior lady, 'and there's no one called Becky Parks lives round here.'

'I think you should go,' says glasses lady.

'Why?' I ask, and now I can see that six more mums have joined the two in the advance party and have formed a resolute barrier like a herd of water buffalo protecting their calves from a mangy old hyena.

'This is a kiddies' playground,' says one.

'We don't want your sort round here,' says another.

My sort. What the fuck does that mean?

'Have you phoned the police, Angie?' says another.

The police, fucking hell, what did they want the police for?

I turn away from them, confused. What have I done? Behind me I can hear muttering condemning voices. 'And don't come back here again,' comes a shout.

I start to walk up the road, my knees seizing in the cold morning, causing me to lurch then limp. I know that they will be standing their ground. I can still hear them, I know that they are watching me as I limp away.

I walk towards The Tollington Perspective. It's midday now and the pub has opened its wonderful doors; in there I would be safe, there would be no confusion. As I reach the pub I look around, the women are still looking at me.

It is an easy decision. I go straight through the front doors, through the heavenly gates and immediately immerse myself in the wonderful warm aroma of the pub with its breathless atmosphere of old fags and yeast and loud nights and spilled beer, sealed in for ever by a lack of light and a sticky carpet.

A man is sitting on his own by the bar, a pint in front of him.

70

As I walk in, he looks at me then looks away. I stand by the bar, breathing heavily and a barman makes his way towards me. The man with the pint turns to me again.

'I know who you are,' he says. 'Ain't you Billy Parks?'

'Yes,' I reply, 'that's me.' And my whole body warms with a feeling of complete and utter wonderfulness.

'My old man used to take me to see you at the Orient back in the day,' he tells me.

'Did he?' I reply. 'You don't get football like that these days.'

'No,' he says. 'I always wondered what happened to you. Do you want a drink?'

'That's very good of you, old son,' I say, and then, without a thought, without a moment's bloody thought for Dr Aranthraman and my new liver and my daughter and Gerry Higgs or Maureen or anything, the words 'I'll have a scotch', slip off my tongue.

10

Tottenham could have had me for free in March 1965, but they said that I was too small. Too small! I went for a trial and scored a hat-trick of goals including one with my bleeding head! Too small: bollocks.

Arsenal could have had me as well; I went for a trial there a few weeks after Spurs, same day as Pat Rice. I quite fancied the Arsenal; I'd heard that they had a marble bath in the changing rooms and that the apprentices got their own tracksuits with their initials on. I sat on the tube to Highbury and wondered if I'd have WP or BP on mine. But, within the first five minutes of the trial, little Pat Rice, who was even smaller than I was, went through me with a clattering tackle that left me on me arse. These days, he'd have got a red card; back then, he got a round of applause and an extra biscuit with his tea at half-time. The tackle completely put me off my game – I just couldn't play, I couldn't run, I stopped seeing the ball early, my first touch went, and then, when my game was going to pieces, I started to try too hard, and this just got me into a bigger fix, running around in a blind panic, up and down, round and round and into pointless positions. It was the first time that a single tackle had done this to me. I'd be lying if

I said it was the last. But you all know that because every critic has said so at some point.

Needless to say, Arsenal weren't interested. I suppose it was fate – Pat Rice went on to play a million games for them, I went home with my tail between my legs and a bloody great bruise on my thigh.

So, when I left school in 1965 I found myself looking for a proper job. Bloody hell. I had no idea; I had no plans, no qualifications and no clue. I'd assumed that I would become a footballer. But that hadn't happened. Not then. Not yet.

On the first morning after I'd left school I took myself down to my local park with the intention of joining in a game, just as I had always done. Somehow, though, it didn't seem right; now I was no longer a schoolboy, playing games seemed wrong, pointless. So instead I sat alone on a swing, contemplating my life, before traipsing back home where I found my Aunty Peggy and Uncle Eric sitting in our lounge. There was an uncomfortable atmosphere.

My mother hadn't made them a cup of tea.

She was sitting there, thin lipped and brimming with violent resentment on the edge of her seat.

'Hello, Billy,' said my uncle as I walked in. He was clearly relieved that I had arrived to warm the room. Aunty Peggy smiled wanly at me. She was still an attractive woman, but, perhaps, had lost some of the exuberant lustre I remembered as a boy. Not as much as my poor mum, though: my mum was four years her junior, but she looked about a dozen years older, sitting there in an old cardigan scowling at the sister who hadn't lost her husband, the sister who didn't need a tonic to get through the day. She sat sucking on the end of a cigarette and looking towards the wall, as Aunty Peggy told her about the twins who were about to do 'A' levels and go off to university to study chemistry or physics or something. I stood there quietly still holding my pointless football.

Uncle Eric, bless him, was desperately uncomfortable. I could tell that he just wanted to move the conversation away from whatever it was that had come between my mother and his wife and go home.

'You still playing football then?' he said and I shrugged; I had been rejected, I had no team and my moments of introspection on the swing had provided me with no answers as to the path down which my future lay. I was clueless.

He tried another topic of conversation. 'Your mother was just telling us how you are looking for work.' The words tumbled out as though the quicker he spoke the sooner he could leave. I told him that I was.

'Well,' he continued, 'how would you like to come and work for me?'

Instinctively I looked at my mum, to see what she thought, to see if she wanted me to take up an offer of work in my Uncle Eric's bakery. She said nothing. Her expression did not change. I shrugged, and nodded and thanked him; it wasn't quite what I had in mind, but it was better than nothing.

After about another twenty minutes of seething bitterness punctuated by poor Uncle Eric trying to make conversation, our guests got up to go. As they reached the door, my aunty turned to my mum. 'If not for you, do it for him,' she said, pointing at me. But my mother didn't react.

When they'd left I asked her why they'd come round, and she snorted derisively. 'They came to save us,' she said, spitting out the words, before disappearing upstairs.

And so, for want of anything better to do, and thanks to Aunty Peggy and Uncle Eric's apparent desire to save me, I went to work in Uncle Eric's bakery. Now, I have to admit that even though I wasn't particularly excited by the prospect of starting my post-school life as a van-driver's mate in a small family bakery in Essex, I look back fondly at the few months I spent there.

I cycled to work every morning and home every night and spent the day loading and unloading the van: it was the best training I could have wished for. I didn't know it, but the act of lugging great bags full of flour in and out of a Humber van, whilst eating more bread and cake than I could ever imagine, swiftly transformed my emaciated form and gave me the strength I needed to make sure that the likes of Pat Rice would never easily knock me off a ball again.

But it wasn't really the food or my inadvertent training regime that lit up my time with Harvey's Bakery; Harvey's Bakery took me away from life in our unhappy house and into a meaningful happy world. Perhaps it was the closest I would ever come to contentment.

On my first morning, I met Uncle Eric in the car park. He led me through the factory, past staring workers wearing hair-nets or white hats that accentuated large, lively, interested eyes.

'Is that the new boy, Mr Harvey?' someone shouted.

'Yes, this is my nephew Billy,' said Uncle Eric.

'He looks like he needs feeding up,' said a giggling female voice.

I smiled as a little coterie of ladies in white coats and hats grinned and cooed at me.

There were proper characters working in that bakery, real people, the salt of the earth. People like Harry Blackstone, who was about 102 and a Master Baker despite only having the two outer fingers on one hand after he lost the others at Passchendaele.

A lovely fella was Harry, a true hero: 'If I hadn't put me fingers in the way,' he told me later, chuckling to himself, as he showed me the space on his hand where the missing digits should have been, 'the Gerry bullet would have ended up in me head.'

I looked at him as he skilfully iced some fairy cakes; a proper hero, who had won the Victoria Cross by taking out a German trench, armed with only a spade – or was it a brush? I can't remember.

Then there was Veronica, who called everyone 'darlin''. She had a deep guttural laugh to go with a filthy sense of humour that would have made a welder blush. And the lovely Tina, who knew full well that her smile and magnificent chest awakened in me feelings I had never had before – the little minx. And the massive Bernie Parfitt, who had a glorious handlebar moustache and mutton chops to match and liked to sing Salvation Army hymns as he kneaded his dough.

But the person who I remember most fondly was Barry Ross. Uncle Eric introduced me to Barry on my first morning. He was sitting in the canteen, smoking a fag and listening to a transistor radio.

'This is my nephew Billy,' said my uncle. 'It's his first day, so make sure you look after him.'

Barry grinned at me. 'Hello Billy,' he said. 'I'm Barry Ross.'

In the space of a few minutes Barry became my older brother, my captain, my mentor: twenty-five years old with a quiffed DA hair-cut that was about five years out of fashion and a pair of skin-tight trousers and beetle-crusher shoes that were coated with a ghostly layer of flour; twenty-five and in the prime of his life, no responsibilities and a twinkle in his eye that would light up the dourest of Essex mornings. Barry Ross was Mick Jagger and Michael Caine and George Best all rolled into one, devouring all that life had to offer out of the back of a baker's van.

He offered me a cigarette – which I took, even though I didn't smoke.

Then, as we sat in the van, he outlined his philosophy on the world. 'You are a very lucky boy, Billy,' he told me. 'You have been given the chance to embark upon the greatest life known to man.'

'What, baking bread?'

'Baking bread! No,' he said, 'the life of a delivery driver.'

'Oh.'

'Unleashed and unshackled, my son, unleashed and unshackled; as long as you do your round, London is your playground.'

'Oh,' I repeated.

And Barry was right.

Over the next few months he introduced me to the wonderful life of a delivery van driver in the midst of the swinging sixties: bloody marvellous.

Each day would start with a trip to the bookie's where Barry would place his bets for the day. 'Never bet too high, and never bet too low,' he told me about the odds and the stake. It seemed incredibly wise advice to me.

Then we would deliver to shops and bakeries and schools and factories, where we would be welcomed by foremen with clipboards and frowning shopkeepers and fawning old ladies who would swoon as Barry flirted with them. We would have breakfast at 8am, a brew at 10 and every lunchtime a couple of pints in some of the finest pubs you could wish to visit: The Copper Wheel in Romford, with its collection of bikers out the front; the William IV in Leyton, where you could get a bacon and egg sandwich served on a piece of wood; the Lord Cecil in Hackney, with the lovely Vera who wore red plastic boots and the tiniest skirt, and Jeremy, perhaps the world's only blind barman. I could go on; each pub came with a comely barmaid and bottle of ale and a collection of lads who would know Barry and welcome him like a brother. In fact, everyone seemed to know Barry, everyone had a tale to recall with him, an anecdote to develop:

'Do you remember that time we were in Margate?'

'What about when we picked up those dolly birds down Walthamstow?'

'I've got a tip for you Barry, my old son: the four o'clock at Kempton …'

Barry Ross sucked the marrow out of every day, and I was his mate, his pupil, his eager little brother. He would impart upon me the wisdom and cunning he had picked up and all I had to do in return was keep quiet about the half an hour or so during every afternoon when Barry would disappear for a bit of 'how's your father' with one of the many women he had on the go, because Barry's greatest pursuit in life was sex.

Without fail, every afternoon, he would happily vanish through the windowed front door of some suburban semi-detached, or into the back room of a shop, or the shadowed darkness of an alleyway, as I sat blissfully content and non-judgemental in the van, reading the sports pages of the *Daily Mirror*. Sometimes I would catch a glimpse of the object of his affections – a woman waiting by the front door or appearing briefly from behind a net curtain.

'How come you've got so many birds on the go, Barry?' I asked him.

'You can't have too many birds, Billy-boy,' he replied. 'It's nature, it's what we are supposed to do as the male species, my son.' And, as with everything else Barry Ross told me, I took that as a piece of absolute unarguable truth even when Barry's afternoons of joy occasionally seemed to leave him subdued and slightly crestfallen or when he got chased by a couple of blokes and had to jump into the van as they hammered the side of it with sticks and bats and we had to tell Uncle Eric that a gang of lads had attacked us for no reason.

Perhaps I enjoyed it all the more for these incidents; after all, these are the memories that stick, these are the moments that made Barry Ross special, these are the events that make life worth all the bother.

Within a few weeks in his company, I had placed my first bet (on a dog called The Ghost who romped home, barking all the way, at the Wednesday evening meet at Romford); I had endured my first hangover after drinking with him and a few of the lads at the Seven Kings in Ilford; and, thanks to Barry, I had enjoyed my first brush with the opposite sex.

We were on our way back from lunch at the Hangman's Noose, just off Bow Road in Tower Hamlets, when he turned to me and announced what was about to happen:

'Do you remember Samantha?' he asked.

I shrugged; all his women were starting to merge into one. 'Yes you do,' he exclaimed, 'the northern bird, from the north, lives above the clothes shop by Bethnal Green Station.'

I was still none the wiser. 'Well, anyway, she's got a friend, and apparently, Billy-boy, this friend's up for anything and wants to meet you.'

The two parts of his statement smashed me in the chest. *Up for anything. Wants to meet me.* I mean, why would any girl who was up for anything want to meet me? I was just a kid; and in any event, I wasn't sure that I knew what 'anything' was.

'Oh,' I said, then I paused, as Barry's white teeth dazzled me in his massive smile.

'You are joking?' I added.

'No,' he said, 'and we're going to see them now.'

'Now.'

'Yes.'

Twenty minutes later, we'd parked the van outside a boutique called Georgina's near to Brick Lane.

'Come on,' said Barry, then seeing my reticence he moved his face closer to mine and repeated slowly and with emphasis: 'Up – for – anything,' and raised his eyebrows.

Minutes later, we were disappearing through the door of a women's boutique. I had never seen anything like it in my life: racks and racks of brightly coloured dresses, blouses and skirts; soft-focus pictures on the walls of beautiful pouting women in fashionable clothes and mannequins with large bosoms wearing just brassieres and panties. In this place I was an alien. Barry was totally at home.

Standing in front of the counter in plastic white knee-high boots and a mini-skirt, was, I presumed, Samantha. She greeted Barry with a high-pitched giggle and a peck on the cheek, before turning to me, as I stood there confused and embarrassed in my oversized delivery overall which had a big smear of cream and jam down the front where I'd earlier spilled a box containing a Victoria sponge.

She smiled, then turned to Barry. 'Ooh,' she said, 'he's lovely, look at that blond hair – he's just like one of the Beach Boys.'

I started to relax and grinned my biggest grin as Samantha

turned the sign on the door to 'Closed' then shouted to someone yet unseen who was behind a curtain in the back of the shop. 'Sandra,' she shouted, 'come out here, Barry's brought a Beach Boy with him.'

Sandra appeared soon after: pretty and brunette with big dark eyes made darker by a fair old coat of mascara. I was petrified. Barry and Samantha seemed pleased.

'How long until his nibs gets back?' said Barry.

'Half an hour,' said Samantha. And with that she took Barry by the hand and led him towards the back of the shop and through the curtain where, I assumed, mysterious pleasures lay in wait. Barry winked lasciviously at me as he followed her.

I was now left alone with Sandra. She looked at me in a rather dismissive way that didn't suggest for one second that she was 'up for anything' or that 'she wants to meet' me.

'What's your name then?' she asked in a northern accent.

I didn't answer. Instead, overcome with nerves, inexperience, and by the fact that I was surrounded by women's underwear, I charged headlong for her and tried to grab her. Adroitly, she sidestepped me, grabbing my arm as she did and placing me in a tight arm lock.

'Easy,' she said, scowling.

'I'm sorry,' I stuttered. 'Barry said you wouldn't mind.'

'Did he now?'

'Yeah. He said you'd be up for anything.'

'Well perhaps Barry should have asked me first,' she replied.

'I'm sorry,' I repeated and she let me go, pushing me away into the middle of the shop.

'You dozy bastard.'

'I'm sorry,' I repeated, pathetically. Then her lips thinned as she considered me.

'What's your name?' she asked again.

'Billy,' I said. 'Billy Parks.'

'And how old are you, Billy Parks?'

81

'I'm sixteen.'

'Well, Billy Parks,' she continued, 'you haven't got a clue about girls, have you?'

She was right.

'You can't just go charging in like a bull in a china shop.'

I felt my head go down.

'You're lucky I didn't hit you with the charity box.'

I spied the box for Dr Barnardo's on the counter; it looked pretty solid. I *was* lucky that she hadn't hit me with it.

'I could call the coppers.'

'Don't call the coppers,' I begged.

'I've got a good mind to.'

'Please,' I said. 'I'm sorry.'

She harrumphed and put her hands on her hips.

'What were you thinking?'

I shrugged as she sighed.

'Look,' she said, 'do you want a fag?'

She took one herself and passed one to me. I took this to be a good sign that she was no longer considering beating me across the head or calling the police. I smiled weakly at her.

'Where are you from?' I asked.

'Oldham.'

'As in Athletic?'

'As in Lancashire.'

'I didn't think you were from round here.'

'No,' she said. 'I've been here eight months.'

'Why?' I asked. 'Why did you leave home and come here?'

She took a big gulp on her cigarette. 'I'm going to be a model,' she said, without a hint of doubt in her voice.

'What, like in catalogues and that?'

'Yes,' she said. 'Something like that. There's a bloke me and Sammy met in Leicester Square, he said he wants to take some photos of us, for a portfolio like.'

I didn't really understand what she was talking about, but she

82

sounded so confident, so utterly at ease with her dream that I just nodded. Upstairs, the bed started creaking rhythmically. We both looked up, then away in embarrassment. It was awkward. I felt I was in a small box surrounded by something I didn't quite understand – sex.

'So how long have you been working with Barry then?' she asked, trying to talk above the sound of Barry and Samantha's rapture.

'A couple of months.'

'And do you enjoy it, delivering bread?'

I shrugged. 'I suppose. It's a laugh.'

'A laugh,' she repeated. I recognised the tone of her voice; it was dismissive and condescending, it told me that delivery boys like me didn't end up with would-be models like her. 'Don't you want to do anything else?' she added.

I shrugged again. I did. I wanted to play football. But somehow, standing there in that women's clothes shop, in my stained overalls, that fantasy seemed ridiculous – I seemed ridiculous. She smiled at me.

'Look,' she said, 'next time, you need to find a girl your own age.'

I looked down at my feet.

'And when you do,' she continued, her voice was now warm and treacly, 'you need to court her, proper like, take her to the picture house, or a coffee shop or summat. Not just grab her.'

I wanted Barry to come back now; I wanted to get away from this conversation more than anything in the world. I wanted to go outside, I wanted to kick a football against my back gate. I knew all about that. That was something I could do better than anyone else. Two hundred times, bang, bang, bang. That was something I understood.

Barry eventually emerged about five excruciating minutes later, minutes in which Sandra had told me all about the types of films that girls would like to go to: *A Hard Day's Night* by the Beatles would be preferable, James Bond would be alright, but definitely no cowboy films and none of those funny foreign films. Barry later told me that that had been a cue for me to ask her out and that I had missed my chance. I wasn't sure.

It had changed things, though; the episode in the boutique had made things somehow different. I had had a little glimpse of Barry's world and somehow I didn't think it would be enough for me.

Thankfully, the next day things changed again.

I was cycling home. It was late August and the nights were starting to draw in. As I approached our road, Johnny Smith, my old mate from school who had masqueraded as Stanley Matthews in my very first game of football, was stood waiting for me. Ah, Johnny Smith, his eyes shining, just as they had in all the games we'd played together. No one else trusted me like he did, the poor tragic bastard. I smiled as I approached him. I hadn't seen him for a while, but I knew that he had been playing regular football for some team up in Hackney and had been for trials with the Orient.

'Hello, Billy,' he said, his face breaking out into its usual wonderful warm smile. I smiled back and returned his greeting.

'How's work?' he asked.

'Alright,' I said, pulling out a box of faulty chocolate éclairs from a bag that was dangling from my handlebars. 'Cake?'

Johnny took one and thanked me.

'Look,' he said, 'what are you doing tomorrow afternoon?'

'I'll be in work,' I said, 'but I finish at two on a Saturday. Why?'

'I've been playing for the Orient,' he said, 'only their reserves like, but they've told me that if I do alright, they'll give me an apprenticeship.'

'That's great,' I said. I was jealous. I was jealous as hell. It was a spiky jealousy – the worst kind. I didn't resent Johnny, no, he was a true diamond; I just resented his good fortune. He was going to be a footballer: I was going to deliver cakes and bread.

'Look,' he said, 'we're short of a player tomorrow, so I told them about you – I told them you had played for London Schools and should have gone for a trial at Man United and everything, and they want you to come along. It's a great chance, Billy.'

I looked at him smiling beseechingly at me, then I looked away – I didn't know. It would mean bunking off work. But it wasn't that that bothered me. I knew, plainly and simply, that if Leyton Orient didn't want me, then that would be the end. I knew that. And that thought was the scariest thought of all.

'I'm too small,' I told him. 'Tottenham said so.'

'Sod Tottenham,' said Johnny. 'What do they know?'

'And I was rubbish when I went to Arsenal for a trial.'

'Everyone has an off day, Billy – even you.'

I snorted. 'I dunno, mate.'

'Yes you do, Billy. Look, meet me at Leyton tube tomorrow – half one.'

I puffed my cheeks out then exhaled slowly. Then I smiled. 'Who are we playing?'

'Good boy,' he said, 'we're playing Tottenham.'

We both laughed.

The next day, I skipped work. I didn't attempt to explain my absence or phone in sick or anything, I just didn't turn up. I feel bad about that – I know that Uncle Eric and Barry and Harry Blackstone and all the others would have been pretty supportive. I know that the girls on cakes would have probably given me a couple of apple and almond turnovers to 'keep me going', and Bernie Parfitt would have burst into a rendition of 'Abide With Me', but I just didn't tell them. Instead I packed my boots in my kit bag and went to meet Johnny Smith at Leyton Station. It was easier that way, no fuss, but, more importantly, no explanations if things didn't go well.

Johnny was waiting for me there.

'Alright?'

'Yep.'

'What did you tell your boss?'

'Nothing, he was fine about it,' I lied.

'Anyway, mate,' said Johnny, grinning at me, 'you won't be there for much longer.'

85

I smiled and we fell into our favourite conversation about what we were going to do when we were famous footballers.

'I'm going to buy a Roller.'

'Yeah, I'm going to go on holiday to Spain on an aeroplane.'

'I'm going to score a goal for England against Brazil at Wembley.'

'And win the World Cup, me and Jimmy Greaves up front.'

We laughed.

Then, as we walked into Brisbane Road, ramshackle home of Second Division Leyton Orient, my excitement suddenly and without warning waned and a feeling of desperation landed on my shoulders: I knew that this was my last chance. The fantasies stopped and thoughts of hopeless desolation took over. That was always the way it was with me; never nerves, just occasionally a black sadness before or during a game, as I grappled with the reality that failure would mean an endless abyss of nothing.

No one ever guessed that I was feeling that.

We walked into the changing rooms. Some of the lads were already getting into their kits, gnarled old men reaching the end of their days and hoping for another contract and young wannabes full of hopes for their future. Two men stood by a door; one wore a tracksuit and a trilby hat and had mad eyebrows, thick hair, and the expression of a lunatic, the other was in short-sleeves and a club tie and seemed quieter, more restrained.

'That's Mr Sexton, the manager,' whispered Johnny.

'Which one?' I asked.

'The one without the hat,' he answered. 'The one with the hat is Gerry Higgs.'

'What does he do?'

'He shouts,' replied Johnny with a grin.

And then, as if on cue, the man Johnny had told me was called Gerry Higgs shouted across the changing room at us. 'Ah, Smith,' he boomed, 'is this your mate? The one who was supposed to have a trial with Manchester United?'

'Yes, Mr Higgs,' said Johnny.

And with this, Gerry Higgs and the other man, Mr Sexton, looked cautiously at me.

'Why didn't you go, son?' asked Mr Higgs.

I shrugged. 'It's a long way from our house, Mr Higgs,' I said but he didn't seem to find it funny. He turned to Johnny. 'Right, son,' he said, 'you'll play outside-right, today,' and he handed him a number 7 shirt. 'You,' he said to me, 'will fill in at right-back. Alright?'

My heart sank. In fact, every one of my organs sank. The despondency that had settled on my shoulders as I walked into the car park now weighed like a hood full of granite: right-back! He may as well have been condemning me to a lifetime of dubious bread-making adventures as Barry Ross's wing-man.

'Alright?' Mr Higgs repeated.

I nodded.

I held the number 2 shirt that Gerry Higgs had handed me; immediately, it became an object for everything that was wrong in my life. It became my dead father and my drunken mother and my joyless lack of experience. I hated it. Number 2. Number 2, right-back, a purely functionary position; the right-back was never the source of adulation. No one ever ruffled the hair of the number 2. Right-backs never scored goals or heard the sound of glorious exaltation; the right-back was never loved in the way I wanted to be loved, the way I needed to be loved.

'Come on then,' yelled Gerry Higgs, and slowly I put on the shirt.

The first half went badly. It was a scrappy affair. Tottenham were obviously trying out some new lads, while most of the Orient boys were more interested in impressing the watching new manager, Dave Sexton, than playing like a team. And as for me, the only thing I did was take a couple of throw-ins and help our goalie off his backside after he'd let in the second goal from a corner.

We traipsed in for a half-time orange – two goals down.

Gerry Higgs gave us a dressing down about us not trying and how none of us were anywhere near good enough to play for the first team and how if it was up to him he'd make us all go and paint the main stand rather than go out for the second half.

Then Mr Sexton took over. He was calm and impressive. 'Look,' he said, 'don't worry about the result for now – what I want to see is a performance. I want to see you get the ball on the deck and start to use it. Remember what we've started to do in training, pass and run, pass and run, pass and run. It's a simple game, gents.'

Gerry Higgs took over again. 'Now has anyone got anything to say?'

The lads muttered negatively and got on with the job of staring down at their laces. I, nervously, put my hand up. 'Mr Sexton?' I ventured.

Gerry Higgs looked scornfully at me. In fact, the whole changing room looked scornfully at me. 'I was wondering,' I continued, 'could I have a half up front? I've played against this centre-half before, he's slow. I think I could do him.'

I hadn't meant to say it. It was the spontaneous last plea of a desperate sixteen-year-old boy. I should have been given a hiding by the more senior players; I know that at every club I ever played at, there is no way that a sixteen-year-old who'd just turned up to make up the numbers would have got away with that kind of request. I heard the words 'cocky little herbert' uttered from somewhere else in the changing room and they were right, my request should have been dismissed, but it wasn't. Lucky for me, an old pro by the name of Tony Fairly, a bloke who was coming to the end of a rather mediocre and uncelebrated career, took pity on me: 'I'll drop back to full-back,' he said, 'give the lad a chance eh?'

Gerry Higgs looked long and doubtfully at me, then he glanced at Mr Sexton, who shrugged. 'Alright, you,' he said, pointing at me, 'start the second half on the right-hand side of the attack, Johnny, you move over to the left; Dave,' he said, referring to big Dave Lamerton, a huge and remarkably lethargic Scottish centre-forward, 'you stay up front with Colin Flatt. Alright?'

I nodded. The rest of the lads seemed uninterested and uninspired by the changes. But for me, it was massively important – for me it changed everything. Tony Fairly changed everything. If it hadn't been for Tony Fairly (376 appearances and 68 goals for Charlton, Aldershot, Brentford and Leyton Orient), I would have left Brisbane Road that day and slipped into an ordinary and inglorious life: there would have been no more chances.

As it was, I took the field in the second half still wearing the number 2 shirt, but playing on the right wing. I was now rejuvenated. I was now mercurial. I was Billy Parks.

Spurs started to press after half-time, but our lads seemed sharper after Gerry Higgs's roasting and Dave Sexton's wisdom. Our centre-half, Paul Went, won the ball in the air and fed Jimmy Scott who passed nicely out to me. Straight away, I noticed that the Spurs full-back was miles away. I don't know if he was confused at the changes we'd made at half-time, but he'd backed off so far that I now had a clear view up the pitch to goal. I put my head down and accelerated into the Tottenham half, running straight at the full-back, the ball never more than thirty inches from my foot. Amazingly, the full-back continued to back off me. I could now see the route to goal. I could hear the cry from Dave Lamerton to pass it, but there was no way I was going to pass. Passing the ball meant surrendering to normality, passing the ball meant a lifetime in the bakery, or with my mother, or being rejected by girls like Sandra the model from Oldham: there was no way I was going to pass. Instead I dipped my shoulder to the right, then, as the full-back bought the feint that I was going to try to take him on the outside, I cut inside to my left and headed towards goal. I was now on my left foot; I could now see the goal. I formed my body over the ball, pulled back my left foot and fired it like a cannon towards the goal. It seared goal-wards, never rising more than three feet off the ground and nestled perfectly in the corner of the Tottenham net.

That was it.

A few minutes later, I had the ball again; this time, the Tottenham full-back was on me, I knew he wasn't going to fall for the same trick twice, so, I did him the other way, dipping my shoulder to my left, then taking him on the outside and charging to the by-line. I would now have to cross with my weaker right foot – I knew I could do it, though; the tens of thousands of times I'd kicked my ball against my back gate meant that I had no concerns about my weaker foot. I even knew the best type of cross, arched and airy, rather than hard and flat or low across the box. I knew that a lofted cross would give big Dave Lamerton more time to get on the end of it, and I was right – I wafted it over and he arrived at the far post and steered it across the line (unfortunately for big Dave, he used his face rather than his head, and emerged from the ground after the goal with a big smile and his nose bloodied and bashed across his big Scottish fizzog). He came over and ruffled my hair. 'Brilliant cross, son,' he growled. 'What did you say your name was?'

'Billy Parks,' I said.

We drew two all, and I was summoned into a small back room by Mr Sexton and Mr Gerry Higgs.

Mr Sexton sat behind a desk. Mr Higgs stood by his side.

'Well,' said Dave Sexton, 'I think your career as a defender is pretty much over, don't you?'

'Yes, Sir,' I said.

'Two footed, eh?'

'Yes, I suppose,' I added, as Mr Sexton placed his chin in his hand and stared at me considering carefully if his instinct was right. He looked at Gerry Higgs who returned a look of resigned encouragement.

Mr Sexton continued. 'What are you doing now, then?' he asked and I told him that I hadn't long started as an apprentice at a bakery. He asked me how much I was on, so I told him, 'Three quid a week, Mr Sexton.'

'Alright,' he said, 'well, if you want to join us, we'll match that.'

I felt my face break into a great sun-beaming smile. Brilliant. I was overjoyed. I shook them both by the hand and I signed there and then, the pen shaking in my hand as I wrote my name: Billy Parks.

Now, I had a professional football club. Now, everything was going to be fantastic.

Details: Match 4, 21 August 1965
Venue: Brisbane Road, Leyton
Leyton Orient Res 2 v. Tottenham Hotspur 'A' 2

Parks	Richards
Lamerton	Weller

Line Ups
Orient: Ramage, Parks, Rofe, Went, Taylor, Street, Scott, Smith, Flatt, Lamerton, Fairly
Tottenham 'A': Brown, Barton, Whisley, Hoy, Jenkins, Low, Pratt, Pitt, Weller, Bartholomew, Richards

Attendance: 92

11

The duvet is crisp and plump and warm and fresh. I know straight away that I am not in my own bed. For a few seconds I feel safe and happy and clean; then my eyes focus on pieces of jigsaw that lie on the floor and something moves in my memory causing a great slag heap of black, slurry-like guilt to slip and overwhelm me. Images form. Horrible ones.

I remember going into The Tollington Perspective and talking, telling stories about myself and Clyde Best and Bobby Moore and Jimmy Greaves as people brought me drinks all the afternoon. Then, other images form in my head: the drinks stopped coming. I remember a taxi journey and being recognised by the driver, who kept telling me that I should go home and sleep it off.

'Come and have a drink with me Mr Taxi Driver old son, come on, I'm Billy Parks, everyone wants to have a drink with me.'

'I think everyone already has had a drink with you. You just go and sleep it off, mate.'

The guilt dances around my consciousness stabbing me as it goes. You stupid, stupid, worthless bastard.

I close my eyes, then move my hand to retrieve a piece of

jigsaw from the small of my back. When I open my eyes I can see that Maureen is standing at the end of the bed.

'You stupid bastard,' she says as though she'd been reading my mind.

'Don't. Please.'

I hold up the jigsaw piece and stare at it; I can just make out the trainers and calves of a runner.

'You brought the jigsaw back here last night,' she tells me, 'but I don't suppose that you remember that.'

I don't.

'You decided that you wanted to do another one. So you could beat the record. Then you staggered around the pub, talking about Poland and Kevin Keegan or something, then you passed out so we brought you up here.'

I wipe my eyes and pain pricks my head – her words also hurt.

'Why are you trying to kill yourself, Billy?' she asks, spitting the question at me.

'I'm not,' I answer. 'Can I have a cup of tea, my mouth feels like a nun's—'

She interrupts my request.

'You stupid bastard. You don't see it do you – if you carry on like this, your liver will pack in and you'll die. It's as simple as that. Just as your doctor told you, just as everyone has told you.'

I nod and look everywhere except at her; at the nice curtains she bought from the haberdasher's in the market, and the slightly aged, but well-kept dressing table, with its bottles and potions of magical renovating creams and liquids, and the pictures of her children on the wall, good-looking kids all of them, and the lampshade that clearly cost a few bob and matches the curtains. Then I sigh.

'Why?' she repeats.

I sigh again and try to create some moisture in my dry mouth before talking.

'I went out to find Becky,' I say slowly, 'but I wasn't too sure of the address, and then some women chased me away from a kiddies' park, threatening to call the police – why would they do that, Mo?'

'Oh, Billy, you muppet, they thought you were an old nonce.'

'What?'

'After their kids.'

'Me, a nonce, a fucking paedowhatsit? Fucking hell!'

Maureen softens. She is now exasperated rather than angry, which makes things a bit easier.

'Why do you want to see Becky all of a sudden?'

'I want to make things right, Mo. I want to find her, but I don't even know where to begin.'

She frowns at me. 'You look terrible,' she says.

I smile, giving her the closest thing to my twinkling smile that I can muster. 'Well don't let that put you off – I'm still more than capable.'

'You must be joking,' she says, 'you've got no chance. First, you can pick up the pieces of that bloody jigsaw that you've strewn all over my pub. Then,' she pauses, and thins her lips before continuing, a friendly reluctance in her voice, 'then, I'll help you find Becky.'

I sit up. 'How?'

'The internet, Billy: you can find anyone these days. But I'll only do it on one condition.'

'Name it.'

'That you'll go to an AA meeting.'

I roll my eyes like an errant teenager. 'Oh come on Maureen, we've had this conversation before, I can't go to one of those meetings, you know what'll happen; someone there will wanna drink with me, talk to me about bloody football, it won't help. It'll just make things worse.'

'That's the deal,' she states firmly. 'If you start going, if you stay dry, I'll help you. Otherwise no deal.'

'Alright, alright, but I tell you, it won't do any good.'

'It will. Now, promise?'

'Yes.'

She smiles, not a full smile, but definitely an improvement. 'Good, there's a meeting on Friday.'

I sigh again.

'You've promised,' she reminds me, 'because Billy, there's no way I'm going to put your Becky back in touch with a drunken bum.'

That hurts.

She leaves the room, leaves me lying there alone – the nice duvet is becoming too hot; the expensive lampshade can't save my eyes from the sharp light that is causing me pain behind my temples. I start to feel uncomfortable. I start to feel ill. I get up and limp into the bathroom and view myself in her mirror. Christ, she is right – I look like shit. My hair is thin and the skin around my eyes seems to hang with the tired-weight of dirty guilt.

A drink would help.

Oh God yes.

The nagging desire creeps into my mind just like it always has, every bloody day, forming itself like an annoying, irritating pain in the fucking arse, tapping and scratching lightly at my thoughts: a drink would help. Just one.

I close my eyes tight and try to chase away the dark thoughts.

Everything's going to be alright, old son; everything's going to be brilliant. Gerry Higgs has told me. I'm Billy Parks and I'm going to get a chance, a second chance.

I try to move my thoughts away from drink. I try to remember that moment before you score a goal, that instant before the ball hits the back of the net. That is the brilliant part, the special second, the immortal moment: the communal inhalation of breath by 40,000 people, the second of stillness, of silence, of hope, of fear – then, then, the roar, that beautiful, bestial roar as the net bulges and they fucking love you. I try to remember that. But even that can't stop the scratching in my head.

I know that I have to get away from Maureen's flat. I can smell the alcohol wafting upwards from the bar; I can sense the movement and noise of people who I know are close by drinking beer and whisky and wine. I have to leave.

I go downstairs, persuade the young Irish barman to pick up the bits of jigsaw that are still lying on the stairs, collect my new jigsaw – 2,000 pieces of Prague Castle By Moonlight (time to beat fourteen hours forty-five minutes) – and start to make my way back home.

Outside, the cool air is initially soothing. I am glad to have left Maureen's pub. Then, as I make my way up the road, my legs start to hurt. By the time I reach my street every step is an effort; sweat cascades down my face and my chest bulges with the effort of still being alive.

Outside my house stands Gerry Higgs.

'Where've you been?' he says without any greeting.

'Hello, Mr Higgs,' I reply. 'I'm glad to see you.'

Which is true; he has promised me everything, and now I want him to deliver.

'I was looking for you yesterday, Billy,' he grunts.

'Why? What's happened? Please don't tell me it's my interview today – I don't feel great.'

'Why? What's wrong with you? You look perfectly well to me.'

'I had a bad night, Mr Higgs.'

'Well, now's not the time for that, Billy – come on.'

'Where are we going?' I asked.

'Park Lane. Café Royal.'

'Blimey – why are we going there?'

'You'll see, Billy, you'll see.' Then he smiles his rather sinister smile. 'Do you remember the last time you were at the Café Royal, Billy?'

I do. But I already know that Gerry Higgs is going to remind me anyway.

'Nineteen seventy-two,' he tells me, and my stomach churns at the memory.

'You were on the shortlist for Player of the Year, at the Orient: we were all very proud.'

'They gave it to Banksy, though,' I say, 'which was fair enough.'

'Gordon Banks was a worthy winner,' he adds, nodding sagely. I wonder if he knows about the incident where me and Alan Hudson and Charlie George were trying to throw stuff into Bill Shankly's soup, and how Shanks had caught me just as I was about to launch a bread roll and came over growling, telling me that I was a disgrace to my club and if I was at his club he'd leave me in the youth team playing in the South Merseyside League, while I was trying not to piss myself laughing.

I regret that now. I bloody regret that now.

We arrive at the Café Royal and sneak in through a back door and down some corridors. I follow Gerry past waiters and workers carrying trays and pushing trolleys.

'Right, Billy,' whispers Gerry, 'this is why we're here: the Council of Football Immortals is having an exclusive lunch in the Gentlemen's Room of the Grill, it's cordoned off by curtains. What we can do is sit behind the curtains, and you'll get to hear what they're thinking through a gap. It should help you.'

This makes perfect sense to me. I would do anything that Gerry Higgs suggested. I nod then whisper to him, 'Gerry, Mr Higgs, do you know when they're going to make their decision?'

'Any day now, Billy. Any day now.'

I nod. This, again, makes sense to me. I question nothing.

We walk up another corridor, into the banqueting suite where, in my beautiful carefree youth, I had cavorted with my mates, then through a door and into the Gentlemen's Room. There, just as Gerry had said, is a heavy, crimson-curtained partition. He leads the way, guiding me quietly, like a child. 'Here we go,' he whispers, pulling the curtains slightly apart and getting a couple of chairs for us to sit on.

'No one will mind, will they?' I ask.

'No,' said Gerry, 'just as long as we're discreet.'

I nod – that was fine by me.

'Can I ask one question, though, Mr Higgs?'

'You can ask.'

'Has Kevin Keegan been here and done this?'

'No, Billy,' he replies, 'he's away in Portugal playing golf.'

'Oh. Right. Of course.'

Cocky, I think to myself.

Gerry has pulled the curtains slightly ajar. I can now see the circular table in the middle of the Gentlemen's Room, around which sit the Council of Football Immortals: Sir Matt Busby, Sir Alf Ramsey, Brian Clough, Bill Shankly and Don Revie. Even repeating their names now sends a shiver up and down my backbone and a tingle in the nape of my neck. The five great generals. Massive beasts all of them. Their decisions had made thousands of men happy or sad. They had created stories that were still remembered, moments of immortality.

From the state of the table, it is clear that they have already finished their lunch and are enjoying their coffee; ghostly waiters busy themselves clearing away bowls that had once contained some kind of chocolate pudding.

I move closer to the curtains; I can't quite hear them, not properly. Don Revie is talking, thrusting his finger in the direction of Brian Clough as he speaks. Clough sits deadpan, a superior smirk playing across his lips. I strain my ears to hear and can just make out Don Revie.

It isn't what I'd expected.

'No, Brian, no, no, no, what's needed is a Nietzschean superman – the type of person, devoid of a conventional sense of morality, who won't be ashamed of the gifts that he possesses.'

'Nietzschean superman?' snorts Clough. 'I don't remember *your* Leeds United possessing many Nietzschean supermen.'

'My Leeds didn't need a superman,' says Revie, sticking his twig-like finger at the table as he talks, 'as you well know, Brian, Nietzsche says clearly in his treatise *On the Genealogy of Morality* that there is only a need for such a person in a weak society, made up of weak people, *rendered* weak by their adherence to

99

Christo-Judaist religion: my Leeds side, which won two League Championships and the FA Cup, was far too strong for that. Sir Alf's England side – no offence, Alf – weren't quite in that position.'

'So, are you suggesting, Don, that my England side, which had won the World Cup only seven years earlier, was so morally weak that only a new superhuman striker could save it?' replies Sir Alf.

'As I said, Alf, no offence meant.'

There is a murmur of response from around the table: Sir Alf Ramsey sits stony-faced; Brian Clough seethes. I turn to Gerry Higgs who is swooning at the assembled greats like a lovesick teenage girl.

'What are they talking about?' I ask.

'Just listen, Billy,' says Gerry without averting his gaze from the Council. 'Just listen.'

Sir Matt Busby speaks next. 'I'm not sure,' he says carefully and quietly, considering every word. 'I think that you might find the dialectical approach as espoused by Hegel to be more useful.'

'I think that we've had enough German philosophers for one night,' says Sir Alf, 'what's wrong with a bit of Hume or Thomas Hobbes, good honest English philosophers?'

'David Hume was Scottish, Alf,' Bill Shankly says.

'Oh bloody hell.'

'Actually though, Matt's got a point about the Hegelian Dialectic,' continues Shanks, 'I always set up my Liverpool teams in a dialectical way: either Peter Thompson or Steve Heighway was the thesis, Tommy Smith or Ron Yeats the antithesis and winning football matches the synthesis.' Bill Shankly seems pleased with this analysis.

I stagger back towards Gerry, whose breath I could feel warm and craggy against my cheek. 'Gerry, what's all this about?' I ask. 'What's it all got to do with the match against Poland, with 1973?'

'Everything, Billy,' says Gerry, his eyes shining in the gloom of the Gentlemen's Room. 'Philosophy is about people, and football is the purest and most successful form of human interaction, my old son.'

I still don't understand, but turn back towards the Council.

'You've got to remember, Alf,' says Brian Clough, 'that there is an awful lot depending on this match.'

'Thank you, Brian, I'm well aware of that.'

'Aye, that's right, Alf, but it goes beyond just football,' adds Shanks, 'if your England team are able to qualify for the World Cup, then the whole history of the country will be different. Perhaps the world.'

'Yes,' says Clough, 'if the goal goes in, and we qualify for the World Cup, we might have a history that doesn't contain Margaret Thatcher.'

'Maggie Thatcher put the backbone back into this country,' bellows Don Revie from across the table.

'I think that's got to be right, Brian,' chips in Sir Alf, 'England was in a terrible mess until Lady Thatcher came along. She did more than anyone to repair the mess.'

The table erupts as Bill Shankly tells them that that woman had done more to destroy this country than even Hitler could have dreamed of, and Brian Clough starts talking about the pit villages of South Yorkshire.

Sir Matt Busby tries to bring the meeting to order. 'Gentlemen, gentlemen,' he says, 'please.'

They quieten, because Sir Matt Busby has that calming effect.

'Gentlemen,' he says, 'let's not lose sight of the aim here: we've got to help Alf make the correct decision in the eightieth minute of a football match and choose the right man to bring on to the pitch. And aye, his decision may, if it's the right one, affect the future of the country. But how that pans out, is something we won't know until afterwards.'

A respectful silence descends on the table as Sir Matt continues, 'Now, we've got just one more meeting in which to get that right, and Alf is correct, the German nihilists are a little, shall we say, stodgy for a must-win match against the Poles in November; perhaps more helpful would be the flair of the Renaissance thinkers

– perhaps we should follow the advice of Niccolò Machiavelli and choose someone who is blessed with a bit of luck and a bit of that indefinable spirit, that unpredictable genius he called *virtù*. After all, whoever we pick will only get the one chance to score the goal that will change everything.'

The rest of the Council murmurs its assent and I look at Gerry whose eyes shine as he stares through the gap in the curtains in blissful rhapsody.

We leave the Café Royal and walk down Park Lane.

I am confused, I don't understand the things that have been said. What was it Sir Matt Busby had called for – luck and a bit of indefinable spirit? Bloody hell. Am I lucky? Do I have that indefinable spirit? What is indefinable spirit?

I turn to Gerry Higgs: 'Gerry,' I say, 'I'm not sure about all of this.'

'What do you mean, Billy? You're not doubting your ability, are you? You, Billy Parks – come on, if anyone can do it, you can.'

I smile weakly. 'It all sounds quite serious, though. I suppose I hadn't realised. Sir Matt said that the goal would change everything.'

'Don't worry about any of that,' Gerry says. 'If they select you, your part is pretty straightforward: you've just got to kick a football. History, old son, will take care of itself.'

I sigh.

'But it will change *my* history, won't it, Gerry? I *can* put things right, can't I?'

Gerry Higgs looks at me. 'Of course, Billy,' he says. 'As I told you, the Service is here to help you. We'll give you the chance,' he pauses in his rather menacing way, 'it's up to you what you do with that chance.'

I go home alone.

My hangover has been sticking to me like swamp mud all day. Various parts of me hurt. I go to bed in the afternoon exhausted and confused. Then awake with the familiar desire for drink clawing at my brain and body, pinching my soul. Bloody, bloody, bloody hell. When will it ever leave me? When will I be cleansed?

I can't do it. I can't allow it. I have to overcome the desire.

Without thinking, I get up, get dressed and walk towards my door. My coat is on a peg. My shoes are waiting by the mat. The Anchor is five minutes' walk away.

I take a deep breath. I can't do it. I can't bloody do it.

I force myself back into my lounge to phone Tony Singh, and put a double-or-quits bet on myself (my odds have increased to 8-1) to beat that fella Staplehurst, from Lloyds Bank, in the race to complete the jigsaw; then I text Maureen to tell her I was starting, dig out my reading glasses from where they are languishing at the bottom of my drawer and start to turn over the pieces of Prague Castle By Moonlight: 2,000 tiny little pieces of bloody grey brick and night time sky.

Bloody hell.

I sigh.

I can do this.

Come on Parksy. I start to imagine that every correct piece, fitting perfectly into the next piece, is being met with a roar of approval by the Green Street End of Upton Park.

Come on Parksy.

12

On Saturday 6 January 1968 the good offices of the Greater London Council moved me and my mum from our house in Scotland Street and into a new flat on the twelfth floor of a high rise on the Carlton Estate in Stepney. It was the same day the Orient were due to play Bury in the third round of the FA Cup.

My mum hadn't spoken for two days prior to the move. She hadn't wanted to leave, but neither had she put up much of a fuss; it just became another miserable thing in her miserable existence.

We packed up the van and watched as the bulldozers massed like warriors at the end of our old street waiting to raze our house to the ground. A noisy, steel goodbye, to the silent lounge, the cold stony hall, the kitchen that would forever be linked with my sad dad, and the back yard – the back yard, God love it; I can close my eyes even now and remember every square inch of that back yard, every rut in the concrete floor, every brick in its insignificant walls, the sound of every ball that I pummelled against the back gate.

Was I bothered by the systematic erasing of that part of my history? Not back then I wasn't; not really. I was nineteen, and things were going well at the Orient; I was in the first team, scoring goals and was thinking about getting my own flat, probably with Johnny Smith or some of the lads.

We got in the removal van and headed for the new estate, my mum, hard-faced, in the front and me in the back with some boxes of our stuff. There wasn't much.

I watched my mother: her lips tucked inside her thin down-turned mouth, her skin yellow and leathery, her hair untidy and speckled with grey – this is what happens when happiness leaves you.

I leaned over. I felt I ought to say something.

'I've heard they've got, like, a club on the estate, Mum, where people can go and have bingo and quizzes and films and that.'

She said nothing.

'And they've got these, like, chutes that you open and just drop your rubbish into – fantastic – it'll be, like, all modern, like in the films.'

The driver chipped in as my mother failed to respond.

'Yeah,' he said. 'My brother and his family have moved into one of the flats – they love it, much better than these old streets, eh?'

'See, Mum,' I said hopefully, 'it's all going to be better.'

I could see the driver looking at me in his rear-view mirror. I could tell he'd realised that a change in the conversation would be better for all of us.

'Big cup game for you this afternoon then?' he said.

'Yes,' I replied.

'Do you fancy your chances or what?'

'Of course,' I said. 'Hopefully get a big crowd. We could get all the way to Wembley this year.' The driver chortled at the thought of Leyton Orient getting to the FA Cup Final.

'How many have you scored this season then?' He smiled as he said it; he knew I was having a good season.

'Fifteen already,' I told him.

'You'll be joining a First Division club then soon, eh? Liverpool or Man City?'

At this my mother turned and looked at me, her eyes were cold and venomous. I expected her to say something, but she didn't; instead she seethed for a few moments at the prospect of me moving to mysterious northern cities, before turning silently back to look at the road.

The van driver slipped his gear, checked his mirror and we drove slowly out of Scotland Street: neither of us turned back to gaze at it. That piece of my life disappeared into the distance without fanfare or sentiment.

The driver was right though; I was having a wonderful season. I had progressed from the reserves and was now in my second full season in the first team and I'd scored fifteen goals in a struggling team. Dave Sexton had left a year or so earlier to manage Chelsea and, though the team's form had dipped after that, I had thrived. I was young and fit and fearless. I would skip away from the clunking defenders of the Second and Third Division – blokes without the speed or the wit to shackle me. I was playing for fun. By the Christmas of the 1967/68 season there were rumours of bigger clubs being interested. I wanted that more than anything. The adulation of a few thousand at Brisbane Road was no longer enough – I wanted more and more. With every maze-like run, with every shot that fizzed from my boot, with every goal that was greeted with cheers and smiles I wanted more: more love, more adulation, bigger crowds, my name being chanted by tens of thousands of people. I scoured the morning papers for rumours of some bigger club coming in for me – perhaps Matt Busby would take a second look, or Dave Sexton would lure me to Stamford Bridge. Every time the chairman, Harry Zussman, arrived at the ground in his Roller with his cigar, homburg and gabardine overcoat, I prayed that he had come to sell me.

There were rumours of Tottenham and Wolves and one of the stewards told me that Malcolm Allison and Joe Mercer of Man City had been seen in the stands a couple of weeks earlier. I'd been so excited I hadn't slept – but nothing came of it.

So, I continued to train hard with the other lads, learning new tricks and skills and having a laugh, and all that was fine because I was still a kid and convinced that everything was going to turn out brilliantly.

We arrived at our block: Rushton House, Carlton Estate, Stepney. We got out of the van and simultaneously looked upwards – it seemed massive and unfriendly. Mum said nothing. I smiled grimly at her as a cold chill blew across a muddy expanse of ground that ran around the front of the flats.

'It'll be lovely when the grass has grown here,' I said, but I wasn't sure she heard me. We made our way heavily into the flats, then into the lift up to the twelfth floor. It was clean in a bleak way – the communal entrance hall smelled of disinfectant and the lift shone like a steel box. There were little pictures of black silhouetted flowers on the wall. At least there were no junkies lying on the floor, nor the smell of piss and graffiti – that would come later.

Mum looked nervous as we travelled upwards, I'm not sure either of us had been in a lift before. I tried to make a joke of living in the sky and her having finally made it to a penthouse like Elizabeth Taylor. But she wasn't having it.

We made our way towards flat 'F'. The door had been left open by the removal men and a biting-cold wind blew into the flat from an open window – it was bloody freezing. My mother started crying.

'Don't cry,' I said. 'It'll be alright.'

But I didn't mean it: my words simply filled a space, spoken because I wanted to leave, get out of there, get into the changing room with the lads, get on the pitch and out to the pub afterwards, get away from this cold flat with its clean, story-less, philistinian walls. My mum sobbed. She seemed so weak; there was nothing of my father in this flat, the last remnants of him had disappeared along with Scotland Street. I should have given her a hug. I know I should've, but I didn't. Instead, I went over to the window that had been left open and found myself peering down towards the ground, towards the patch of brown earth you would hit if you fell out of this window and plummeted through the air towards its muddy infinity.

I turned back to my mum who was sitting quietly on the edge of the settee that had been brought from our old house in Scotland Street.

'Look, I'd best be off,' I said. 'Third round of the FA Cup, Mum, it's a big game.'

She nodded and I smiled weakly at her. 'You'll be alright, won't you?'

'Yes, Billy,' she said.

'OK. Perhaps we could go to a film later, or try out the club where they have the bingo and stuff.'

She nodded and I walked towards the door.

'Billy,' she said, and I turned, 'you will be back later, won't you?'

'Of course,' I said.

I didn't come back that night. I quickly forgot about my promise in the frenzy of our triumphant cup victory over Bury.

We fought out a tough 1-0 win. Our triumphant goal came late on after eighty craggy minutes on a freezing cold pitch. The Bury full-back, a portly young lad by the name of Archie Winters, had chased me all around the pitch, chuffing like a bleeding steam engine as he did; fair play though, for an hour he did a cracking job, God bless him, but after that he was knackered and I was able to get behind their defence and lay the ball back across the eighteen-yard box, where Roy Massey stuck it in the net. I ran over and hugged him like I'd never hugged anyone before, gripping his body and burying my head into his neck, close, like a lover, in the overwhelming excitement of a winning goal.

We were in the fourth round of the FA Cup.

Brilliant. Bloody. Brilliant.

Thirty-two clubs left.

Four games away from Wembley. Four bloody games. That's three hundred and sixty minutes – that's nothing.

We celebrated like we'd landed on the moon.

We sang naked in the big bath: *We're on the way to Wembley, we're on the Wembley Way.*

Harry Zussman came in and stood at the side of the bath and made a speech: 'When we get to Wembley, boys, I'm going to take you all to Savile Row for a new suit.'

'What kind of suit, Harry?' asked Johnny Smith.

'One that fits, my boy,' shouted Harry and we pulled him into the bath with us, and sang, *Ee aye ai-de-oh we're going to win the cup.*

Then we were straight into the Birbeck Tavern, singing all the way.

Fantastic; all the lads were together that night and with every drink, with every slap on my back and ruffle of my hair, I forgot about my mum and our colourless fatherless new flat in the sky. We ended up in a dance hall in Southend: me, Johnny Smith, Vic Halom and Roy Massey. Johnny pulled a brunette called Susan while I had to talk to her plain friend.

I got back to our flat the next day after crashing at Johnny's. I was pale, tired, a bit dirty, but still elated: back then, beer was fun and guilt-free and we were still going to Wembley.

My mother was in the kitchen.

To my surprise, she didn't ask me where I'd been and she didn't tell me off, which is what I'd expected. Instead she was busying herself in the kitchen, putting cutlery in drawers and cups in a cupboard.

I looked at her from the doorway.

'We won,' I said awkwardly. 'We're through to the next round of the FA Cup.'

'That's nice,' she said with a smile that perplexed me – I had expected sulking. 'Will you help me put these plates in that cupboard, they were a wedding present from your Aunty Elsie.'

I moved towards her and picked up the best china plates from the sideboard.

'If we get to the final, we all get a new suit, you'll have to have a new hat.'

She smiled again, but it was a distant smile; she didn't believe me, I was just another man who was promising her things that he would never deliver, another man who was letting her down. Then she gave me a look I'd never seen before – it was resigned, cold, devoid of love, devoid of the last semblance of gentleness that my father's love had given her – he was long gone now.

'When we've finished, we should have a little drink,' she said.

This was the first time that she had invited me to have a drink with her. It was a significant moment. She had smelled the alcohol on me; she had sensed her weakness in me and now she would invite me to drink with her. It was her next step, her acceptance of the way things were: she would no longer drink in secret – she would drink with me. The world had stripped her of her love and her youth and her beauty and put her here in this antiseptic flat in this monstrous tower, and now she no longer cared if I knew of her pain and the way in which she coped with that pain; she had given up trying to protect me, I was just another man who let her down, I was a fellow drinker.

'A drink?'

'Yes,' she said, 'just to mark the new flat, eh?'

'OK.'

'Good,' she said, 'pop into town then, and get us some wine and perhaps a bottle of gin.'

So that's what I did. I 'popped' up the road to an off licence and wine merchant on Stepney High Street. I did it happily, because it seemed the right thing to do. I didn't understand. Not then.

We were drawn out of the hat to play Birmingham City away in the next round of the cup. Birmingham City, we could beat them, I knew we could. They were only one division higher than us, but this was the FA Cup where a plucky mouse can triumph over the indignant cat. We could overcome all the indignant cats – we could go all the way.

We trained hard. Gerry Higgs put us through our paces and

manager Dickie Graham set up a plan that he thought would beat Birmingham City – lovely man was Dickie; we all played our hearts out for him. He reckoned the way to beat Birmingham was to expose their flanks. 'They've got the slowest full-backs in the known world,' he said. 'Parksy and Johnny will hog the flanks and get down the by-line for Roy and Vic, to apply the finish. I want every ball diagonal and early to the wings.'

I listened. Enthralled. It was brilliant. Me and Johnny were going to propel the Orient to the fifth round, every ball was going to come to us, we would provide the ammunition. It would be just as we had imagined when we were kids, me and Johnny lifting the cup at Wembley. Birmingham would lie down before my wing-wizardry.

After our final training session, our chairman Harry Zussman came and spoke to us. He promised us that we would all get brand-new handmade shoes to go with our new suits if we won.

'What kind of shoes, Mr Zussman?' asked Johnny.

'You can have fucking clown shoes if you get to Wembley, my boy,' said the chairman and we all cheered and chucked bits of mud at him and Johnny smiled his warm wonderful mischievous smile.

Fantastic.

Birmingham would lie down before my wing-wizardry and I would cop a pair of handmade shoes into the bargain.

We lost 3-0.

We lost 3-0 in a one-sided game, in which I had the ball twice in the first minute, then only one more time in the next eighty-nine. They cut out every attempt the lads made to play a diagonal ball to the flanks. They saw us coming. Still, I did as I was told and stayed on the wing, but all that meant was that I was in a better position to hear the jabbering, brainless chump in the Birmingham crowd who insisted on telling me that I was a 'blond-haired Cockney poof', for the entire ninety minutes.

I didn't mind that – that kind of abuse was part of the game as far as I was concerned – it just made me more determined to make him look like a cunt. What I did mind, though, was when the same bastard cheered and laughed when they took Johnny Smith off on a stretcher just before the end. The fucking bastard. I could have waded into the crowd, I could have pummelled him until he cried like the coward he was. But thankfully Jimmy Bloomfield, who'd played 200-odd times for the Arsenal pulled me away. 'He's not worth it, Bill,' he said, and he was right.

We watched Johnny. He was in agony. He'd broken his leg. We didn't call it a cruciate ligament then, we just called it the end. And it was, he wouldn't play again. Poor, poor bastard, poor poor Johnny. I didn't know. I just didn't know how important it was to him. Not until later.

We traipsed back on to the bus. There was no singing. I sat at the back with Peter Allen and Vic Halom as Jimmy Bloomfield took all our money in a game of pontoon. After about twenty minutes I was called down to the front of the bus. There sat Gerry Higgs, Dickie Graham and Harry Zussman.

'Sit down,' said Harry, his cigar in his mouth. I looked nervously at Gerry Higgs and Dickie Graham; I had no idea what was coming.

'We've had a couple of offers for you, boy,' he said, and my heart started to beat faster.

'Offers?'

'Yes,' said Harry, 'it's up to you. I've arranged to meet with Ron Greenwood of West Ham at the Corby Services and Dave Sexton of Chelsea at Watford Gap. They've both met the asking price, so it's up to *you* who *you* want to meet, son. You'll sign for one of them tonight.'

I gulped: West Ham or Chelsea. West Ham or Chelsea. Bloody hell. This was everything I'd ever dreamed of. West Ham or Chelsea. Chelsea would mean Dave Sexton, who I'd liked and admired, but West Ham, West Ham were my dad's team, West Ham were Bobby

Moore and Martin Peters and Geoff Hurst – West Ham were legends.

'How long have I got, Mr Zussman?' I asked.

'How long until we get to Corby, Harry?' Zussman shouted at the driver.

'About forty minutes, Mr Zussman.'

'There's your answer, Billy – forty minutes.'

I nodded and started to walk down the centre of the bus – by the time I reached the lads at the back, I'd made up my mind – I would be a West Ham player.

I signed that night, sitting in a hard plastic chair in the café of the Corby Services with a plate of egg and chips in front of me. I'd forgotten all about Birmingham City and the FA Cup; I'd forgotten all about lovely Johnny Smith and his cruciate ligament; I'd forgotten about my mother alone in the high-rise flat.

Billy Parks was about to play in the First Division.

Yes. Bloody yes.

Details: Match 5, 6th January 1968
FA Cup Third Round
Venue: Brisbane Road, Leyton
Leyton Orient 1 v. Bury 0
Massey

Line Ups
Orient: Goddard, Howe, Jones, Mancini, Taylor, Smith, Bloomfield, Allen, Parks, Halom, Massey
Bury: Ramsbottom, Tinney, Anderson, Turner, Winters, Parnell, Farrell, Kerr, Grundy, Arrowsmith, Jones

Attendance: 9,265

Details: Match 6, 27 January 1968
FA Cup Fourth Round
Venue: St Andrews, Birmingham

Birmingham City 3 v. Leyton Orient 0
Vincent (2)
Pickering

Line Ups
Birmingham City: Herriot, Thomson, Martin, Page, Foster, Hockey, Wylie, Vincent, Murrey, Pickering, Vowden
Orient: Goddard, Howe, Jones, Mancini, Taylor, Smith, Bloomfield, Allen, Parks, Halom, Massey

Attendance: 27,876

13

I pick up the last piece: a detail of Charles bloody Bridge. I pick it up, check the time – 4am: fourteen hours and seventeen minutes! I am inside Thingy Staplehurst from Lloyds Bank's time by nearly half an hour – get in! I pick up the last piece and imagine a roaring crowd – Billy Parks, goes past one Czech defender, goes past a second Czech defender, he's now into the Czechoslovakia penalty area, the goalkeeper comes out, but Parks shimmies to his right and pummels it into the top corner! Get in: England 1 – Prague Castle 0.

I take a picture of the massive completed jigsaw, note the time and send a text to Maureen. Next I phone the bookie Tony Singh and remind him that he now owes me four large ones.

I go to sleep, sober and triumphant and dream of castles with grey brick walls and no door. Then, I wake up cold with sweat and a new pain in my cheekbones. A new pain that feels like slivers of steel are shunted under my skin. I take a couple of pills – that should do the trick.

By noon I have arrived for my check up at Dr Aranthraman's liver clinic. I walk through the door into the dull yellow doom-laden light of the NHS waiting room; on the walls are posters telling us about the perils of smoking and drinking and why it is better to breast-feed. I get the feeling that most of the collection of jaundiced and decaying losers who are already sitting silently in the hard-back chairs of the waiting room know full-well about the dangers of fags and booze, and probably aren't that bothered about benefits of breast milk. This is a place of failure and illness and death, a waiting room for the sad, the dependent, the dying. Poor old souls. It smells of hopelessness. I take a seat and sit quietly and alone, and allow myself an occasional glance at my fellow patients. Some of them are with silent loved ones; you can tell the difference: the patients' faces are yellow, the loved ones' faces are just grim, they are the ones who know that the vicious battle is coming to an end, one way or another.

Poor bastards all of them. I wonder if any of them are about to be given a second chance by the Service.

A bloke walks past carrying a clipboard. He looks at me, then twists on his heels and lollops over like we are old friends, his fizzog oozing into an ecstatic gurn.

'Don't tell me,' he says, thrusting his hand towards me, 'you're Billy Parks, aren't you?'

I smile. 'Yes, that's right. For my sins eh?'

He leans over and whispers in a voice that everyone can hear, 'So what are you doing here, then?'

'Oh, just a check up, you know, make sure I'm in peak condition and that.'

'Quite right too,' he says, and looks at me with a concerned facial expression that tells me that he is making a qualitative assessment of my health.

'I used to watch you back in the seventies at White Hart Lane.'

'Did you?' I say. 'Happy days eh?'

'I always thought that you were a bit past your best when you came to us – you know what I mean? We should have had you a few years earlier.'

I smile in a thin-lipped, grimacing way. How am I supposed to respond to this? What the fuck does he want me to say? I know he doesn't mean anything by it, I know that he doesn't realise that what he is actually saying is that by the time I had reached my mid-twenties I had, in fact, gone past my usefulness, or perhaps he does realise that and he's just a horrible man with a clipboard. I sigh; as a footballer, I have to take it, and normally I can, but not here, not in Dr Aranthraman's liver clinic, not among these poor jaundiced old sods.

Thankfully, he shakes me firmly by the hand, wishes me well, then takes himself and his clipboard and his rude health to wherever he was on his way to.

Some of the deathly-faced yellow people and grim-faced loved ones look over, then quickly look away.

I sigh again and wait for my call.

Dr Aranthraman's room is warm and smells like clean-scrubbed flesh. He greets me like a brother with his beautiful white teeth and mahogany skin.

'Billy Parks, how are you?'

'I'm fantastic, Doctor; absolutely top notch. I feel like I could do ninety minutes against Leeds.'

I decide not to tell him about the pains in my legs and the overwhelming fatigue or the funny poo or the excruciating and constant ache in my stomach or today's new pain in my cheekbones.

'Excellent,' he says, then adds with a wagging finger, 'No drinking I hope?'

'Absolutely not, Doctor. Not a drop. I've taken to doing jigsaws. Did you know that it took the Czechs 600 years to finish Prague Castle?'

My lie is camouflaged with an unnecessary throwaway fact – I've become good at doing that. He looks at me like I'm mad. Then picks up my notes.

'Well, Billy,' he says, 'I've got the results from your tests.'

'Very good,' I say, but in actual fact I'm shitting myself.

He licks his lips, then makes a strange slow rasping noise with his tongue before he eventually speaks.

'Well,' he says, 'there is some good news and some bad news.'

'Very good,' I repeat – I've always liked good news.

'The good news is that the liver has not got any worse.'

'Brilliant.'

'The bad news is that it hasn't got any better either.'

I ignore the bad news.

'So it hasn't got any worse then?'

'No.'

'Well that's good, isn't it?'

Dr Aranthraman looks at me, a pained expression forming across his face.

'Well, it does mean that I'd like to keep you on the tablets that you are currently taking, perhaps with a little bit of a bigger dose. And it does mean that you will stay on the liver-transplant waiting list.'

Ah yes, the liver transplant: the plan to remove my liver and replace it with a new one. I still wasn't sure about that. It just didn't sound right to me. I didn't really want part of someone else's body in mine. I felt my face scrunch up at the doctor's mention of the word transplant.

'When will this transplant happen, then?' I ask.

'Not for a while I'm afraid – the average waiting time is about five months.'

Five months: that suits me just fine. In five months' time everything will be very different. There will be no need for liver transplants after the Poland game. I will be cleansed.

Dr Aranthraman picks up on my earlier concern. 'Don't worry,' he says, 'the operation is now very successful, with most patients going on to live much-improved lives.'

I nod.

'For you, Billy,' he says, 'it will be like a second chance.'

Second chance: suddenly everyone is offering me a second chance.

'A second chance, eh?' The words just come out. I am not sure why or what I mean by them, or whether they are a question or a statement.

'Of course,' he says, 'we surgeons deal in renewal. It is my job to give second chances.'

'And what do your patients do with their second chance?'

He smiles confidently. 'The second chance makes people aware of how precious this life is,' he says. 'Most people try to make up for the mistakes they've made first time around.'

I nod. 'So, some put things right, then? Do many do that? You know, mend the mess that they made beforehand?'

'I'm sure they do, Billy,' he says.

I nod, 'Thanks.'

We end the consultation with the usual warning about how just one more drink could kill me and how I'm not to eat fatty foods and that I'm to stay fit and all the rest, and I thank him, because he is a good doctor and a very nice bloke.

I leave feeling relatively happy and confident and make a spontaneous decision to get a bus to Oxford Circus, which is very unusual; in fact, apart from my trips with Gerry Higgs, I can't remember the last time I'd been up West. I decide that I want to get a football top for Liam, though. That seems like a good thing to do. After Maureen has found them for me, I will present Liam with a Hammers shirt. That is a proper thing to do. The type of thing normal granddads do.

I go into one of those massive sports shops where trainers and football shirts and bikes and footballs of all different colours, shapes and sizes overflow from shelves. I spy a bucket full of leather footballs for a couple of quid apiece. Christ, in my day, you had to sell your grandmother to buy a leather football.

I go up to the counter; a young girl is standing there.

'Hello,' I say. 'I'm after a West Ham football shirt.'

'Next floor,' she says, without looking at me while pointing to an escalator.

'Thanks,' I say and traipse towards it, ignoring the pains in my knees as I go.

On the upper floor, a little kid kicks a bright-yellow football towards me. I trap it and consider a trick or two, but the pain in my knee shoots up towards my thigh, telling me that I have no place trying to kick a football. Not now. That has gone. That is over.

I look at the ball for a second, then side-foot it back to the boy, but he ignores it and me and goes back to his mother, leaving the ball to collide gently with a rack of golf clubs.

I find a West Ham shirt and approach the counter. A young friendly-looking Asian lad is standing behind it beaming at me.

'It's for my grandson,' I say.

'Is he a fan?' asks the Asian boy.

I stop, my mouth open. I don't know. I have no idea if Liam is a West Ham fan or not.

'I don't know,' I say, then add quickly: 'They were my old club.'

The Asian lad nods at me. I want him to ask me about that. I want him to recognise me; tell me how he's seen me on the TV, on ESPN Classics or on his computer or anything. I want him to remind me of a bit of skill from my glorious beautiful past – but he doesn't.

'Would you like his name on the back?' he asks.

'Yes, please.'

'What name would you like?'

And I stop, my mouth open – is he Parks or Leadbetter? I don't know. I don't bloody know the surname of my own bloody grandson.

'I don't know,' I stutter and the Asian lad looks suspiciously at me. 'Well, do you know his first name?'

'Yes,' I say. 'Yes, of course, his first name's Liam, like Brady.'

'Shall I put Liam Brady on it then?'

'No, his name's not Liam Brady – that would be ridiculous – his name's just Liam.'

'Just Liam?'

'Yes. Thank you.'

I pay and leave, a plastic carrier bag in my hand.

I get the bus from outside Oxford Circus Station. It is full of the usual happy tourists and excitable kids and mournful workers on their way home. I look at them as they get on, each with their own lives and problems and secrets and passions. I could change the lives of all of them. I could change all of their personal history. My goal could make people sad or happy or rich. Christ, as a result of my goal, babies might be conceived, families made – people might do wonderful things.

Or they might do stupid things.

Buildings could be built or destroyed. Roads and cars might come into existence that wouldn't have done before – it was *that* important. In my mind I imagine the ball hitting the back of the Polish net and, instantly, the world changing before my eyes. Things moving and disintegrating, changing and evolving, progress and regress and life and death and all because of me. Fuck. I close my eyes and the pain in my cheekbones starts again, cold and high-pitched.

I have to stop.

I have to stop looking out of the window and using my imaginary powers. I have to stop thinking about the possibilities I have at my disposal. The overwhelming hugeness of it starts the scratching, gnawing ache in my head. Drink. It would be so easy, so bloody easy, and so bloody wonderful: a nice afternoon in a dark inner-city London pub, one of the ones you find in a backstreet, that has clearly stood there for ever, but somehow, you've never been in it before. Just one or two; after all, Dr Aranthraman had said that my liver had not got any worse, so a few liveners isn't going to make any difference. And anyway, none of it matters, because I am getting a second chance. I am going to change everything.

I look forward, out of the bus, towards the road. I close my eyes tight hoping that the scratching will stop. But it doesn't. It never bloody does.

I get off at Monument. I hadn't planned on doing that. I get off, and walk down towards that massive building, the one that looks like a gherkin. I'm not sure why. I half expect Gerry Higgs to come and join me as I go.

I enter the building, go through the security and take a lift to the top floor: a sign reads '40/30 Restaurant Gallery'.

The lift stops and I step out into a fantastic bar and restaurant. It is quiet and I am able to find a corner in the viewing gallery and look out over London. I can see everything. I look at the mass of grey buildings and the tiny teeming cars and buses and people and think about my goal. What *would* happen if I scored the goal? Would everything change? Would it be better? Perhaps it would all end up worse. I feel my head thicken and my thought processes blur, as though little confused people had started to run up and down the blind alleys of my brain, confusing me in the process. I want to scream.

A group of businessmen are having dinner at a nearby table – you know the type, 'City Gents', all suit and money and no common sense or manners. Normally, you see them pissed up with an attitude and a big wallet, laughing at their own jokes, but these particular fellas are glum and tense. One of them keeps repeating over and over in a quietly aggressive voice, 'I can't help you Stu, I can't help you.' He seems cold and hostile. As the bloke, who I assume is Stu, keeps trying to butt in, the other man keeps repeating his aggressive phrase, 'I can't help you, I can't help you.' Eventually, Stu gets up, pushes his plate towards his tormentor, tells him to fuck off and storms out.

As he is leaving, both men catch me staring at them, so I look away.

Could I change that – whatever that was?

Gerry Higgs had said that I should just let history take care of itself. He was right wasn't he? That is all I can do. All I can do is score the goal and let history run its own course. Yes, I have to forget about everything else, and concentrate on doing what I can do; make it right in my life, make it alright for Becky and all the others. I just need to score the goal. That's all.

But what if I miss?

I hadn't contemplated that before. After all, I am Billy Parks; I am supremely confident of my ability: there is no way I could miss. Is there?

In the shop, though, I had hardly been able to kick a ball. Sure, I realise that Sir Alf wouldn't be bringing on the old and knackered me from today; but the pain of trying to kick the ball, makes me contemplate for the first time, the possibility that, even if I was selected, I might not score. Gerry Higgs had warned me, *all you've got to do is score, Billy.* He'd kept saying it. He was warning me.

Shit. What if I miss?

At the moment, no one even remembers that I was in the squad, but if I came on and missed, that would be it, that's all anyone would ever remember me for, just like poor old Kevin Hector. Billy Parks, the bloke who missed the open goal that would have put England into the World Cup Finals of 1974. Billy Parks, the man who fucked it up for everyone.

No, I won't miss, there is no way I'll miss – I'll score the goal and then everything will change. I will undo all the bad stuff. There is no way I am going to miss.

In the reflection of the window another face forms behind my own. I don't turn around. I know it isn't real. I know that it can't really be the face of Johnny Smith – he is definitely lost. No one has seen Johnny Smith for nearly twenty years.

'Hello, Billy,' says the face of Johnny Smith.

I chuckle to myself.

'Now I know that you don't really exist, Johnny, old son,' I say, still chuckling.

'Of course I exist.'

'Oh yeah, don't tell me you're part of the Service as well?'

'The what?' he replies.

'See,' I say, 'I know the difference between people and ghosts and immortals and figments of my own imagination.'

The cherubic face of Johnny Smith breaks into that sweet chubby mischievous smile that I knew so well.

'Are you going to make everything right for us, Billy?' he asks.

And now I turn to him. 'Oh yes, Johnny,' I say. 'Of course I am. One of the first things I'm going to do is make everything right with you, old son. You and me are going to the World Cup together – West Germany, 1974: Holland, total football, Gerd bleeding Müller, the lot.'

The face of Johnny Smith breaks into a big deep smile.

'You think you'll beat Kevin Keegan then, mate?'

'Yes, I'm due for an interview any day – and I've got a few tricks up my sleeve to beat that scouse git.'

'The Council's not stupid you know; you managed to piss them all off back in the day.'

'Ah, yes, but as Sir Matt Busby says: this is an important match, it goes well beyond the stuff that happened years ago. History depends upon it, mate. History depends upon me.'

'But, Keegan's quality – twice European Footballer of the Year. Sixty-three caps for England, European Cup – the lot.'

'I don't deny that, my old friend – but Kevin Keegan was all about perspiration, you know what I mean – with me, it's inspiration, you never know what you're going to get. I have got *virtù*.'

'*Virtù*?'

'Yes, that's Niccolò Machiavelli, mate – it means excellence, but with that certain unpredictability. Well, I think it does.'

The face of Johnny Smith looks into my soul. 'I think we all had a good idea what we were going to get with you, Billy.'

I know what he means. I know what he means and it hurts.

'Yes, I was meaning to say about that – I'm sorry mate.'

'You ignored me, Billy. You forgot all about me.'

'I know, I'm sorry.'

'Why, Billy? Why didn't you come round?'

126

I close my eyes tight. I want Gerry Higgs to be here to explain everything to me. I open them; the face of Johnny Smith is still there.

'I'm sorry,' I say. 'I couldn't help it, Johnny, I was busy, what with West Ham and then Spurs and England and everything.'

'I know,' he says, 'I watched you on *Match of the Day* and read about you in the papers, and saw that advert you did for Burton's that was always on the telly. I was so proud of you, Billy, and my Mrs kept saying, "When's he going to come and see you?" And I kept saying, "Soon, he never forgets a pal does Billy Parks, he's one of us, a proper East End boy. He won't forget who got him into the Orient in the first place."'

I close my eyes again and this time tears explode through the tight skin and down my cheeks.

'I'm sorry, I'm so sorry,' I say. Then I look into the eyes of the face of Johnny Smith. 'Why did you do it, Johnny?' I implore him. 'Why did you just leave? You had so much going for you. You had your boys and your Mrs and everything.'

'You're right, Billy,' he says. 'I had everything, but all I wanted was to play football like we used to.'

I shake my head. 'I'm going to make it all better for you, mate,' I say, 'just you see.'

He looks at me doubtfully.

'I took a ball with me,' he says, 'when I left. I went to the woods round the back of our estate. I took a ball, one of my boys' footballs, a leather one, black and white patches, and I put it down on the ground, and I said to myself, if I can kick it against that tree, I'll go home back to the family, if I can't, I'll just carry on walking. I said that to myself. After all the operations and the false hopes and recuperation and then being told that it was all over, then not getting a job, and being told that the only job I could get was pushing pens with the council. I used to put ticks in boxes and stamp forms – stamp bloody forms, Billy. Stamp. Stamp. Stamp. Stamp. No one ever remembers the bloke who stamps a form, do they?'

'But I remember you, Johnny.'

The face of Johnny Smith ignores me and looks slightly away into the distance.

'So,' he continues quietly, 'in the end it was as simple as that: could I kick a ball against a tree.'

Tears are now streaming down my face. 'You daft bastard,' I say. 'How did you miss? You were the best crosser of a ball I ever played with. How did you miss a bleeding tree?'

'The pain,' he says. 'The pain in my bloody leg and the black pain in my head that just wouldn't go away.'

I know all of this. I know it all, but I tried to forget it. I know that Johnny carried on walking and that, the first time around, they had found him with his ball in Holland or Belgium or somewhere; I know all this because his Mrs, Christine, had come to me and asked me to help. 'Acute depression,' she'd said, and, God bless her, she'd organised a charity match, a load of Orient old boys versus an All Stars team. She wanted to raise money for his treatment. I turned up the first time, quite a few of us did, because he was a diamond; we'd hoped he'd play, but he couldn't, he just watched for a bit, an ashen face on the touchline.

'He just needs to get his leg better,' I'd said to Christine. 'He'll be fine then. Get his leg better and get him out on the piss with a few of the lads.'

I didn't know anything.

After his treatment, he walked away again only this time, no one found him. This time he stayed lost. My lovely Johnny Smith, the best of boys, the bloody best of boys. Lost. And I did nothing to find him.

'I'm going to make it all better, Johnny,' I say to him. 'I've been given a second chance. I'll be able to see you afterwards; perhaps we can get you to a specialist in America, get your leg sorted out. Go to the World Cup – everything.'

He shakes his head. 'It's not my turn for a second chance, Billy,' he says, 'not that kind of chance. And anyway, Billy,' he adds, 'what if you miss?'

'I won't bloody miss,' I shout. 'You'll see, Johnny, I'll score, I'll do it for you. I'll find you.'

But the face of Johnny Smith has gone and in his place is a man in a shirt and tie. 'I'm afraid that I'm going to have to ask you to leave if you're not going to order anything,' he says.

'I will order something,' I tell him, 'I'll have a drink. I'll have a scotch please, a large one.'

'Not in here, you won't, Sir,' he says.

14

Bobby Moore intercepts Peter Houseman's pass: a touch of under-stated class from a man at the top of his game. The crowd react with a hearty round of applause – different from a cheer, a clap: we pros like that, we know that when they give you a full-bodied clap you've done something technical and clever that they admire, something that they know they couldn't do themselves.

Moore then passes it carefully to Billy Bonds who plays it across the deck to Trevor Brooking – all nice carpet-slipper football, just how Ron Greenwood likes it. The crowd like it too; they can see that Chelsea are a bit slow on to us and that Trevor's got a bit of space. They react: 25,000 hearts beat a little quicker, 25,000 voices increase slightly in volume – this is the excitement that they paid their money for, this is why they watch twenty-two men kick a football. Trevor plays it to me. I'm in the inside-right position, about thirty-five yards from goal, I feel the noise of the crowd grow again, changing from a buzz to more of a fervid and urgent growling prayer, willing me to do something.

I look up and see that Dave Webb and Eddie McCreadie are coming at me – why are they both coming towards me?

What are they thinking?

The ball bounces perfectly just before it reaches me and I am able to loft it between McCreadie and Webb then skip round them – two Chelsea rent-boys taken out of the game in one go: genius! I can now see the goal: fuck me, Peter Bonetti's in the wrong position, he's in the wrong bloody position! He expected McCreadie and Webb to skin me, so he's standing by the edge of his six-yard box close to his near post.

He's got it totally wrong.

I know this. I know this without even thinking. I know that this is my chance.

In an instant, in a bloody-tiny fraction of a second, I change my body position, and I wait for the ball to drop on to my right foot. The crowd wait for the ball to drop on to my right foot too, and it happens: that millisecond of hush, that communal intake of breath – come on, come on, come on.

And in that instant I know exactly what to do, I know that I can't hit it too true because it'll carry over the crossbar and into the stand; I know this, I can't tell you how I know this, I can't explain the physics or the geometry or whatever it is that makes me know that I have to get under the ball in such a way that it will drop over Bonetti and into the back of his goal.

The ball falls on to my foot and I clip it towards the vast open space of Peter Bonetti's improperly guarded net.

I've caught it just right. Perfect.

Bonetti back-pedals, his right hand thrust upwards in desperation as he tries to get a glove on it, 25,000 pairs of eyes on the ball, get in, get in, get in.

Then. Pause. The roar. That roar, as the net ripples and the ball nestles into it for a goal.

I feel every part of my body surge with the excitement – this is the best thing ever, this is better than sex, better than love, better than the birth of your kids, better than the best drink or drug. This is perfection.

I raise both my hands in the air and turn towards the terrace and watch the bestial gush of orgasmic ecstasy, as 25,000 men roar in acclamation of my goal and surge violently down towards the pitch, towards the goal, my goal. Me. Billy Parks.

Yes. Yeeees.

That was my first goal for West Ham. It was my fourth game since I'd signed from the Orient. The first three had been largely forgettable, the odd flash, the odd trick, but nothing to justify my place in the team – but the fourth game changed everything, with this goal, the manager, the lads and the fans knew that I could do it.

I lay on two more goals – one for Geoff Hurst, the other for Brian Dear. Me, laying on a goal for Geoff Hurst – fucking hell. He ruffled my hair at the final whistle: 'Nice one kid.'

The next week at training I was invited to join a few of the boys for a beer. 'Win, draw or lose, we're on the booze,' said John Charles, a coloured lad, lovely boy, who was one of the first black boys to play professionally; captained England at youth level he did; fast as a whippet, brave as a bastard and, as I was about to find out, he could drink like a camel, as could most of the other lads at the club.

'What we do,' Bobby Moore told me, 'is take it in turns to pick a different pub each Monday, Tuesday and Wednesday and go and have a few beers after training.'

'Why do we go to different pubs?' I asked innocently.

'Bloody hell, Billy,' said John Cushley, a gruff, quick-witted Scotsman, 'if people get to hear that the Captain of England goes to the same pub each day, then we'll nae get a moment's peace.'

'Oh,' I said grinning, 'I get ya.'

My months in the delivery van with Barry Ross meant that I knew dozens of good east London and Essex boozers. So, each Monday, Tuesday and Wednesday (rarely on a Thursday, never on a Friday), as soon as Ron Greenwood had finished teaching us how to play football in the way God intended, we would scoot off to some pub or other and drink solidly for most of the day. It was a magical time; these boys were legends, Bobby Moore, Harry Redknapp, John 'Budgie' Byrne, Brian Dear, John Charles, John Cushley. When we'd finished in the pub, some of us would go up West to take in a club – Blondes or Tramp or Annabel's, wherever was flavour of the month.

Moore was the Captain of England, he had lifted the World Cup: every door was opened up to us, drinks were bought; we were given the best seats and introduced to the most exciting people. We would see Georgie Best and Mickey Summerbee, surrounded by dolly birds and drinking champagne. I met Michael Caine and Mick Jagger and Peter O'Toole and Jimmy Tarbuck and Tommy Steele. I even met Telly Savalas once, or was it Yul Brynner? Bloody everybody was there.

And girls: loads of them, with white lipstick and tiny skirts and knowing smiles. Bobby would introduce me: 'This is Billy Parks,' he would say, 'watch out for him, he's going to be special.' And I would grin like the happiest bastard in the world, because everything was so bloody fantastic.

I scored five goals in that first season and sixteen in the next, which wasn't bad as I was playing either wide on the left or in midfield – only Geoff Hurst scored more. People were now talking about me being a future England prospect.

I lapped it up. I drank more. I stayed out later. I chased girls wherever I went – lovely, young, forgettable girls. Oh how I wish I could remember them now; how I wish I could still feel my hands on their soft skin, recall the touch of their lips, the taste of their mouths. Christ, I can't remember half of their names: Melinda, was it? The waitress at the Embassy Club; Deirdre the air-stewardess, who I met when I was out with Billy Bonds; Carol (or was it Karen?), the Irish girl, who kept getting me mixed up with Harry Redknapp; Tanya, the model; Daisy, the model; Sharon, who I shagged in the back of my car near Buckingham Palace. For a few seconds I loved them all, then they would evaporate into the growing carbuncle that was my ego, drunk on alcohol and adulation.

Nothing mattered. Everything was so easy.

On the opening day of the 1969/70 season I scored a hat-trick against Crystal Palace: the first, a drive from outside the box; the second, a tap in from a Martin Peters corner that their goalie dropped; the third, a penalty that Geoff let me take to complete my treble. Three goals in the first game of a season that would end up with a World Cup in Mexico; I was only twenty-one, but already people were saying that Sir Alf should take me.

That afternoon, the crowd chanted my name, a rhythmic clap, followed by a deep tribal, '*Parksy!*' It rang out across the east London skyline: *Parksy*. And, later someone wrote: 'Billy Parks Is God' on the wall of the stadium in bright claret paint.

Billy Parks Is God. I bloody loved that. I still bloody love that.

I stared at the claret paint, then I got into my Triumph Stag and drove back to the flat I was sharing with a new friend; Ray Harley his name was, he owned a nightclub in Chingford and wore Paisley slacks and a fur coat. Christ, I'd left my mother on her own in her high-rise tomb to share a flat in Bethnal Green with a bloke who wore a fur coat.

I regret that now. Of course I do.

I had to get out though. My mother had settled into a devastating routine: every morning she would visit one of the three off licences that were within quarter of an hour's walk from our flat. She would rotate between them in an effort to maintain the respectability she believed that she still had. I'd come home from training or after a match and even then I still had no idea what kind of state or mood she would be in; occasionally, it would be euphoric, 'Here he is, my little superstar,' she'd say. 'How proud your dad would be of you, son,' she'd tell me. Then, the next day, I would be 'the little bastard who hated her' and who had let her down. Just like every other man.

It was easier if I drank with her, so, if I was home, I'd make sure that I brought a few bottles of beer or some wine, then we would sit in uncomfortable silence and watch TV, drinking out of mugs, with me thinking of ways to escape.

When Ray Harley offered me a room in his flat, I jumped at the chance; a room of my own meant more birds and more booze, and now these would come without the burden of going home and explaining where I'd been.

I bought my mum a colour TV in an effort to make her feel better and rid me of my own prickly guilt.

'You can watch the *Eurovision Song Contest* in colour, Mum,' I told her. 'Lulu's for us.' As though being able to watch a collection of foreign singers in full and glorious colour would somehow compensate for the fact that I was leaving her.

She refused to have the telly in her house, so I left it outside the front door. Amazingly when I came round a week later, it was still there. When I came round a month after that, someone had nicked it.

Once I was ensconced in Ray Harley's flat, I stopped going around as often as I should. I made up excuses: that I was too tired after training, or that I needed to prepare for the next match. I told myself that she was best left alone to sort her problems out, and make new friends; I even told myself that she deserved to be alone. In fact, if I'm going to be honest, I told myself that quite a lot – that she had brought her suffering upon herself and I wasn't going to let it contaminate my beautiful, perfect life. I'm not proud of that. She was lonely and on the run from the awful misery that fate had bestowed upon her, and I was too stupid to see it. So what does that make me?

By the night of the 1969 West Ham United Christmas Party at the St George's Hall, Dagenham, I hadn't seen my mum for weeks, but I had added another five goals to the three I got against Palace on the opening day of the season.

The West Ham United Christmas Party: that was the night I met Sandi Leadbetter.

You need to know about this.

The West Ham United Christmas Party of 1969: I feel myself letting out a sigh, just thinking about it.

The night I met Sandi Leadbetter.

Sigh.

Now, I don't know if they still do it, but back then, they used to mix the tables: youth and reserve team boys sitting with the first teamers. I was on a table with Harry Redknapp and Martin Peters, John Cushley, John McDowell and a few of the kids. Sitting in-between me and Harry was a lad called Wayne Bernard, who'd been Captain of England Youth or something. He was a big huge centre-half with a great big hairy back, and a massive opinion of himself because someone once said he was the new Duncan Edwards. Yeah, right – only if Duncan Edwards had been more interested in his hair than his footballing and had been as slow as an Eastern Dairies milk float.

After a few drinks, Harry started to wind Wayne up: 'So Bernie, you must be fantastic, being the youngest player in the reserves and all that.'

'Yes,' said Bernie proudly.

'Reckon you'll be in the first team this time next year?'

'Hope so, Harry.'

'I hear that you're the new Duncan Edwards.'

'I'm not sure about that.'

'You do realise, though, that as the youngest player sat around this table you have to carry out the Christmas challenge.'

Wayne Bernard looked suspiciously at Harry, but noticed that Martin Peters was nodding sagely by the side of him, and no one ever questioned Martin – I mean, you just didn't; Martin Peters had scored a goal in the World Cup Final, his status was messiah-like.

'Oh yeah?' asked Bernard. 'What's that then?'

'Well,' continued Harry, 'we all put ten quid in the pot, and that's all yours, if you successfully carry out the challenge.'

'What if I lose?'

'If you lose,' said Harry, 'you have to clean every car in the first team car park once a week until the end of the season.'

'Bloody hell, Harry,' stuttered Wayne Bernard. 'That's quite a forfeit that.'

Harry turned to Martin Peters. 'Has anyone ever turned down the Christmas challenge, Martin?'

'Never,' said Martin Peters.

'Alright,' said Bernard. 'You name it. What's the challenge?'

Harry looked at me so I took my cue. I stared into the face of the young lad and adopted a grave and serious tone. 'Before midnight, my son, you have to get the phone number of the best-looking waitress.' We all looked around. 'Her,' I said, pointing at a petite, dark-haired girl of about eighteen.

Wayne Bernard smiled – 'Alright, boys,' he said, 'leave it to me. No problem. It'll be a pleasure taking your money off you and giving that bird a right good seeing to.'

His reaction to the challenge was too cocksure to be fun. He was too low in the pecking order to be worthy of serious banter. The challenge was quickly forgotten and ignored as we drank and revelled in being young and carefree and oh-so-very-very male.

About two hours later I found myself doing a drunken meander from table to table, aimlessly starting conversations, making jokes and slapping backs. There was a band and some of the lads were dancing. The chairman's table was closest to the dance floor. I could see that all the senior staff had their jackets off and that some of them were wearing paper hats. I briefly considered going over and asking Ron Greenwood what I'd have to do to get Sir Alf Ramsey to pick me for England – that would have been a conversation I'd have regretted in the morning. Instead, I decided to go for a leak. A tiny and, on the face of it, insignificant decision, but, as it turned out, one of those little moments of fate that makes me believe that perhaps life is all too amazing to be true and that perhaps everything really is controlled by the Service, and maybe my sudden desire for a Jimmy Riddle at that precise minute was pre-ordained, meant to be, written in the bloody stars. Oh I don't know.

I walked from the main hall and into a quiet corridor where about twenty yards from me big Wayne Bernard was standing menacingly in front of the young waitress who I'd earmarked for him a few hours earlier. She seemed to be pinned against a wall. My first instinct was to leave it, walk on by, mind my own business, after all, this was a football club and young men sometimes get a bit frisky, but, as I turned to go, she looked at me, her eyes bright and wide with fear.

I couldn't walk by. She was scared. I couldn't walk by. I stopped. I had to do something.

'Hey, Bernie,' I shouted, and Wayne Bernard moved a step backwards and looked at me; he was a young lad, pissed, frustrated and losing control.

'John Lyall's after you, mate,' I said, making up a plausible lie. Bernard grunted, but didn't seem to want to back off.

'John Lyall, mate,' I repeated, more forcefully. 'You don't want to let him down, do you?'

'Why? What does he want?' Bernard was slurring.

'How the fuck should I know – probably, something about how brilliant you are. Come on now, leave the young lady alone; I'm sure she'll still be here when you get back.'

Reluctantly he stepped away, staring at the young girl as he did.

'He's through there, mate,' I prompted. 'Best not keep him waiting.'

Wayne Bernard staggered off for a meeting with the assistant manager that would never happen, leaving me alone with the girl.

'You alright?' I asked and she nodded. She didn't seem alright. 'I'm sorry, you know what young lads are like when they've had a drink.'

A smile flickered around her mouth and she looked away from me. I could see now that she was beautiful. I could see that she was innocent. Pure. I was mesmerised. As I stood there looking at her, time slowed. I didn't feel my masculine need to consume her at breakneck speed. I didn't feel the anxious desire for instant physical gratification and love and adulation before running off for the next hit. Somehow, here, in this corridor, with this girl, I felt the weight of potential contentment and a deeper feeling of human contact – I wanted to know everything about her, I didn't just want her to be a fleeting, disposable part of my existence, but something better.

'Can I get you anything?' I asked.

'No, thanks,' she said and then she walked away.

I paused for a second, one of those seconds that you remember years and years later, because it was a moment in which my body and mind welled up with an instinctive, overwhelming desire to act. 'What's your name?' I shouted as she walked away. But she didn't answer me.

After the dinner, a few of us went over to Ray Harley's nightclub in Chingford. I don't remember much about it: no doubt we drank more booze and pranced around like peacocks because we were footballers, knights of the round table, the untouchable dynamite dealers of Saturday afternoon and any other night we wanted; no doubt there was banter and girls and silenced young men who couldn't compete with us, because they weren't footballers – but I don't remember. What I do remember, was that the first thing I wanted to do when I woke up the next morning, was find out about the girl I had saved from big Wayne Bernard.

I thought about her for four sober days and on the fifth day, I picked up the telephone in the players' lounge at Upton Park and phoned the number for the St George's Hall, Dagenham. I then had an excruciating conversation with a receptionist.

'Hello,' I said, 'it's Billy Parks here, from West Ham, we were there last week for our Christmas Party, and I'm trying to find out the name of one of your waitresses.'

'Oh yes?' came the reply.

There then followed a futile exchange between me and a nice

140

middle-aged woman on the other end of the phone in which I tried to describe the girl who had been harassed by Wayne Bernard, and she said things like, 'Ooh, that sounds like Debbie, or Angela. Did she have a Dusty Springfield hairdo?'

Eventually, I hung up. I felt embarrassed – things weren't usually this complicated.

Bobby Moore, who had been sitting reading a newspaper nearby, smiled at me. 'Why don't you just drive down there, Billy,' he suggested, 'then you can make sure you've got the right girl.'

I was even more embarrassed now; I hadn't meant anyone to hear this, let alone the club captain, but Bobby's advice was wise, of course it was, he was the Captain of England, he had held the World Cup aloft, he was the wisest man in the universe.

That evening I got in my car, picked up a massive box of cream cakes on the way, and drove over to the St George's Hall.

I got there about six o'clock, the dining room was being prepared for some kind of function. I stood at the entrance. It was a massive ornate room from a time long gone. It contained about thirty circular tables, and the only sound was the clunking of cutlery being placed on top of brilliant-white tablecloths by brilliant-white-and-black-clad waiters and waitresses. I stood at the door clutching my box of cakes and scanned the room for the damsel I had saved from Wayne Bernard. I couldn't see her. I felt stupid. Normally things were so much easier, normally women just happened in the fug of drink before disappearing the next morning.

'Can I help you?' came a male voice.

'Er, yes, er, I don't know.' I was stuttering like an imbecile. A man in a waistcoat walked towards me clutching a handful of forks. I could see that he was squinting as he tried to work out who I was – he looked suspiciously at the box of cream cakes. I felt my mouth dry. I had no idea what I was about to do or say. I wanted to be far away.

The man's face brightened.

'You're Billy Parks, aren't you?' he said. I could have kissed him.

'Yes,' I said, 'that's right.'

'Blooming Nora,' he continued. 'Hold on, I'll just get some of the lads from the kitchen.'

Seconds later, as I stood there, the man returned from the kitchen with about half a dozen lads in chef's whites.

'Billy Parks, lads,' said the man.

'Hello,' I said, uncomfortably. I wasn't sure that I'd come here for this. For once, I hadn't wanted to be feted and stared at and adored.

They started to fire questions at me, as others gathered around:

'Are you going to win the cup, Billy?'

'Is Martin Peters going to Spurs or Arsenal?'

'Are you going to go to Mexico for the World Cup?'

'What are you doing here then?'

What are you doing here then?

That was the tricky one, the pertinent one.

'I've come to deliver these cakes, from the lads like, to say thank you for the party last week.'

Someone took the box off me, and everyone cooed and thanked me and told me that it was nothing. And as they spoke, I looked at the assembled throng, which now numbered about thirty, waiters, waitresses and various staff. I couldn't see *her*, it was just a mass of smiling staring happy faces none of which was hers – none of these people could slow down time.

'Right then, I'd better get off,' I said, and I turned around and walked back out of the dining room and into the foyer. The man in the waistcoat followed me telling me about how he used to know Malcolm Allison and I nodded and grunted in what I hoped was an appropriate way.

'Right,' I said. 'Cheers, I'd better be off.'

I turned to go.

And there she was.

Stood by the front door, wearing an olive green coat and matching hat.

I stood still. This was what I had come for. By my side the man in the waistcoat's prattling voice blurred.

'Excuse me,' I said, and walked over to the girl.

'Hey.'

She turned to me and smiled.

'Sorry,' I said, though I'm not sure why I was apologising, then there was a pause during which I grappled with my own existence. 'Are you alright?' I added.

'Yes.' She looked puzzled.

'I mean after the other night.'

She looked down at her shoes. 'That was nothing,' she said, then she looked up at me, her teeth shining brightly, as she started to realise what I was doing there. And as she smiled, it happened again; time slowed, the usual uncontained and barely understood physical desires that engulfed my life diminished and were replaced by something strange, something more substantial, something I wasn't used to and didn't understand.

I started to laugh. Then I looked away in dumb embarrassment, still laughing. When I turned back to look at her, she was laughing as well.

'What's your name?' I asked her.

'Sandi,' she said, her voice soft like a feather floating on a warm current of air. 'Sandi Leadbetter.'

'I'm Bill Parks, Sandi Leadbetter.'

'Oh,' she said, still smiling.

That Saturday I took her to see *Butch Cassidy and the Sundance Kid* at the Odeon in Leicester Square. We sat in the darkness surrounded by the fog of cigarette smoke. I felt a human contact like no other. I didn't touch her. She didn't touch me. We sat only inches from each other: the desperate physical desire was immense. I couldn't concentrate on the screen. I wanted to look at her, so I kept sneaking glances, taking in the shape of her face and her cheekbones as she quietly smiled at the film. Time ticked by with a beautiful contented sluggishness.

For eight months and one week, I allowed myself to be happy with her. For eight months and one week, I wallowed in the effect she had on me. We made plans. I would propose that Christmas and we would get married in the summer of 1971. I was happy. Time was slower. She made time slow down.

Eight months and one week: how can I pinpoint the duration of my happiness so precisely? How can I possibly know exactly when that feeling ended?

Because that was how long it took for me to fuck everything up.

It was 26 August 1970: the first game of the 1970/71 season. We were at home to Leeds. It was a dirty, nasty affair; they went ahead with a Sniffer Clarke goal early on, then, for the next hour they hammered us in the brutal clinical Leeds way, which was a combination of muscle and forensic passing. Leeds were like that, they'd kick you if they had to, but they had players like Johnny Giles and Billy Bremner who could pass a ball all day long. They should have scored four or five – but they didn't.

Then, in the last minute, Ronnie Boyce put a long hopeful ball into the box and Leeds' Jackie Charlton only managed to head it straight to me. I advanced into the area and he steamed towards me with his massive legs and dived in.

I went down like an old lady on a frosty morning, even though not one single part of Jack Charlton touched me. There, I've admitted it. I dived. It was a cheat. I'm not proud of it, but it was the last minute of a game and against Leeds. The ref gave a penalty, and Geoff Hurst duly put it into the back of the net: 1-1.

After the game, Don Revie and Jackie Charlton came after me, with Don Revie storming into our changing room to call me a cheating little bastard and Jackie Charlton threatening to kick my arse, which led to a bit of scuffle between some of their lads and some of ours.

And that is why I remember it. That's why I know, because that night I went out. It was the night I had dived to get a penalty against Leeds.

We ended up in some trendy bar. Pissed.

It was the first time I'd been out without Sandi for ages. She hadn't fancied it much that night, and perhaps I didn't press it.

We drank champagne and cocktails and I have sketchy images in my head of speaking to George Best and Bestie being more pissed than I was, and then, a tap on the shoulder and a voice.

'Hello, you don't remember me do you?'

And me squinting at the girl standing in front of me. And she's laughing. And I'm laughing too.

'I see you're not delivering cakes any more then.'

And now I'm smiling at her, because it's the bird from the boutique who Barry Ross set me up with. And I'm pissed in a way I haven't been for a while and the music in this club is merging with the colours of the lights and the taste of the girl's mouth on mine and the smell of her perfume wraps itself around my brain and my manhood. And I don't care about Sandi, my lovely Sandi and all our beautiful plans. Bloody hell, the girl's mouth on mine. And then a taxi back to hers.

I thought that it wouldn't matter, I thought that everything would go back to how it was, and I would never do anything like that again, but it wasn't: after that, Sandi would never be able to make time stand still again.

It took eight months and one week. Then I spoiled everything.

Details: Match 7, 19 March 1968
Division One
Venue: Upton Park
West Ham 3 v. Chelsea 0
Parks
Hurst
Dear

Line Ups
West Ham: Ferguson, Bonds, Stephenson, Moore, Lampard,

Redknapp, Brooking, Peters, Parks, Dear, Hurst
Chelsea: Bonetti, Harris, McCreadie, Webb, Hinton, Hollins, Cooke, Houseman, Birchenall, Osgood, Baldwin

Attendance: 35,876

Details: Match 8, 28 August 1969
Division One
Venue: Upton Park
West Ham 4 v. Crystal Palace 0
Parks (3)
Hurst

Line Ups
West Ham: Ferguson, Bonds, Cushley, Moore, Lampard, Redknapp, Brooking, Peters, Boyce, Parks, Hurst
Crystal Palace: Jackson, Loughlan, Hynd, Blyth, Taylor, Payne, Hoy, Kember, Lazarus, Tambling, Queen

Attendance: 29,876

Details: Match 9, 20 August 1970
Division One
Venue: Elland Road, Leeds
Leeds United 1 v. West Ham 1
Clarke   Hurst (pen)

Line Ups
Leeds United: Sprake, Reaney, Charlton, Hunter, Cooper, Bremner, Giles, Gray, Lorimer, Clarke, Jones
West Ham: Ferguson, McDowall, Bonds, Moore, Lampard, Redknapp, Brooking, Boyce, Parks, Hurst, Best

Attendance: 42,349

15

Maureen looks at me, the beautiful furrows and creases of her face forming themselves into an expression of sadness and disappointment.

It is two days since I went to see Dr Aranthraman, two days since I spoke to the face of Johnny Smith.

They hadn't been a happy two days.

'Oh, Billy.'

Her dark eyes focus on me.

'What have you done?'

'Nothing.'

I stand at the door of her pub as she stares at me from behind the bar holding a tea-towel in one hand and a warm, clean pint glass in the other.

'You look terrible, what did Dr Aranthraman say?'

I drum up as happy an expression as I can muster. 'Good news, actually,' I told her, 'he says that my liver is definitely getting better.'

Her expression changes into one of suspicion and disbelief.

'Are you sure? You don't look better. You look worse, you look terrible.'

'No, I'm fine. I think I've picked up a cold that's all.'

'Really?'

'Yeah.'

'Where were you yesterday? I was calling you all day.'

Ah. Yesterday. Yesterday. The truthful answer is that yesterday I woke up at dinner time, with gravel where my throat should be and my chest tightening as sweat dripped from my matted hair into my stinging eyes. Shit. Yesterday, I woke up at dinner time and I lay there, knowing that I couldn't go and see anyone, especially Maureen, as I retched up the bile from the day before and battled with the evil spirits that were swimming around and around in my head, reminding me in their dark whispers about the wasted life that was Billy Parks.

'I went up West,' I tell her. 'I wanted to buy Liam a football shirt.' It was a good lie as it was partly true. I was just a day out. She didn't need to know about my lost day. I wanted to shut that out, toss it on to the scrap heap with all the other lost days.

I didn't blame the barman from the Gherkin bar either. He was just doing his job – alright, he was a bit of a wanker, but, I suppose, he was right: you can't go drinking in a place like that on your own, it's just not done.

I'd left his precious bar without any fuss.

I'd got in the lift and watched the numbers descend. I told myself that the barman had actually done me a favour. It was good fortune, he had prevented me from drinking and now I was going to leave the bloody Gherkin and go home and maybe get another jigsaw or something. That is what I told myself as the lift descended and the numbers went from 40 down to 30.

But.

I already had the taste of alcohol in my mouth.

And I needed to make sense of the face of Johnny Smith. I needed to make sense of everything. I was scared. I wanted to think and make sense of all the things I could change.

Only drink would help me.

And, after all, Dr Aranthraman had told me that things weren't

148

getting any worse, so a few quick scotches wouldn't do me any harm. Would they?

By the time the lift reached floor 10, I had made up my mind; or rather I had waved a little white flag of surrender. Again.

There was one of those massive modern City pubs up the street; not really my type of boozer, too light, too noisy, the ceiling too high. But it was close, so I went inside in search of someone to ruffle my hair and tell me that I was Billy Parks, tell me a story of a goal or a piece of skill; anything.

I drank alone all afternoon. I spoke to no one. No one recognised me. I went from pub to pub in search of company and kinship and someone to talk to me about the past, but I drank alone and woke up hateful and jaundiced and in pain.

And a day later, the alcohol that had made me a twat, made me weak, is now making me a liar because that's what it does.

Maureen looks at me. 'Look, why don't you go upstairs?' she said. 'Will's up there, I'm sure he'd love to see you.'

Will is Maureen's son: a fine young man. He's studying biology at Leeds University. Really clever lad.

I nod and make my way upstairs.

'I'll come up after we've done the lunchtimes,' she says.

I make my way upstairs and find Will in Maureen's lounge doing something on one of those laptop computers.

'Hello, son.'

He looks up at me – there is a pause and a change of facial expression. 'Hello, Billy, how are you? You look like shite, mate.'

'Shite! Is that a Yorkshire expression?'

He smiles at me. 'Do you want a cup of tea?'

I want vodka. Vodka makes the lunchtime shakes go away. Vodka cures me.

'Lovely,' I say. 'Two sugars please.'

He gets up and says, 'I've got something to show you actually.'

He really is a good boy, Will. I've known him since he was a kid. He passed all his exams. Mind as sharp as a new pin. I used to take him occasionally to kick a football about in the park – he wasn't half-bad either.

Perhaps my grandson could meet him? That would be good. Perhaps Liam's good at exams as well. Perhaps he's going to be a doctor or a lawyer, go to university, do something really worthwhile with his life.

Will comes back with a cup of tea in a Millwall FC mug, emblazoned with the words, *No One Likes Us!*

I lift it up to him and give him a mocking look. 'That's because you're rubbish,' I say referring to the slogan. It's a joke we've had going on for years. He really is a good boy: not sure where he got the Millwall thing from, though, perhaps his father.

'Right,' he says. 'Look at this,' and he picks up the laptop computer and comes and sits by me. 'One of the lads I live with found you on YouTube.'

'YouTube?'

'Yes, it's like a massive online library of video clips – music, sport, all kinds of stuff.'

'Oh yes.'

I don't really know much about all that; I am slightly wary about being 'found' in a library of film clips. Will taps something on his keyboard and the familiar, beige-suited figure of Brian Moore pops up on his screen. It is a clip from *The Big Match*, years ago.

'Well I'll be—'

Then, suddenly, there I am, me, in my claret and blue, with my blond hair lovely and luxuriant and my massive sideburns and my twenty-three-year-old twinkling smile. We're playing Derby County – I know this because the pitch is like a swamp, which is the way Brian Clough wanted it if the Hammers were coming to town, the wily old bastard. I watch intently, my face breaking into a smile as I score a goal from a Trevor Brooking pass. Oh it's lovely it is. I don't remember the goal. I don't remember the game. I can see that David Nish is marking me, but I get in front of him because I'm twenty-three and so, so bloody fast, and I

150

hit it first time and the ball flies into the back of the net and the camera pans on to me and I'm so happy, so bloody happy, my face bursting with the most fantastic ecstasy as big Clyde Best comes over and gives me a smacker.

For a few seconds the transportation back in time has left me deliriously joyful.

'Nineteen seventy-two,' says Will. He clicks a few more buttons and I pop up again in a different clip from around about the same time. Again, another goal, this time in an FA Cup match against Cardiff City. I remember this goal, a lovely curling shot from outside the area. Then another clip of another goal, and another: I don't remember these; I don't remember smiling that effortlessly; I don't remember feeling that fantastic. Suddenly, it's as though my youthful smiling happy self is mocking me. Suddenly, all I can remember are the rows at home with Sandi and the silences and the feeling of wanting to be somewhere else; and the guilt, the desperate black bloody guilt when I'd come home, after two or three days on the piss, smelling of some other bird, and pray that she'd shout at me, because it was easier for me to deal with her anger than her pain. The images started to scare me. My young beautiful self seemed to goad me.

The truth isn't contained in the clips.

I want Will to stop.

'Crikey, Will,' I say, 'it's like looking at a bleeding ghost, mate.'

'I'm sorry, Billy.'

'That's alright, they're amazing. I'm just a bit shocked –' I pause. 'Sometimes things weren't always as easy as they seem.'

I'm not sure why I said that.

'Shit, Billy, I'm sorry.'

'Don't be daft, son.'

I have an idea. A bloody good one.

'Look, can you find any match on there?'

'Well, not any match, but most of the big ones, you know, cup finals, England games and that.'

'What about England versus Poland; you know, the one in 1973.'

151

'The Jan Tomaszewski game?'

'Yes.'

'Sure. I'll have a look.'

It comes up at the touch of his keyboard. It has Polish commentary. I've never seen it before, but the gloomy, dank north London October night is unmistakable. I sit and watch as Will's screen shows England hammering at the Polish goal.

'You weren't playing, though, were you Billy?'

'No,' I said. 'I was on the bench. I didn't get the nod. I just want to see something.'

There they were: all the chances, just as I remember them; all the failures, all the saves by the great Polish Clown; and all the misses by the great English strikers: Allan Clarke, Micky Channon, Martin Chivers. I can see now what Gerry Higgs had meant – the Polish keeper saved a couple he shouldn't have.

I watch as Kevin Hector makes his way on to the pitch. I watch as he takes his place on the six-yard line and Tony Currie puts the ball down to take the corner. I watched as the Clown finally makes a mistake and poor Kevin Hector does everything right apart from put the fucking ball in the back of the net. I ask Will to play it again. I study it carefully. More carefully than I've watched the flight of a football in years: Kevin Hector's moment of immortality. He couldn't be blamed, God bless him, he did everything right. I feel my mouth drop open as I stare at the ball moving slowly from the striker's head then rebounding off the legs of the perfectly positioned Polish defender.

It *had* been a textbook header: putting the ball back against the direction of the cross downwards towards the corner of the goal. The poor bastard had done everything right. It wasn't his fault. He had been unlucky. The Polish full-back had positioned himself perfectly.

How the bloody hell am I going to score? I have never been known for my heading. How am I going to put the ball in the back of the net? How am I going to change everything? Change bloody history. How can I help my mother and Johnny Smith and everyone else? How am I going to make everything better?

I rub my eyes.

Gerry Higgs and the bloody Service might actually make everything worse. *I* could become the person who missed the open goal that would have taken England to the World Cup. I sit back on the chair as Will looks at me with concern.

'What's the matter, Billy?'

'I've just realised that for years everyone has said that Kevin Hector missed an open goal – but really it wasn't quite straightforward.'

'Didn't Kevin Hector score loads of goals for Derby?'

'Yes,' I reply, 'hundreds. But it's not easy to steer the ball past the defender on the line. Not with a header.'

I feel myself sucking air into my mouth as I consider the incident again and again. It isn't going to be easy.

Maureen's appearance at the door breaks my concentration.

'The AA meeting is tomorrow night,' she says.

I turn around to face her. Bloody hell. As if I don't have enough to worry about.

I smile feebly. 'Oh good, I'm looking forward to it.' That was a lie.

'Will, could you go downstairs to the bar and help Finn for a little while – there's a bit of a rush on.'

'Sure, Mum,' Will says, getting up. He really is a good kid.

I start to tell Maureen what a fine young son she has, but she isn't listening.

'Right, Billy, no bullshit. I want to know: where were you really yesterday?'

I sigh. 'I told you, Maureen, I went up West to get a Hammers shirt for Liam, Oxford Circus, if you must know, cost me thirty knicker.'

She looks at me unconvinced.

'Christ,' I say backing up my lie with a firm voice, 'if you want

153

to see, I'll show you the top; it's got his name on and everything. I'll even bring the bloody receipt.'

I know that she won't want to see the receipt. I know that my firm voice will probably do the trick and end the cross-examination. It is a technique I've been successfully employing for thirty years on different people.

Her lips thin as she decides to take my word on trust.

'You really don't look that great,' she continues, softening. 'Are you sure that Dr Aranthraman is happy with you?'

'Yes,' I said, 'I told him all about doing jigsaws and going to AA meetings, he was absolutely tickety-boo.'

'Because ...' She pauses. 'I think I might have tracked down Rebecca.'

My heart leaps with unbounded last-minute goal joy.

'That's brilliant. Where? Where is she? What have you said? What did she say? When can I meet her?'

Maureen looks at me, an expression of mature seriousness on her face.

'I've found her using the computer,' she says. 'One of those social networking websites.'

'How do you know it's her?'

'Rebecca Leadbetter, yes?'

I nod.

'Date of birth 13 December 1973, in Ilford?'

I nod again.

'One son – Liam?'

'That's right,' I say. 'That's absolutely right. What has she said?'

'Nothing yet,' says Maureen. 'But now I know where she is, and how to contact her, all you need to do is carry out your side of the bargain.'

I smile.

'I will,' I say. 'I will. Tomorrow night, AA, I'll be there.'

I sit back in the chair and feel a wave of excitement pass over me.

Maureen stands smiling by the door. She still looks lovely when she smiles. Her brown eyes have a warm calm to them – if only I'd met her years earlier.

'You are a diamond,' I say. 'An absolute diamond, I knew I could count on you.'

I sit forward and look at her.

'Where were you in 1973?' I ask, trying to muster up some of the twinkle in my eyes.

'Christ, Billy, 1973: I was living out near Heathrow with a couple of friends. We were working at the airport.'

'Right,' I say. 'After I've scored the goal against Poland, I'm coming to find you.'

She looks at me. 'Billy, what on earth are you talking about? You keep going on about bloody Poland!'

'After Poland everything's going to change,' I say. 'I'm going to make everything right, for everyone – you'll see.'

She shakes her head dismissively. 'Some of us don't need any repairs, Billy.'

She looks at me with a soft pity, before adding quietly but with increasing firmness, 'I'd better get back to the bar. You just make sure you're here tomorrow night by seven, if you're not, or if you've been drinking, I won't help you any more.'

I grin at her. 'On my honour.'

She looks dubiously at me then turns to go away.

'Oh and Maureen,' I shout.

She turns back to me, and I ask, 'Have you got another jigsaw?'

'No, but I'll get you one.'

'Thanks, how about something that doesn't have bricks in it this time?'

'You just make sure you're here at seven o'clock tomorrow – I'll take you to the AA meeting myself.'

Her words left me feeling suddenly tired.

16

I hang around Maureen's for a little while, and then walk back to my flat. I feel terrible: tight chest, runny nose, pounding throbbing head and a deep, tight pain in my stomach. I must have picked up some kind of bug or flu or something.

Worse though, much worse, was the cold fear that had started to rush round in my head as soon as I'd left Maureen's pub. I can't stop it: fear of the shadowy Polish defender on the line; fear of being unable to save my friends and my mother, of not being able to put everything right; fear of the next drink and the pain in my stomach; fear of being rejected by Rebecca or Liam; even fear of the bloody AA meeting. It just keeps surging round and round, like some kind of demented wet slavering greyhound endlessly chasing a rabbit round a small room.

And the more fearful I get – the more the bloody dog goes round – the greater my thirst.

I knew this would happen.

I wish I had one of Maureen's jigsaws.

When I get back to my flat, I check the time: it is about three o'clock in the afternoon. I have no plans whatsoever for one day and four hours – that's twenty-eight hours. Twenty-eight hours without a drink. I'd promised Maureen that I wouldn't drink – so I can't. I have some sleeping tablets which I hope might knock me out for a bit, but, that is later, and I need help now. I needed to make the bleeding dog stop running now.

I put the telly on: crap afternoon TV. I turn it off and think about the bookie's. Yes, that's what I'll do, I'll go down the bookie's. But even that is fraught with danger, because the walk to the bookmaker's on the High Street will take me past O'Hara's Irish Bar, the Speakeasy and the Mitre, and a few hundred yards from the Castle – I especially like the Castle. I put my coat on and walk towards my front door. I know what will happen if I leave. I know it. I *want* it to happen. I want it to happen and I hate myself. I've told Maureen, I've promised Maureen, it's the only way she'll help me, I know that if I get pissed up now, I won't see Rebecca, I won't see Liam – I won't see Maureen ever again.

But the dog runs round and round and round.

I put my back against the door and slowly feel myself slide down to the ground, tears running down my face; me, Billy Parks, sitting on the floor against my front door, crying like a lost toddler.

Eventually I take myself back to my couch.

I don't remember falling asleep. But I must have, because when I open my eyes Gerry Higgs is sitting in the armchair across the room.

'You shouldn't go leaving your door open like that, old son,' he says. 'Not round here. I've heard of people nipping to the khazi and when they come out, someone's nicked the telly. You need to be more careful.'

'I'm sorry, Mr Higgs.'

I still have my coat on.

'I was going to go out for a walk, but I must have come over a bit sleepy.'

I look at the digital clock on the video player: 17.32. I've been asleep for a couple of hours.

I feel a bit better; the presence of Gerry Higgs and the sleep have made me feel better. The dog has stopped.

I get up and start to take my coat off.

'What are you doing?'

'Just taking my coat off.'

'No, don't do that, Billy, come on, we're going out.'

'But, Mr Higgs, I don't feel very well, I've got a cold or something.'

'Don't give me that, you look fine to me – come on, let's go and watch some football.'

'Football?'

'Yes, Billy, you remember, football, twenty-two players, one ball.'

We walked to a floodlit football pitch not far away to watch a youth game – under 18s, Gerry Higgs tells me.

The pitch is smooth like a billiard table and all the kids have got the look of supreme athletes about them. Around the pitch stand a cordon of men and dozens of bottles of those special sports drinks. There are dads and scouts, coaches and just men of a certain age who need the thrill of football. All of them watching intensely, kicking every ball in their minds.

'Bit different from your day, eh, Billy?' said Gerry Higgs.

I don't want to talk about football; I want to tell him about my fears.

'Look, Mr Higgs,' I start, but Gerry Higgs is too intent on watching the game.

'I'm told that the centre-forward for the blue team, that's Southwark Juniors, is a good prospect, fast I'm told, and strong – mind you, they're all fast and strong these days.'

'Mr Higgs,' I say, 'about this Poland game, I'm not sure.'

He continues to ignore me. 'It amazes me, all these young lads are so bloody big and strong, yet hardly any of them can tackle properly and none of them can stay on their bloody feet.'

I try again: 'It's not that I'm not grateful or anything, I just don't think I can do it.'

Now, he turns to me.

'Nonsense, Billy, course you can do it. You've been especially picked, old son. The Service doesn't just give this type of chance to anyone.'

The word *Service* resonates with a distorted echo through my head as though Gerry Higgs has shouted it in my ear using a megaphone.

'But, what if I fail?' I say, 'and what if I mess it all up? I mean, are we even supposed to go back and change stuff that we got wrong? Isn't that a bit like, well, a bit like cheating?'

At this Gerry turns sharply towards me, his eyes ablaze. 'Cheating!' he exclaims. 'It would only be cheating if we made sure that you scored. Believe me, Billy old son, if you're lucky enough to be picked over Kevin Keegan, you've still got to put the ball in the back of the bloody net. No one can help you there – that's not cheating.'

'But, bringing me on in the first place, isn't that—'

'That's simply correcting a mistake. And everyone should have the chance to correct a mistake.'

I shrug. I know all about mistakes.

Gerry Higgs continues, 'Just look around you, Billy, what do you see?'

I shrug again. 'I don't know, sky, trees, those blocks of flats over there.'

'No, Billy, other than that, here, now – what do you see? In-bloody-front of you.'

'A football match.'

'Exactly, a football match: two junior sides – twenty-two young lads, all of them with one dream, to be a professional footballer, to be a hero, to feel the joy that only very few people can ever get to feel. To feel that love, that adulation.'

I nod, as Gerry Higgs gets into his stride: 'And watching them, Billy, standing on the touchline, who do you see? You see old men, dads and granddads and uncles, all of them living their own failed dreams through the young lads out there. Nearly all of whom will also, one day, pore over their own failed dreams and watch some other kid play and wish to God it was them. Do you understand, Billy?'

I shrug, I did. But I wasn't sure that it would get rid of the fear.

'You, Billy, were born with talent. You, my son, had what all these lads dream of. And now you might have a chance to finally fulfil that talent. Do you understand?'

I nod again.

'A second chance, Billy,' he continues, his voice firm and gravelly, his eyes watering with the intensity of his words. 'A second bloody chance.'

I sigh, he is right.

'And not only will you have a chance to help yourself, you will have a chance to help your country. Believe me, Billy, our country is better off with a successful football team.'

'Alright,' I say.

A cheer goes up from the crowd as the blue centre-forward charges through the middle of the defence and drills the ball past the goalkeeper.

'Now I don't want to hear any more about not being sure.'

'Alright, Mr Higgs, I'm sorry. It's difficult that's all.'

Gerry Higgs ignores me and goes back to watching the game: he was never one for the arm-around-the-shoulder or the cuff-to-wipe-away-the-tears approach.

'Look at that,' he says, gesticulating towards the pitch. 'The bloody full-back has just hoofed the ball fifty yards up the pitch to absolutely nobody, when the wing-half was there crying out for the ball. These lads, they've no idea about the subtleties of the game. No idea how to pass a ball simply from one player to the next. Dave Sexton wouldn't have let *you* do that, would he? Or Ron Greenwood?'

I ignore his question. 'So, when is it all going to happen then?' I ask. 'When will I know?'

'Next week,' he tells me, without averting his gaze from the match.

161

'Next week?!'

'Yes, the Council are meeting next week. I don't know what day, so don't ask me.'

'Bloody hell. And what will happen, you know, what will happen if I get the nod over Kevin Keegan – will I go up in some kind of spaceship or something?'

Gerry Higgs looks at me. 'Spaceship? What are you talking about? This isn't bloody *Star Trek*, this is the Service putting right a mistake that was made in the past – this is the hand of history being given a chance to rewrite itself. There's no bloody spaceships involved.'

'So how will it happen then?'

He looks at me, exasperated. 'I will be there with you. I'll take you to where you will have to go. It's part of my job. Alright?'

I nod, this sounds better; this was a more concrete proposal: Gerry Higgs would be my guide.

Then I remember that I was due to meet Rebecca and Liam.

'I might be meeting my grandson,' I tell him.

'Very nice, Billy. I'm very pleased to hear that.'

'What worries me, Gerry, is what will happen if I score against Poland and that leads to him not being born?'

'You're talking about the vagaries of fate, Billy.'

'Yes, I suppose I am.'

'Well, you can't do nothing about that, you can only score your goal, and let fate and history take over. If you want my advice, just relax, go and see the boy and make sure that both of you have a wonderful time.'

'Will I get the chance to do that, Gerry? What if the Council meet before I get the chance to see Liam?'

'That's up to you, Billy.'

17

Parksy for England (clap-clap, clap-clap, clap);
Parksy for England (clap-clap, clap-clap, clap).

That was what they sang.

Every time I scored a goal, every time I went on to the pitch with my sunshine hair bobbing and my face smiling at the adoration. They even shouted it if they saw me in the street or in the pub. They loved me, or the person they thought was me: Billy Parks Was God.

They ignored the stories about me missing training a few times due to mysterious colds and ailments. They ignored the stories about me being found drunk and incapable in my car in a churchyard in Chadwell Heath. They ignored the fact that I played against Nottingham Forest that season with two black eyes after a bloke had taken offence at me talking to his Mrs.

They even forgave me when I got sent off against Coventry City.

It was in December 1971. We were struggling in mid-table. The great West Ham side of the 1960s, the side that had won England the World Cup, was in the process of being dismantled: Geoff Hurst was on his way to Stoke City; Martin Peters had gone to Spurs;

Greavsie, Ronnie Boyce and Brian Dear had all gone in various directions. Even Harry was on his way out, and the younger lads, the Trevor Brookings and Billy Bonds and Frankie Lampards, were finding it hard to cope. Bobby Moore was still there, but, dare I say it, Bobby was starting to show signs of age.

The game against Coventry had been a boring Sunday pub-team type of affair played on one of those dark winter afternoons when there's moisture in the air even though it's not raining and the sky goes from dark to hateful cold grey and then back to dark again.

I don't remember if I had a hangover when the game started – probably – but I do remember that Coventry had put a little fella on me called Nolan. Horrible little Irish bastard he was. I never heard of him again, but that afternoon he had been given one task – hurt Billy Parks. Every time he came near me, he raked his studs down my Achilles, every bloody time.

The silly fool didn't have to hurt me, I was playing shite as it was. I was tired and slow and cold and uninvolved and disinterested, but still the little cunt kept trying to hurt me. Rake, rake, bloody rake, and if he couldn't rake me, he pinched me, the little bastard, and after each assault he laughed in a sneering way. I turned to him after a corner and pushed him in the chest – he laughed at me again: 'Is that the best you can do, yer wee ponce?'

So I hit him.

I am not a fighter, I'd never successfully hit anyone in my life – I prided myself on staying well away from any rough stuff on the pitch – but in that moment, as the little twat stood there laughing at me, I chinned him, a great big haymaker that landed perfectly on his nose and exploded across his face like a smashed egg.

Everyone looked at me in eerie dumbfounded silence. Even the nutcases who would normally wade in once a punch had been thrown just stared at me. No one said a word.

The ref – old Fitzpatrick, good ref he was, nice bloke an' all – came running over. 'Parksy,' he said, 'what the bloody hell you playing at?'

'Sorry, Ref, he's been at it all afternoon.'

'But you hit him?'

We both looked down at the prone Nolan who was clutching his face and muttering something in a thick Ulster brogue about his nose being broken.

'You're going to have to go off, son.'

'I know, I'm sorry.'

I walked off, my head down, as the Coventry fans treated me to wolf-whistles and two-fingered salutes. I don't blame them for that. I can't, can I?

I waited alone in the changing room. Far away I could hear the occasional muffled roar of the crowd. I breathed deeply and slowly took off my boots and shin-pads.

I stared at my teammates' clothes, which hung silently and haphazardly on pegs. The items seemed to mock me: *when these trousers are filled you're going to get it.*

We lost 1-0 to a Willy Carr goal. I knew what to expect: Coventry City were rubbish, and with eleven men we'd have murdered them.

Billy Bonds laid into me first. 'What were you thinking, Billy? You stupid, stupid cunt – getting yourself sent off.'

'The bastard was kicking me all afternoon.'

'Well he wasn't kicking you hard enough, was he? I've got a good mind to show him how it's done.'

'I'm sorry, Bonz.'

'You twat. It's about time you realised that there's more to this club than you.'

'Leave it Bonz.' Bobby Moore came to my rescue. The changing room descended into a screaming tortuous silence as my team-mates quietly got dressed and contemplated the frustration of an avoidable defeat.

Billy Bonds was right. I knew he was right.

I sat there quietly, making sure that my face retained a suitably remorseful expression as the rest of the lads got changed. But, deep down, I wasn't as bothered as I should have been. I didn't care as much as I ought to. I *was* starting to care more about myself and my appetites and desires than anything else.

Later, on the team bus, as I sat alone with my head resting against the window, Bobby Moore came and sat by me. 'Billy,' he said, 'I think it's time you settled down, mate, isn't it?'

I nodded shyly. Bobby Moore: the wisest man that ever lived. He was my Captain. I'd have done anything for him.

'Why don't you get married to that girl you've been seeing, the pretty one with the dark hair?'

I couldn't tell Bobby Moore that ever since I'd shagged Sandra the northern girl from the boutique, my beautiful Sandi no longer had the ability to contain the mischievous sprites that danced around in me; I couldn't tell him that she had lost the ability to make time slow down or lead us both into a dreamy, warm, happy, languid, contentedness – blokes just didn't say that.

So I nodded and told him that we were making plans – which was true.

I served my ban and got back to playing at the top of my game. And in the spring of 1972, me and Sandi got married. Chingford Registry Office: she wore a beautiful yellow dress and a wide-brimmed hat with flowers on it. I stood in front of the registrar as she walked down the aisle between two sets of plastic chairs, gazing at me as she did, her beautiful full lips slightly open, her hazel eyes beseeching me: please, please, please make me happy.

And I looked away – because I knew then, even though I loved her, even though I knew how lucky I was, even though I knew that I didn't deserve her, I knew that I wasn't capable of making her happy.

I kissed her and smiled as they pronounced us man and wife, then I turned to the congregation and invited everyone to the pub for 'a proper booze-up'.

'Where's your mum?' asked Sandi.

She'd tried valiantly to get my mum interested in the wedding:

'It's important that your mum is there,' she'd said. 'You'll regret it if she isn't.'

So, dragging my heels, I'd gone to see my mum on my own on the Friday before the ceremony. Her flat was cold yet clean, the TV was on. She'd acquired a vicious little poodle with bad breath and that horrible matted fur poodles have that leaves you wanting to wash your hands if you ever touch them. Horrible curly bastard he was. She called him Peppy and he made her flat smell of old wet dog. He and the telly were her constant and only companions.

When I arrived at her flat she was rubbing a brass vase. I'd never seen it before.

'Where did you get that from?'

'It was your Uncle Wilf's,' she said. 'He brought it back from India after the war.'

'What? Fat Uncle Wilf? I never knew he'd been in the war?'

'Oh, yes, he fought at Verdun before going to India. Apparently, he stole this from some maharaja. I've had it in a cupboard for years, thought it needed a polish.'

I was surprised by this information; until then, long dead Uncle Wilf was someone who sat in my memory as a portly, red-faced man who had featured fleetingly during my childhood. But now, within the space of this short exchange, he'd been reinvented as a war hero and cunning thief.

Peppy sniffed at my trousers and I tried to move him away without touching him. 'I've just come round to check on the arrangements for tomorrow,' I said. She didn't answer, she just rubbed Uncle Wilf's stolen vase even harder and I knew that I wouldn't be seeing her at my wedding.

I felt relief, but out of a sense of duty, I tried to chase that feeling away.

'Come on, Mum,' I said, knowing that I had to go through the charade of encouragement. 'It'll be brilliant.'

'I've nothing to wear,' she said curtly.

'Yes, you have, you've got lots of things to wear.'

Actually, I had no idea what lay in my mother's wardrobe. For years, I had only seen her in old cardigans and dowdy skirts: the days of her youthful flowery dresses and red lipstick had been washed away by gin and barley wine. (God, how I longed for the days of her long flowery dresses and red lipstick: she had smiled then.)

'Have you invited your sister?' she asked.

'Carol? No, I hardly ever see her. It's not going to be a big affair. Just a few mates from the football club and that.'

'What about your Uncle Eric and Aunty Peggy?'

'Jesus, Mum, course not, I haven't seen them in years.'

'I'll have no one to talk to.'

She had stopped rubbing the vase; I could see that her hands were shaking uncontrollably. They were thin.

'There'll be no one to look after me,' she said. 'You'll just leave me on my own. I know you will.'

I sighed. For her, the act of coming to my wedding, sitting in a registry office and then some kind of function room afterwards with the strangers from my life, would have been excruciating. I knew that, and I knew that the only way she would have coped would have been to drink and then God knows what she would have said and done. I didn't want to be shown up by my drunk mother. I didn't want to have to watch her to make sure that she wasn't embarrassing me. There, I've said it, I'm not proud of it – but it's true.

I tried half-heartedly to persuade her, and then went to leave. As I did, she gave me her customary look of wilted wretchedness. 'Billy, you will keep calling on me won't you? You won't forget me now you've got her.'

This annoyed me, what did she mean by 'her'? Sandi deserved better than to be referred to so dismissively.

'Why, Mum? Why do you want me to keep coming round? You don't want to have anything to do with my life. You never have. Even when I do come round, you just watch the telly or carry on drinking that crap cheap wine you've got.'

'I need you to keep coming, Billy.'

'Why?' I repeated. 'Why?'

The bloody dog started barking.

'Because you're the last thing I have left of him,' she said. 'The closest thing I have to him.'

'But Mum, I'm not him,' I said. 'I never will be. You can't punish us both for that. He jumped in the bloody canal – not me, and not you.'

She went back to rubbing her vase. The dog stopped barking at me and went to sit by the telly.

I inhaled a mouthful of air into my exasperated lungs. I should have said more. We both should have said more. This was our chance. This was our chance to say how we felt after all these years. To have a right good ding-dong-clear-the-air barney. To admit that we both just missed him. But we couldn't. Because to admit our fears and our loves, to let loose our emotions, would have taken us far too close to a conversation about drink, and neither of us wanted that, the drink didn't want us to do that – it was our unspoken connection, the weakness we both shared.

'*Will* you come to the wedding then?' I said softly.

And my mum smiled weakly at me as though nothing had passed between us, as though there had been no words at all. 'I don't think it'll be my sort of thing, Billy.'

We got married without her.

I told everyone that my mother was ill, which wasn't far from the truth. No one said anything and we did have a right good knees-up.

Sandi was disappointed, though. Sandi was patient with my mother and made excuses for her even when she was pissed and abusive, even when she accused Sandi one drunken afternoon of being a 'gold digging little whore'.

Sandi reckoned that my mum had never got over the death of my dad and that perhaps both of us should think about counselling. I had laughed and grabbed her round the waist and swung her around. 'Counselling? Don't be daft, why would I need counselling – I'm Billy Parks, I've got everything I could ever wish for.'

Sandi had smiled and pouted and pretended to be infuriated – it was fun then. The real hurt hadn't started.

Oh, her pout.

Oh, her beautiful lips. God in heaven, how I wasted my life with her. How I threw it all away. I'd listened to the evil voices that told me that my thirst and hunger were natural, that blokes were designed to chase as many women as possible and that what she didn't know wouldn't hurt her.

She did know.

It did hurt her.

I didn't deserve her.

For the first few weeks I tried to be a good husband. For a few weeks I did as Bobby Moore had suggested and settled down. We moved into a semi-detached house in Chelmsford. Brand new. Lovely it was. It had its own garage and a little patch of grass at the front and a nice garden at the back. It had its own happy ding-dong front door bell and a lovely clean-and-untouched smell. We bought G Plan furniture and a pretty swinging bench for the back. Sandi planted flowers and shrubs.

Helpfully, the drinking culture at the club had been curtailed after a notorious Blackpool incident when a few of us had left the team hotel and gone out on a booze-up in Jack London's nightclub the night before a cup game. That had been the final straw – the chairman got involved and a few more of the lads had been moved on as a result.

But I missed it. I missed the feeling of power when we all walked into a pub and people immediately started to nudge each other and point. I missed having the ability to hide behind it, to make the real me invisible behind the outlandish and impenetrable spectacle of me out on the piss with my mates.

I started to go out again. I told Sandi that it was a bunch of us and that I couldn't let the lads down, that it was a team thing; I told her that it was important for me to be seen about in public. Then, I would drag some of the younger lads out with me, and if I couldn't find any of them, I'd go on my own, or with my other mates like Ray Hartley or Tony McGarry who was a record producer who'd worked with Mud.

I'd leave late and come back in the early hours of the morning – still drunk and smelling of other women.

It was on one of those nights that Brian Clough arrived on my front doorstep.

I was getting ready to go out and Sandi was sitting in the lounge watching TV. The happy doorbell rang.

Brian Clough stood there on my doorstep holding a bag of chips, a couple of bottles of brown ale and a box of Cadbury's Milk Tray.

'Don't just stand there, young man,' he said, 'let me in.'

'Who is it?' shouted Sandi.

'Er, it's, er, Brian Clough,' I shouted back.

'I've come to sign you for Derby County, lad. The Champions of England.'

'He's come to sign me for Derby County,' I shouted out.

I opened the door fully and in walked Brian Clough, looking around approvingly as he did. Sandi appeared round the lounge door.

I wasn't sure what to do or say.

'Have you spoken to the board at West Ham, Mr Clough?' I asked. Brian Clough ignored my quite reasonable question.

'Next year, young man, Derby County are going to win the European Cup. We're going to be the biggest team in the world. And you're going to play down the left-hand side. Providing the service for John O'Hare and Kevin Hector to score the goals.'

'But Mr Clough, I'm not sure that I want to sign for Derby County. I quite like it at West Ham.'

Again Brian Clough ignored me and turned to Sandi, who he had now spotted peeping round the corner of the lounge door, giving her a slightly lascivious smile. 'Hello love,' he said, 'would you put the kettle on? I've driven all the way from Derby. I don't know how you people can live down south. Have you ever been up north, love? You'll love it there. Friendliest people on the planet. Here, have these.'

He handed her the chocolates and chips and Sandi gave me a look, which suggested that she had no idea whatsoever what Brian Clough was going on about.

I wasn't entirely sure myself.

For about twenty minutes he talked at me, telling me that, with his help, I was going to be a great player who was going to play for England, and what a great team he had at Derby, and how he was going to make me the most expensive player in the country by paying £300,000 for me, and how money wasn't a problem and I could pick my wage.

'I don't normally go for Cockneys, young man,' he told me, 'but myself and my pal Peter Taylor think that you've got what it takes to be a great player. What do you think about that?'

I didn't know what to say. I was confused. I hadn't thought about leaving West Ham. I felt guilty just talking about it.

'I'm not sure, Mr Clough,' I said. 'This has come as a bit of a shock.'

'I'll tell you what,' said Brian Clough. 'I'll kip down on your couch and you go upstairs with your young lady and sleep on it. And we'll finalise things in the morning.'

'Er, OK.'

I then watched as Brian Clough took himself into our lounge with a quilt that Sandi had given him and closed the door. I put one foot on the stairs; I didn't know what to think. I wasn't sure that I wanted to go to Derby County. I wasn't sure about anything. I remembered that I was supposed to be going out. So, I turned around and tiptoed out of the front door, picked up Ray Hartley and went off into town. When I got back the next morning, Brian Clough was gone. Sandi was furious – I told her that it was the only way I was able to get away from him, and that otherwise we'd have had to sell our little house and move to Derby, which was practically in Scotland. It was never mentioned again.

West Ham couldn't sell me, though; I was Billy Parks, I was God and the crowd at Upton Park urged Sir Alf Ramsey to pick God for England.

And after a run of good games towards the end of the season, the newspapers joined in the campaign; I was the bee's bloody knees. The *Daily Mirror* reckoned that I was the closest type of player England had to one of the Brazilians who'd won the World Cup or the Germans who'd hammered us at Wembley in a European Championship game: *Is Billy Parks the Rivelino of Upton Park?* they'd asked. *Is he the nearest thing we have to Günter Netzer?*

The Times even made a virtue of my sending off against Coventry City saying:

> We can understand why Sir Alf might be wary of the fragile talent
> of Alan Hudson or Charlie George, but Billy Parks has shown that
> he is not afraid of getting his hands dirty when it comes to playing
> Association Football – we're not condoning his assault on Coventry
> City defender Tommy Nolan, but it showed a gritty side to Parks that
> should in some way be commended – he wouldn't let Sir Alf down.

They got their wish. I got my wish. The fans at Upton Park got their wish. The letter arrived, the bloody fabulous letter:

> Mr William Parks, you are instructed to attend at the Hendon Hall
> Hotel, Hendon at 4pm on the 13th May, to meet up with the England
> football squad in preparation for the 1972 Home International
> Championships.

That was it. Four lines. One sentence. Bloody hell. The most amazing sentence ever. You have been called up to the England squad. You are now an England International Footballer.

The elation.

The surge of power as you realise that all your dreams and ambitions have been fulfilled.

The sheer bloody happiness of it all.

Then, the fear.

The same fear that had strangled me all those years earlier when I had walked into Brisbane Road, the Orient, with Johnny Smith. The same heavy, slate-grey fear that had gripped me so many times as I had sat in various changing rooms and contemplated rejection, contemplated insignificance and irrelevance and oblivion and normality and the canal.

I arrived early to meet up with the squad. Sir Alf didn't seem particularly enthused by my presence. He stood at the door of the hotel with Harold Shepherdson and Les Cocker.

'Come this way, William,' he said. William, Christ, nobody ever called me William. 'Now,' he said, 'you're here for us to see if you've got what it takes to play for England. Do you understand?'

'Yes, Sir,' I replied, smiling at him, because, despite the fear, I was as excited as a four-year-old on Christmas Eve.

'And playing for England calls for different types of players, playing a different type of game. Do you understand?'

'Yes,' I nodded. But I don't think that either of us was entirely convinced by my response. Sir Alf didn't much like smiling footballers.

'Very well then,' he said. 'You'll be sharing a room with Emlyn.'

'Fantastic.'

He looked mildly perturbed at the animated way I'd reacted to the prospect of sharing a room with Emlyn Hughes.

Training wasn't at all as I had expected. In fact, the whole England experience was a bit odd. To me, it felt like prison – there I was, surrounded by the best players in the country – Gordon Banks, Colin Bell, Norman Hunter, Rodney Marsh, and others – but the atmosphere was one of incarceration: it was as though we were all imprisoned by the same desperate dread, the dread of

174

letting the country down, the dread of losing, the dread of looking stupid in front of the others, and, most of all, the dread of not living up to the gigantic tag: England International.

We were *the* chosen. We were the elite and we knew that every bastard who supported us, who wanted desperately for us to succeed, also wanted to *be* us.

The dread permeated everything. In training the players ran around with haunted looks and hunched shoulders, clearly playing within themselves as they tried so desperately hard. Even when the likes of Rodney Marsh and Alan Ball tried to lighten the atmosphere with a joke, we laughed, but it was a nervous laugh.

One night a few of us escaped and went to the pub for a few beers, but even that wasn't particularly pleasant as we spent the whole night looking over our shoulders like convicts on the run.

I wasn't picked for the first game against Wales, but got the nod for the second fixture against Northern Ireland at Wembley. 'William Parks, you'll play on the left of midfield,' said Sir Alf. 'Peter Storey and Colin Bell in the middle and Michael Summerbee on the right.'

The words, my name, then the absolute total fear that cascaded through my body like a plummeting stone from my head down to my boots. I would be starting for England.

It was an evening kick off, 19.45, and every minute, from the moment I woke up with my face fixed with blood-pumping fear to the moment we left the hotel and travelled to Wembley, felt unbearably long. I'd never experienced anything like it before; I would have killed to run away, find a pub, get talking to a couple of girls, drink.

We walked into the Wembley changing room as the crowd started to chant, *England, England, England.*

Bloody hell: the chanting like a baying animal; the chanting and that changing room and my shirt – number 11, white, and not just any white, England white, with three lions on the chest – hanging up waiting, like the gallows. Even now, after all these years, the very memory makes my heart hammer against my rib-cage with utter fear.

Bobby Moore took me to one side. 'Enjoy yourself and play your natural game,' he said. 'This is special.'

I nodded.

Sir Alf had different ideas: 'In the England team, William,' he told me, 'the full-backs play far up the pitch – which means that you, as the left-sided midfielder, must play deep to cover and track back. When you're playing for your country you have to work that much harder. Do you understand?'

I nodded. But, I was confused. Bobby Moore, the wisest man ever, the man who had lifted the World Cup, had told me that I should play my natural game and enjoy myself – that didn't really include tracking back and playing deep.

'That means,' Sir Alf continued, 'I don't want to see any of the unnecessary showboating you're used to doing at Upton Park. Do you understand? There's none of that carry-on with England.'

I nodded again, but really I was just wondering why he kept calling me William and why he was talking with a strange posh voice when he was born not far from me, and why did he keep asking me if I understood, as though I was suffering from some kind of mental disability?

The game was nothing short of a disaster. I felt as though I had the devilish voice of Sir Alf on one shoulder, telling me that I should keep tracking back, and the angelic Bobby Moore on the other, telling me that I should enjoy myself. The result was that I ran up and down and round without making much impact on the match. The only moment I remember of any note was just before half-time: I got the ball from a clearance by big Larry Lloyd, and as the ball dropped for me who should come steaming into the tackle but Pat Rice, the same full-back who had put me on my backside in my trial at Arsenal all those years earlier. This time, as Pat Rice approached me, I lobbed it over his head, caught it perfectly on my foot, did a couple of kick-ups as the crowd roared, then beat him again as he chased me. Then, the dread took over and, against every instinct to attack the Northern Ireland goal, I stopped, turned and played it infield to where Colin Bell was calling – the sensible pass.

Terry Neill scored the winner for the Irish not long before half-time. The Irish boys jumped for joy and we just stood and stared at each other in terror.

After the game, Sir Alf collared me again. 'What did I tell you about being a useless showboating circus pony, William?'

What was I supposed to say?

I just shrugged and thanked him for picking me. I meant it. I was grateful. He had picked me to play for England. I think he thought that I might have been taking the piss.

The next day we travelled up to Glasgow for the game against Scotland. I wasn't picked; I wasn't even on the bench. I was glad. I could relax.

We beat Scotland 1-0 in a vicious encounter.

Afterwards, we were allowed to go out; I drank like a man who had been released from a life-sentence. With each pint, with each small dram, the fear left me, and I felt my own usual exuberant hunger return, inflating me, pumping me back up into Billy Parks.

I got back to our new house in Chelmsford. Sandi had put bunting up around the door. When I saw it I wanted to cry.

Later as we lay in bed she turned to me and asked, 'How was it then? The newspapers were saying that you were the only one who did anything.'

I snorted gently in response to her tender loyalty. 'It was brilliant,' I replied. 'I absolutely loved it.'

I looked up at the shadows on the ceiling and lost Sandi in the dark jungle of the bed and her own sleep. Thoughts filled my head in differing degrees of devastation about my life, my existence. I had everything – so why did I feel like this?

I could make sense of nothing.

I would only get one more cap for England.

Details: Match 10, 16 December 1971
Division One
Venue: Highfield Road
Coventry City 1 v. West Ham 0
Carr

Line Ups
Coventry City: Glazier, Coop, Blockley, Parker, Catlin, Nolan, Carr, Mortimer, Machin, Hunt, Chilton
West Ham: Ferguson, McDowell, Taylor, Moore, Lampard, Redknapp, Brooking, Bonds, Parks, Best, Hurst

Attendance: 22,648

Details: Match 11, 23 May 1972
British Home International Championship
Venue: Wembley Stadium
England 0 v. Northern Ireland 1
Neill

Line Ups
England: Shilton, Todd, Hughes, Storey, Lloyd, Hunter, Summerbee, Bell, McDonald, Marsh, Parks
Northern Ireland: Jennings, Rice, Nelson, Neill, Hunter, Clements, Hegan, McMordie, Dougan, Irvine, Jackson

Attendance: 80,000

18

I hold the betting slip in my hand. I have decided that if Jumbo McLean comes home, I will buy myself a laptop computer like the one Will had.

Yes. I will go straight from the bookie's and buy one. Then, I will be able to go on to that internet and study things, and relive things and improve myself. Confront myself. Yes, that's what I will do – straight to one of those computer shops and set it all up at my flat. Then, when Maureen comes to pick me up for the AA meeting, I'll be able to show her the computer and tell her that I bought it to help me learn things and see things, understand things. Distract me from myself. It's the type of positive act that would please her. I might even do a course.

Jumbo McLean romps home, 8-1: I had £100 on him – easily enough for a computer.

Get in.

The cashier counts out the tenners: lovely, crisp, warm ten pound notes. Ninety of them.

I don't leave the bookie's.

I put each and every ten pound note on Japanese Boy.

Bloody, three-legged, overweight donkey. Couldn't beat an egg.

But, still, what the hell. It doesn't matter. It's all going to change in a couple of days – Gerry Higgs had said so – I can buy a computer another day. There will be loads of computers, loads of time, and anyway, what do I know about computers? I wouldn't even be able to turn one on let alone find footage of Brian Moore introducing my goal of the month for February 1973.

And at least my afternoon in the bookmaker's has kept me from an afternoon in the pub.

I make to leave.

I walk towards the door of the bookie's.

Three hours until the AA meeting.

The Irish Bar is across the road. I can see it through the glass door. I still have enough money in my pocket. I have three hours until Maureen is picking me up. I can see the movement of the world outside the bookmaker's. I can see people and life and everything that lies beyond the door. It seems cold.

I take a step towards the exit, but suddenly the front door blurs and I feel a strange retching in my stomach and chest. I swallow hard and find myself doubled up in pain and starting to cough; deep, disturbing, uncontrollable coughs.

A couple of people grab hold of me and someone puts me on a chair. I can't stop coughing. I try to tell them that I am alright, but I can't get the words out.

I can see concerned screwed-up faces and pairs of distant eyes. I can't stop bloody coughing. Someone shouts to get me a glass of water; someone else mentions getting an ambulance. I don't want a bloody ambulance; I just want the coughing to stop.

Eventually it stops. Eventually the pain and retching stop. It's left me tired.

'Are you alright?' asks one of the girls who works behind the counter – nice-looking girl, always well turned out. I try to smile at her.

'Yes, I'm fine, love, absolutely fine. Coughing fit. That's all.'

My chest heaves. I stand up and go to leave.

'You know who that is,' says a voice behind me, 'that's Billy Parks, that is.'

'Bloody hell no.'

I don't turn round to confront the faceless voices. I don't turn round to show them that they are right – I am Billy Parks. I am still Billy bloody Parks. I am still Billy Parks, England International Footballer.

I stagger out into the street.

Three hours until the AA meeting.

I stand outside for a few moments. The Irish Bar across the road beckons me like a womb. I would be warm in there. Safe.

Instead.

I buy a bottle of vodka from the corner shop. I walk home with guilt and loathing laughing at me, almost bringing me to tears.

When I get home I put the bottle in the middle of my kitchen table and sit quietly, looking at it, contemplating it.

Beautiful.

The clearness of the glass, the clearness of the liquid. This beautiful pure liquid can do me no bad, only good.

I look at it. My whole body is cheered by its presence. I watch it.

There are two and a half hours left until the AA meeting.

19

'The Boss wants to see you, Billy.'

'Me?'

'Yes.'

I nodded and made my way from the treatment room down the corridor to John Lyall's office. September 1974. Two months after the England-less World Cup. West Ham hadn't started the season very well. John Lyall had taken over as manager from Ron Greenwood. He'd been with the club for years, had John. Nice man. Good footballing man. Handsome too, and I don't mind saying that, it's true: there was an elegance to him. And, fair play, he went on to build some great Hammers teams.

'Billy,' he said. 'Sit down son, how's the hamstring?'

'Fine thanks, Boss. I'll be fit for Saturday.'

'Good,' he said, but I knew by the tiny infinitesimal delay in his response that I wouldn't be here on Saturday.

'Look, we've accepted an offer for you from Spurs.'

'Spurs?'

'Yes.'

'How much?'

'One hundred and ten thousand.' He paused to let me take in

the news about my worth. One hundred and ten grand – a lot less than Brian Clough was going to pay for me.

'It's a good move for you,' he continued. 'Spurs are a cracking team.'

I wasn't sure. I wasn't sure I wanted to leave. It wasn't as if I'd been angling for a transfer. I felt my head go down as I wilted in my chair with the pain of rejection.

'You've given this club, what, eight years of good service?' he said.

I nodded again.

'But, perhaps, son, it's time for you to move on now, make a new start with a new team. If you start to take care of yourself properly you could still have a good four or five years left.'

Four or five years, and then what? I exhaled slowly. Then looked up at him. He was probably right. It was the way of footballers. We were like cattle. I was being sold, and there was no point in arguing or sulking. I didn't blame John Lyall; he was building a new team. I knew that.

'Alright,' I said.

'Good man.'

He stood up and thrust his hand over the table and that was the end of my time at West Ham United. My dad's club.

A car took me to White Hart Lane to meet Terry Neill, the Spurs boss.

'Hello Parksy, welcome to Spurs,' said the man at the players' entrance. And I smiled and looked around me; Tottenham Hotspur, what a lovely big club, reeking of history and tradition: Bill Nicholson, Danny Blanchflower, Jimmy Greaves. I *was* lucky. Yes, they wanted me. Here I could be loved.

Terry Neill's office was bigger and grander than John Lyall's. Perhaps this was a good move. He greeted me warmly: 'Ah, hello, Billy,' he said, shaking me by the hand. We then talked about the club and his plans for it and his winner for Northern Ireland against England. Then he handed me the contract. I hardly read it; it was long before the days of agents and lawyers and all that.

Terry Neill told me what my wages would be, and that was good enough for me.

'Look,' he said once I'd signed. 'I know that you like to relax and enjoy yourself, Billy.'

I smiled. 'Don't believe everything you hear, Boss.'

'Well, I'm fine with that Billy, I understand that, remember, it's not too long since I was playing myself. But,' he said, 'if you ever miss training, or if you ever turn up to the club too relaxed, if you know what I mean, then I can't play you. You do understand that?'

'Of course,' I said. That was good enough for me – the boss was fine about me being *relaxed*.

And things started really well. Terry Neill played me in a quite central position, just off Martin Chivers – this was new and I liked it. He told John Pratt and Stevie Perryman to win the ball and give it to me, which was brilliant.

We beat Derby County 2-0 and Leicester City 2-1. I found myself a little coterie of lads to go out for a beer with and a very good bookie just off the Seven Sisters Road. Rebecca was born now, and I was able to tell Sandi that it was better for me to stay over in town if we had important matches so that I could get a good night's sleep.

'I've got to get back into the England squad,' I'd say to her. 'This is my big chance.'

Then we played West Ham at the Lane in my third match. Confidence was high after two wins. I remember the feeling that day. I remember arriving at the ground, the sky a beautiful autumnal azure, the pubs heaving, already you could hear the chanting of *We are Tottenham, super Tottenham* ringing out. I felt no dread that day. I felt a calm and complete confidence in my own ability. It was like being back at school playing for Taffy Watkins. No one would get near me that day.

And it wasn't just me, you could sense the atmosphere in the changing room – that afternoon we were going to be part of something special. We were a team. We were together. It is a tremendous feeling, that natural masculine primeval enjoyment of being in the pack.

West Ham scored early on through Bobby Gould, then their new young keeper Mervyn Day pulled out a string of fantastic saves as we threw everything at them. We were playing sublime football – fast, direct, skilful, attacking.

At half-time we were still 1-0 down, but Terry Neill told us not to worry. 'The goals will come, lads,' he said, then he winked at me. 'Billy,' he said, 'I want you to roam around even more, look for the ball; West Ham are still expecting you to play on the left – let's surprise them.'

Going into that second half I felt at peace. I felt perfect. I felt that there was nothing I could not do with a ball. No player I could not beat.

Fifteen minutes into the second half, I got the equaliser. And if I say so myself, it was a pearler. We had a free-kick after Tommy Taylor had pulled down Jimmy Neighbour. I screamed at Martin Peters to leave it for me. Then I placed the ball and curled it past Day into the back of the net. The Park Lane end went mad. I lifted my arms, my head pointed towards the heavens, as ripples of humanity rejoiced on the terrace behind the goal.

Ten minutes later, I got the ball again, just outside the centre circle in the West Ham half. I could see their goal. I knew exactly what to do. In that moment everything went quiet. I could hear nothing. Silence. I was aware of nothing and nobody else, only me. My body and my mind and my history and my weaknesses and the fear and dread and the arrogance and whatever talent I bloody well possessed merged into one thing: me. I started to accelerate towards the goal. Past Billy Bonds, past Tommy Taylor, past John McDowell, into the penalty area where the kid Mervyn Day had advanced quickly and decisively and stood tall as the last thing between me and the goal – but this is my moment, this is my fate, this is my history. Me, me, me. I tucked the ball into the side of the goal. Oh God yes. I raised my arms and looked up to the still cloudless blue sky. For a fraction of a second there was stillness, quiet, and then – the noise of the crowd bursts through the air like an explosion and fills my brain.

That was it. That was perfect.

It got no better than that.

Ever.

In the next game up at bloody Everton, I got my ankle stuck in a piece of mud and, as I turned to meet a pass, I broke my tibia. I heard it snap. Snap. I felt a rush of pain like no other move from my ankle up my spine to my mouth that contorted in agony.

'Are you alright, Parksy?'

'Yeah, I'll be fine, just gone over on my ankle. I'll be fine.'

I wasn't fine.

Five months off.

Five months with nothing to do except drink and seek my moments of glory and excitement in other ways. It was never the same. All because of a piece of mud, a piece of bloody mud. There's no philosophy that can explain that is there?

Details: Match 12, 1 October 1974
Division One
Venue: White Hart Lane
Tottenham Hotspur 2 v. West Ham 1
Parks (2)   Gould

Line Ups
Spurs: Jennings, Kinnear, Knowles, England, Naylor, Pratt, Perryman, Neighbour, Peters, Parks, Chivers
West Ham: Day, McDowell, Taylor (T), Bonds, Lampard, Lock, Brooking, Holland, Paddon, Gould, Taylor (A)

Attendance: 38,657

20

Maureen has found me asleep on my couch. I have my yellow and blue anorak over me. I can't remember doing that. She rouses me gently by calling my name and patting me softly on my shoulder. I awake terrified. I can feel my eyes widen and bulge with a cold shapeless fear and I start to shake uncontrollably. What am I scared of? I have no recollection of a dream. I have no idea what was making me shake. It isn't the delirium tremens this, no – I know all about the DTs – this isn't them; this is terror.

'It's alright, Billy,' Maureen says, 'you're alright. Shhhh. Everything's going to be fine. Shhhhh.'

I hold her, tight, like a little boy. I feel her warmth and slowly my eyes relax and my face thaws; the scary darkness starts to brighten.

'I'm sorry,' I say, my body still convulsing. 'I must have had a dream or something.'

'It's alright,' she repeats. 'It's alright. Are you cold? You're shaking like a leaf.'

'Yes, I'm bloody freezing.'

She looks at her watch. 'I'll make us a cup of tea.'

She gets up and walks towards the kitchen area. The bottle of vodka was still on the kitchen table.

Unopened.

We both look at it.

'I bought it on the way home,' I tell her. 'I wanted to drink it, but I didn't. I'm sorry. At least I didn't drink, though, eh? Check it, it's unopened.'

She looks at me with sad-eyed disappointment.

'Home from where?'

'I went into town. I wanted to buy one of those laptop computers, but I ended up in the bookie's.'

She smiles at me, then averts her eyes upwards. 'God Billy, what would you know about a laptop computer?'

We drive across south London to the AA meeting; it is drizzling and the liquid sky causes the colours of the shops and car headlights to merge into one another, giving the city a seedy, dirty, impure quality. I am still cold when we arrive at the venue, a church hall in Streatham. The church is massive, unused and unloved; it casts a sinister shadow across the already-murky unhappy evening. Alcoholics Anonymous. A bloody A. I have no interest. I don't want to be here, this is too stark, too real – there is no glory to be had here.

Maureen parks outside a kebab shop on the other side of the road.

'I'll be waiting here for you.'

'Thanks,' I say. 'I don't know how long these things last.'

'It's alright. I'll be here.'

I nod at her then turn and open the car door.

'Billy,' she says and I look back to her. 'This *is* important you know.'

'Yes, I know, absolutely.'

'You do feel OK, don't you?'

'I feel great. It's all worth it.'

'You understand, I'm doing this for your own good – Rebecca won't see you otherwise.'

'I know.'

I leave her car and walk towards a light that is coming from a side door that leads into a hall. Inside the church hall there are rows of chairs and stacked-up tables, and a little corner packed full of well-used cast-off toys. The walls are adorned with children's pictures and notice boards advertising things to do with starving children in Africa and courses that will help you understand the meaning of life.

It is alien to me; I haven't been inside a church hall for years.

On the back wall is a large sign telling me that *God So Loved The World That He Gave His One And Only Son.* I look at it and repeat the words slowly to myself. Underneath, in vibrant childish colours, is a depiction of Jesus on the cross; Jesus, with pink skin, red cheeks, black hair and massive oversized hands nailed to a thick brown-and-black felt-tip pen cross, being adored by a little array of odd malformed people who look up at him with wonky smiles. I find it strangely disturbing. I've never really been one for God and religion and all that – don't get me wrong, I respect people's beliefs, I've just never had much cause to believe myself.

On another wall are the words: *The Wages of Sin is Death.*

I feel my brain ache and I look away.

Nearby is a table with five or six people standing round holding cups and saucers. These are the alcoholics, I know that straight away: unhappy people, standing far apart from one another, making quiet small talk, all probably wishing they were in a pub somewhere.

A man wearing a grey suit but no tie comes up to me. 'Hi,' he says, offering me a hand. 'I'm Karl.'

'Hello, I'm, er, Billy, Billy Parks.'

My name prompts no sign of recognition. I am not sure if tonight, here, that is a good or bad thing.

'Welcome, Billy,' he says. 'You're new aren't you?'

'Yes,' I answer.

'Ever been to one of these meetings before?'

'No.'

'Well, you're very welcome. It's a closed meeting, as you know. We'll start,' he looks at his watch for effect, 'in about five minutes. There's tea and coffee over there and some leaflets which you might find helpful.'

'Thank you.'

I want to run.

I want to slalom in and out of all of them, a ball at my feet, never taking my eye off the ball, my ball, always knowing where the defender is, always one step ahead, never, never, never being bloody well caught, not by anyone.

'I'm a trained AA counsellor,' continues Karl.

Counsellor. What do I need a counsellor for? What am I doing here? I bet Karl the counsellor has never had his name chanted by 50,000 fans, I bet Karl has never walked into a pub and had the whole place stand up and applaud him for the goal he'd scored earlier in the day. *Billy Parks Is God* they use to say.

'There's no agenda here whatsoever, Billy, OK? You don't have to join in if you don't want to. The twelve steps are steps that you ultimately make yourself – we're just here to help you.'

I nod weakly. 'Thank you.'

We sit down. In a semicircle. Ten of us, with Karl at the apex of the circle making eleven. I sit there holding a drooping leaflet in one hand and my reading glasses in the other. I am not even sure why I've brought them – perhaps I thought they would make me more anonymous.

I look around. All of humanity has been thrown together: next to me is a bloke in his fifties with neatly combed hair and a roaringly loud purple V-neck sweater; next to him is an Asian guy with a big belly and a sad sweaty face; beside him sits an ageless woman in a woolly hat and a scarf that she wears over her mouth, perhaps as some kind of barrier to stop the gin from getting inside her; then there is another bloke in a suit wearing rimless glasses, who looks considerably fitter and healthier than everyone else; by him is an old black chap, who seems significantly happier than the rest of us;

then there are a couple of kids, both skinny with bad teeth and crew-cut hair and an air of jail about them; and beside them, scowling, is a large bloke who looks about forty and wears a checked shirt and jeans – he looks ordinary, like the type of bloke who comes round to do your plastering, the only thing that betrays him is a slightly bulbous nose; then, finally, there is a middle-aged woman, quick with nerves, she is wearing a skirt that is far too short for her and her skin is ravaged with the shovel marks of booze, but she was clearly pretty once. God love her. God love all of them. For a second, I try to put my mother amongst them, sitting here, in her cardie, simmering with quiet resentment and hating each and every one of them for simply existing in a world that had forgotten her.

I don't want to be here. I am not meant for this. I don't want to be an anonymous alcoholic. I want to be back in front of the faithful at West Ham, with my fingers raised up to the sky, then in some boozer afterwards with the lads, loud with drink and the possibility of the night. I want to be in Maureen's arms. I want to be in anyone's arms. Anywhere but here.

Karl stands up first. 'Good evening, everyone,' he says, and everyone mumbles a response. 'Nice to see you here on this awful night – and especially nice to see two new faces – Billy,' he looks over to me and I nod, 'and Ryan.' At the name, Ryan, one of the youngsters with bad teeth, smiles without a trace of self-consciousness and I know immediately that he is too young to be here – despite his bad teeth, he still has a long way to fall, his suffering is all still in front of him. Lucky bastard.

'As I've said to both of you,' Karl continues, 'there's no pressure here, no one is judging you, no one is going to lecture you – we're here to offer help, because we are all alcoholics.'

I want to scream: *I'm not! I'm not an alcoholic, I'm Billy Parks. Drink is just part of being Billy Parks. It's part of being a footballer. It's what we all did.*

'We all know,' he adds, 'what it's like to reach the bottom, and we know that it isn't easy to get back on your feet.'

'No way,' says the happy black chap, which I assume is an expression of his agreement with that proposition.

'Now,' continues Karl, 'before I open the floor, I'd just like to thank those of you who took part in the seminar on alcoholism and violence at Parkhurst Prison last week; everyone who was there commented on what a positive response we all had from the inmates.'

Prison? Alcohol and violence? Fucking hell. I shouldn't be here. This has nothing to do with me.

'There will be a similar meeting at the Young Offender Institution in Feltham next month, so anyone wishing to take part, please contact me.'

Christ, he looks at me as he says this – as if I am going to go into a prison full of young hooligans and talk about drink and violence. I put my head down. I will sit patiently until this has finished. I will listen politely. I will nod when necessary, then I will go back to Maureen. Gerry Higgs said any day now, any bloody day now.

Then all this will be over.

Karl continues to read out various announcements and I wonder if Maureen has got rid of the bottle of vodka. I don't think that she has, but I am not sure. Then I start to think about when I will get to meet Becky and Liam; after all, that is what this is all about, that is why I am here. I will stomach this, then I will go home and drink vodka. I sigh to myself. The thought makes me want to weep.

Karl says something and everyone claps politely interrupting my fantasy, so I join in.

The bloke in the purple jumper next to me stands up. He smiles at us all. He has a nice face, gentle and slightly effeminate, like a kindly teacher or a social worker, the type of face you'd say yes to, the type of face that has never seen the inside of a boozer or been on a football terrace; his soft gloopy lips have never called a referee a wanker.

'My name's Lee,' he says, then adding with a smile, 'which I've always hated, I always wanted something with another syllable in it. Like Billy or Ryan,' he says, looking at me and the other young fella. There is a murmur of laughter, not too much. I smile politely.

'And I'm a vicar, which you may not have guessed, as I'm not wearing my dog collar. And I'm an alcoholic.'

The word alcoholic slips lubricated and harmless from his mouth: alcoholic. That most dreaded of words; from him it comes out as easily as if he was saying, I'm an accountant, or I'm a Chelsea fan, or I prefer butter to margarine. He has my attention, though. I listen to his each and every individual word.

'I haven't had a drink for three months and six days,' he continues, 'or ninety-eight days to be precise'.

The room claps and I join in. You couldn't help it – the sheer thrill he had obviously got from each sober day exhilarates us all.

He continues. 'I'm hoping that if I can make it to twelve months, then I can go back to my parish, which is in Wimbledon.'

He pauses now, looks down for a second then continues. 'Karl has asked me to share my own experiences with you. I realise that we're all different. Different backgrounds and different experiences. For my part, I was never someone who was particularly interested in drink; I never went out to the pub as a teenager, a bit at university, I suppose, but not much. I was a bit square really. Well, vicars are, aren't they?'

The laughter has muted, but it doesn't matter, all the alcoholics sitting in the little semicircle are now mesmerised by Lee the vicar. The two toothless kids' mouths have dropped open, giving them a look of unbelievable gormlessness, and the lady with the woolly hat has removed the scarf from around her mouth. Lee is impressive, a natural performer: there was nothing anonymous about his alcoholism.

He goes on to tell us how he had become a vicar because he wanted to help people, and how he had become confused as the lines became blurred between the desire to help and the need for praise.

This makes sense to me.

'At first the admiration was enough,' he tells us. 'I suppose, that was *my* addiction for a while, but then, when I didn't get enough of it, I turned to wine and then vodka, because we all believe that no one can tell if we've drunk vodka, don't we?'

We all hum with approval and understanding; we'd all also convinced ourselves of that little pearler.

Lee the vicar then tells us a series of tales from his life as a drinker, which had stopped ninety-eight days ago; amusing tales, such as when he got his congregation to sing the same hymn 'Be Thou My Vision' twice because he was too pissed to remember that they'd already sung it, and we smile because this is alcoholism in a nice, light Sunday-evening-entertainment type of way. No one got killed or hurt in Lee's life.

Then he adopts a more sombre tone to tell us about the day he reached rock bottom: 'I was supposed to be taking a funeral,' he tells us. 'I was totally blotto, I realise that now. It was a lovely old lady, she'd been a parishioner for years, used to make the most wonderful jams – she deserved a good send-off. But, as I was putting on my surplice, a couple of elders came to me and told me to go home. One had his arm round the old lady's daughter who was crying. They said that they couldn't take it from me any more.'

Lee's face is cast downwards and shadowed. He smiles weakly to himself, and repeats the words 'They couldn't take it from me any more', then he looks up at us again. 'That was three months and seven days ago. Because the next day, I drank like a fool, waiting for the Bishop to relieve me of my duties. Which he did. And I haven't had a drink since.'

We clap. We nod. We offer our solidarity. Lee was a good turn. He has brought us together.

Karl stands up, still clapping.

'Three months and six days,' he says. 'That's fantastic, Lee, fantastic, a few years to go to catch up with Bob, who's been dry for, how long now?' He looks at the happy black man.

'Seventeen years,' choruses Bob.

'Seventeen years,' repeats Karl, 'but, three months and six days is a good second step, and we applaud that and support you.'

'Thank you,' says Lee quietly.

Next up is the ordinary-looking bloke in the checked shirt. 'I'm Chris,' he says, clearly nervous, very different from the polished Lee, 'and I'm an alcoholic.'

We all clap again at this admission of weakness. Chris *is* very different from Lee. Chris isn't a vicar who had become confused by his own wonderfulness, Chris is a former squaddie whose lager-fuelled anger had put his wife into intensive care.

'I was just back from my second tour of Basra,' he tells us. 'Two of the lads had been killed in a roadside bomb.'

This is immediately more serious than Lee. We look up at Chris, but we know that there are not going to be any funny anecdotes, no heart-warming stories about dead old ladies; he had come home from the hell of war and beaten up his wife with his drunken fists, as his kids cried cowering in the corner. Our faces adopt stern yet understanding expressions.

'I couldn't cope with the pain of knowing that I had lived. But it was more than that,' he says, before pausing to concentrate on finding the right words. 'It wasn't just that, there I was with this lovely home and this lovely wife, but I knew that I was happier out in Iraq with my mates, and I just thought, how can that be? How can that horrible, sweaty, piss-stinking place be better than this? Then I realised that I had a purpose out there. Back home I was just nobody. Drink helped me cope. Drink made everything alright. Or I thought it did. Right up until my wife and kids left me. I haven't seen them in three years. She got sick of my moods and –' He pauses '– the beatings.'

Chris's head goes down and I know that he is crying. One of

the lads with the bad teeth gets up and puts his arm around him, and helps him back to his seat.

Lovely.

Bloody lovely.

All these lovely weak, injured people sitting in this room, supporting one another. And for a few minutes, as Lee the vicar speaks and Chris the soldier who'd beaten up his Mrs cries, I feel a kinship with them: happy Bob, the fat Asian bloke, the old girl with the short skirt, the toothless kids, rimless-glasses man, the woman with the scarf – all of them, even Karl the counsellor, we are a team. We are taking on the ravages of life and drink and we are going to play them off the park with our slick passing game and passionate defence.

'Would anyone else like to speak?' Karl asks. No one says anything. The two kids look down at their rancid trainers. 'What about you, Billy? You don't have to. But it might be a good first step.'

I feel that I can't say no.

'Alright.'

I stand up and take my place at the front of the semicircle.

'My name's Billy,' I say.

And there is a murmur of applause, not Upton Park, not White Hart Lane, not Anfield, or Old Trafford or Wembley, but enough.

'My name's Billy, and I'm …'

The words freeze in my throat. I can't say it. It is as though everyone who has ever touched my life is waiting for me to utter the words, but I can't. No way. I can't say it. It would be a betrayal. Suddenly I picture the back of my dad's head as he is sitting there looking up at the sky. How can I admit in public that I am a bloody alcoholic? I know they'd clap if I said the word – and that just makes it worse, I don't want that, I am not deserving of that.

'My name's Billy and I'm …' I repeat. I can sense Taffy Watkins and Johnny Smith and my mother and the Council of Football Immortals. For a second I think I see the shadowy figure of Gerry Higgs standing by the front door. I can't do it.

'Take your time, Billy, there's no rush, we don't give out prizes at the end of the session.'

'... and I'm a footballer,' I finish.

The room looks at me in shocked silence.

'Yes,' I continue, 'I'm Billy Parks and I used to play for West Ham and Spurs and England a couple of times as well.'

'Oh yeah,' says the healthy-looking man in the rimless glasses, 'I remember Billy Parks.' His words sound as though he has successfully disconnected me from my former self. I look at him for a second, thinking that he might say more, hoping that he might say more – but he doesn't, instead he sits there with a smug grin on his face, as though he is bursting to tell everyone a really funny joke at my expense. I ignore him. I have to. Bastard.

'I can't speak as well as Lee,' I say. 'And I don't have a story that's moving and sad like Chris.'

I feel uncomfortable. I find myself pausing and looking instinctively sideways to where a glass of scotch would have been if I were addressing one of my sportsman's lunches or dinners. I want to slip my hand effortlessly and thoughtlessly around its lovely glass neck and lift it to my lips and take myself away from all of this. Instead, I look down at my shoes then up again, sneaking a look at rimless-glasses man, who, thankfully, has stopped grinning. The semicircle is growing uneasy – they want to hear about my weakness. They want me to confess – that would make them feel better. That would make us all feel better.

'I just kicked a football,' I say. 'I've had it easy really.' I am stumbling around now. It is like one of those dreams where you're in front of your school assembly naked; yes, I am naked because I wasn't able to use the word, utter the net-busting phrase – I am an alcoholic. For a second, I contemplate telling them a couple of footballing anecdotes, perhaps the one about me accidentally kissing Tommy Smith after scoring a goal up at Anfield, or the one about us gluing up the doors of Frank Lampard's new Ford Capri. Oh, the bloody happy stories from a time when I would walk toweringly into a pub and order whatever I liked without any guilt. Again, I look sideways for the non-existent tumbler of scotch – was it wrong to want a drink, now, here?

'I had this games master when I was at school,' I continue, as my alcoholically anonymous teammates stare up at me. 'Lovely fella he was, a Welshman, Taffy Watkins we called him. Well, anyway, Taffy used to take me training on my own after school, and he said to me once, Billy, he says, great footballers have got an instinctive first touch because they can see the ball before anyone else does.'

The semicircle gawp and I find myself looking over their heads towards the picture of Jesus on his cross dominating the back wall of the hall – the childish faces mock me. The two blue spots that make up Jesus's eyes bore into me. *The Wages of Sin is Death* – childish Jesus was telling me that I was a total twat.

I continue to tell them about Taffy Watkins. 'He said,' I explain, 'that he could teach anyone to kick a ball, or trap a ball, or head a ball, but that first touch, he said, that ability to see the ball coming towards you quickly before anyone else has seen it and then put your body in exactly the right position to control it and do something with it, without even thinking, that, he said to me, that is a gift given to you by the gods of football. That you cannot teach. That is instinct.'

I smile as a little image of Taffy Watkins forms in my mind: I see him, murky grey, telling me to pull my socks up as he puts me through my paces on the school football pitch, just me and him, hour after hour, cross after cross after cross, until I could find the head of any striker, until the sun goes down, before I never went to Manchester to play for Sir Matt Busby. Before I let him down. Before everything.

'My problem,' I tell the semicircle, 'is that I always believed that as my first touch was God-given, then everything else in my life would be just as perfect, just as brilliant, just as easy. I'd be, what do you call it, infallible, untouchable? And, when you're a kid, when you're a footballer, every bad touch, every stupid thing you do, every mistake you make, is excused. So you think you can get away with everything. You think that you are above the way in which normal people live their lives. So you do what you like. And you forge this lonely existence where nothing is real and proper. For me, I drank as much as I liked, because everyone forgave me, everyone made exceptions for me –' I pause '– but now, it's not so easy. Now, I know I shouldn't drink, I know that it will kill me, I know that it upsets people who love me – but from the moment I wake up, it's so bloody hard because every emotion, every minute from my life, every success and every failure rushes towards me like a train, telling me that it'll still be easier if I have a drink. And I feel so powerless, like I'm just standing in the middle of the track holding out my hand to try to stop it, but I'm not strong enough to stop it, so I just get pushed out of the way. And then, I go out, I find a pub, hope I'll find people who still love me, and drink until nothing matters. And the next morning there's the pain, as you hate yourself ...' I stop. I can hear my own voice tailing off. I don't want to go on. '... And that pain just makes the train go even faster.'

No one claps; they just look up at me with sad eyes, then look away. I continue, I know I have to.

'Lee and Chris mentioned their lowest point, well, I've had lots: we'd be here all night.'

I sigh. This is hard. I hate myself. I've said more than I'd planned to.

'I've got a second chance, though,' I continue, trying hard to give them my twinkling smile, to sound as though I wasn't defeated yet. 'I've got a chance to put a few things right. I've got a daughter I haven't seen in years and hopefully I'll see her soon if I can stop drinking; she's got a son, too, my grandson, a young lad called Liam. I want him to think well of his granddad – you know what I mean.'

They nod. That was it, I can't think of anything else to say. I can't actually blame it on the drink. I can't admit to being a big failure. I can't confess. I can't say the word 'alcoholic'.

I look at the semicircle: they are uncomfortable, wondering if I am going to say any more.

One of the young lads with bad teeth breaks the silence. 'Did you really play for Spurs?'

'Oh yes, son. You ask your dad.'

'My dad supported Palace.'

'Nothing wrong with that,' I say. 'Palace are a fine football team with a great tradition.'

I feel a surge of happiness now as nice images of Selhurst Park and my mate Stevie Kember who played for Palace in the seventies and had a lovely left foot push the miserable images of confession and drink away.

'What about the rest of you?' I ask smiling. 'I suppose you all support Arsenal or Chelsea?'

The smug fella in the rimless glasses speaks first: 'Charlton Athletic actually.'

'Well done, son,' I say. 'Another proper club – I once scored a hat-trick at the Valley.'

'I know,' he says. 'I was there. Nineteen sixty-six. You gave Johnnie Hewie a right seeing to.'

This is wonderful; this is the most wonderful thing I've heard all night. This means that I am still alive. This means that it doesn't matter that I can't confess. I am still Billy Parks. I was eighteen when I scored that hat-trick and everything was still sparkling and fantastic.

'Yes,' I say. 'I cut in from the left, they didn't expect that did they; poor John Hewie was nearly forty, he couldn't get near me.'

The smug man smiles. And I smile too – I had given him pleasure. We had shared that moment. That was the meaning of my life.

Karl gets up and intervenes, clapping with perhaps a tad too much enthusiasm. The others follow his lead and clap as well.

'Thanks, Billy,' he says, 'wonderful stuff.'

Wonderful stuff. What did he mean by that? Which part?

He comes up to me at the end of the meeting. 'Billy,' he says.

'Yes?'

'You mustn't worry about not being able to admit you're an alcoholic – it's the first step and probably the hardest step, admitting you've got a problem, but not being able to say the word is not a bar to recovering.'

'Thank you,' I say.

But it doesn't matter to me. Not really. He doesn't understand: the wonderful stuff was not my admissions about drink; the wonderful stuff was the memory of forty years earlier.

'Will you come again next week?'

'Oh yes,' I lie with enthusiasm. But next week, I'll be in a different place, basking in the glory of my second chance, by next week I'll be Billy Parks again. Gerry Higgs had said so.

Karl smiles at me. 'Good,' he says. 'I really liked what you said about the locomotive; I understand, the difficult part is resisting that locomotive when it comes towards you.'

'Oh yes,' I say, trying to meet his enthusiasm with my best concerned expression.

'But in time, and with our help,' he continues, 'you learn to see it coming down the line – I suppose a bit like *you* see a football – and you're able to put into place the mechanisms that will help you get out of its way. Keep you sober.'

'Thank you, Karl,' I say. 'That's very helpful.'

Then he looked at me for a second before continuing, 'One other thing, Billy.'

'Yes.'

'I couldn't help noticing, and I only mention this because I'm obliged to and I'm trained to, but you seem quite jaundiced, are you seeing a medical doctor?'

'I am, but don't worry, Karl,' I tell him. 'I'm fine, you should have seen me a few weeks ago. I was in a right state then. I'm a lot better now. This has helped. Being here tonight.'

'Good,' he says. 'I'd hate to see you stumble towards some kind of liver disease.'

'No chance of that,' I tell him.

I leave the church hall and spot Maureen's car still parked across the road. It has stopped raining. I feel liberated. I take a big breath of the night air. It is all going to be alright.

'Billy.'

I turn to see Gerry Higgs standing in the shadows by some railings. He is holding a plastic bag that contains some kind of food.

'Mr Higgs, what are you doing all the way over here?'

'I'm after you, of course.'

Of course.

'I've been to a meeting,' I tell him. I won't use the words Alcoholics Anonymous. 'About my drinking and that, you know, it's time to rein it back 'n'all – you know what it's like when you reach a certain age.'

'You always did have a thirst on you,' says Gerry, but I know that he's not that interested in the meeting or my drinking. 'We've got a date, old son.'

'A date?'

'Yes, the Council will be meeting you the day after tomorrow.'

'The day after tomorrow,' I repeat, my face breaking into a bright smile. I am ready for it now. All I want is to go back to being Billy Parks, to get my second chance, score the goal, score that bloody goal that will change everything.

'Fantastic, where? When?'

'Be ready at midday,' says Gerry. 'I'll come and find you.'

'That's fantastic, Mr Higgs, absolutely fantastic – day after tomorrow?'

'Yes, Billy, it's important, so get an early night.'

'Yes, of course.'

We look at each other. I want to hug him from the excitement that is now coursing through my veins, or give him a big post-goal kisser – but, instead I grapple for something to say.

'So, what will happen then?'

'Then you'll know your destiny, Billy old son. You'll know all

204

of our destinies, one way or another.' His mouth drops open to form a slow and slightly ominous smile as he emphasises the words '*all of our destinies*'.

'Yes, destiny,' I repeat for no good reason, nodding to him as I do, as though all of this is absolutely clear.

'What should I wear then?'

It is a ridiculous question and I immediately regret it; there I am, being given the chance to do what every human being that has ever lived probably craves, the chance to go back and make it all better, live it all for a second chance, and I am asking whether I should wear a tie.

'Best bib and tucker I'd have thought, Billy,' said Gerry Higgs. 'A bit of self-respect never did anyone any harm, did it?'

Again, we look at each other and I mumble my agreement, smiling earnestly at him.

'Look, Mr Higgs, would you like to come and meet my friend Maureen, she's parked over there in that Peugeot – I've told her all about you. She'd love to meet you.'

'That's very nice of you, old son,' says Gerry, 'but I'd rather keep the work of the Service strictly between the two of us.'

'Oh yes,' I say as though this makes perfect sense. 'Of course. So then, midday, the day after tomorrow.'

'Yes, Billy.'

I start to rush over to Maureen, but I have to stop – Gerry's use of the word Service caused a rush to my temple, and the same retching in my chest and stomach that had struck me down earlier. I hold on to the bars of the church wall for a few seconds, until it passes. Everything is going to be alright, I tell myself. Everything is going to work out. Gerry Higgs has said the day after tomorrow.

I get into the car and grin at Maureen. She smiles back at me. 'Well?'

'Great,' I say, 'everything's going to be great, Mo.'

'Brilliant,' she says. 'Did you have to say anything? Introduce yourself to the group and everything?'

'Yes,' I say.

'And how was it? What did you tell them?'

'Not much, really,' I continue. 'What can you say?'

'Well, that doesn't sound very good, Billy – you must have said something.'

'I told them I was a footballer, Maureen. I told them I was lucky.'

Her face starts to drop now. 'Well, surely you spoke about drink too?'

'I did, but don't worry, Mo. Don't worry about anything. It's all going to be better.'

'But, Billy, you've got a problem, the whole point of AA is that you accept that you've got a problem.'

I look at her. 'I'm the luckiest man in the world, Maureen,' I say. 'I've got a second chance, a chance to put things right.'

'But, Billy, if you carry on drinking, you won't have any chances. That's the whole point.'

'Don't worry,' I say. 'Next time, I'll know – it's all about getting out of the way of the train.'

'The what?'

'The train. The train that's carrying all my baggage with it, coming towards me, making me drink. After I've had my chance, scored my goal, there won't be a train, and if there is, I'll learn how to see it coming and get out of the way.'

'Oh,' says Maureen.

'Yeah, Karl, he's a counsellor, lovely man, very clever, he told me all about it, he reckons that my ability to see a football early will help me with this as well.'

'Does he?'

'Oh yes, Maureen, it's all connected, I just needed a bit of help, someone to point it out to me. There's no need to worry.'

We drive home, with Maureen asking me questions about what was said and who the others were and what they had said, and me hiding adroitly behind the curtain of their anonymity: 'I'd love to tell you, but we're all sworn to secrecy, that's why it's "Alcoholics

Anonymous", isn't it? All I can say is that they are all lovely people, Mo, very helpful, very caring.'

She parks her car outside my flat and I turn to her.

'So, will you do it, then?' I ask. 'Will you arrange a meeting with Rebecca?'

'Yes, Billy,' she says. 'I've already spoken to her. It's arranged.'

'Arranged?' I exclaim. 'Already? I didn't know, I wasn't sure. When? What has she said?'

'She lives in Sidcup, Billy. If you want to meet her, I've arranged for it to happen the day after tomorrow.'

'Sidcup? The day after tomorrow?'

'Yes, I couldn't tell you before, and, Billy, I mean this, I won't take you there if you get pissed between now and then.'

'No, of course not,' I reply, my mind attempting to work out the logistics of meeting up with her and making sure that I am ready for Gerry and the Council.

'I'll take you to a location to meet her,' continues Maureen. 'She's ready to give you a second chance, but, Billy, you've got to realise, she's very, very wary of you – she's still very raw about one or two things.'

'Yes, I won't let you down.'

'Don't worry about me, it's her you've got to concentrate on.'

I look straight into the distance. My little girl is living in Sidcup, bloody Sidcup, just up the road; things don't get much more real than Sidcup. I will meet her; I will put everything right.

As I look out at the road ahead of me, I feel the elation and emotion of the evening ebbing away, to be replaced by a tiredness that overwhelms my bones and brain – I dismiss it as nerves.

'What time?' I ask, rubbing my eyes. 'What time will I meet her?'

'Ten o'clock.'

That is OK; I can easily be back at my flat for Gerry by midday.

'One more thing you should know, Billy,' says Maureen. 'I got rid of that vodka.'

'When?'

'Never mind when, it's gone, and I've put a new jigsaw on your kitchen table with some food.'

I smile at her.

'I don't deserve you,' I say. 'What's the jigsaw of?'

'It's a football one,' she says. 'I think it's one of the England World Cup Squads; 2,000 pieces, it took Brian Staplehurst ten hours.'

I grin.

Inside my flat on the kitchen table, the bottle of vodka has indeed been replaced by a jigsaw of the England 1982 World Cup Squad, Ron's twenty-two. And there, in the middle of the front row, with his thick tanned thighs and heroic dark locks, is Kevin Keegan. I start to laugh. Everything is going to be fine.

21

Let's face it; my time at Spurs was a bit of a disaster. The piece of mud up at Goodison Park put paid to the 1974/75 season, and when I finally got back for pre-season training, the first thing to happen was my hamstring went. My body was turning against me – the muscles and blood cells and veins and organs had got together, had a meeting, and decided that enough was enough.

I finally got back into training around the end of September 1975, but, by then, I had been out for nearly a year – a year with nothing to keep my mind and body occupied. I was underweight and out of condition.

The team had started the season badly; by October we'd only won once. Terry Neill was under pressure and was losing patience with me; until I was fit and firing, I was useless to him.

He came to see me after training and put his arm around me.

'Billy,' he said, 'you are without doubt one of the best players I've ever seen with a ball.'

'Thanks, Boss.'

'We've been drawing a lot of our games recently.'

'I know.'

'What we need is a player who can provide the spark, the imagination, to turn those draws into wins.'

'Yes, Boss.'

'We need you, Billy.'

'Thanks, Boss.'

'How are you feeling?'

'Not bad, Boss: Brian, the physio, reckons I'll be back in about three weeks.'

'Good, you'll play against Liverpool on Saturday.'

'Liverpool!'

'Yes, Billy, Liverpool. Our luck has got to change sometime, and I tell you now, I can feel it with every inch of my being that it will change this Saturday, and that this will be the start of your climb back into Don Revie's England squad.'

We lost 4-0.

I'd felt terrible before the match. I'd sat in the changing room and looked at my legs; they seemed skinnier than they used to be, skinnier and slower. I didn't trust them. I didn't trust my own legs. They were clearly in on the conspiracy. I had a hip-flask in my bag, full of vodka. I took it into the toilets and had a little sip, nothing too much, just enough to take the fear away from my legs, just enough to get rid of the black feeling of desperation that was hanging over me.

I went back to the changing room and sat down. Stevie Perryman, lovely Stevie Perryman, the best pro you could ever wish to meet, was giving us a pre-match pep talk about the history of the club.

'This isn't about all of us,' he said quietly. 'This isn't about eleven of us who are about to run out on to the park, this is about the hundreds of thousands of men who have supported Tottenham Hotspur for the last ninety-odd years. Men who have gone without food to buy a ticket for the match, men who would die to have the chance we have to play against Liverpool on a Saturday afternoon, men who wake up thinking about Spurs and go to sleep thinking about Spurs, that's what this is all about.'

I slunk off as Stevie scowled at me and went back to the toilet where I took out my hip-flask and drank the rest of the vodka.

We lost 4-0.

We lost 4-0 and I contributed nothing. I was slow. I ran with slow heavy legs and flat feet. I saw the ball a second later than I usually did, and when I had it I couldn't even bloody kick the bloody thing straight; all those hours kicking against my back gate, all those hours practising crosses with Taffy Watkins, and all I could do was keep putting the ball into the groaning crowd.

Parksy, you overpaid fucking piece of shit.

We lost 4-0. Kevin Keegan scored Liverpool's first goal. He didn't look slow. He looked bloody sharp with his wonderful balance and strength and lovely bouncing curly barnet.

Amazingly, Terry Neill picked me for the next game. Again, he came to see me before the match. This time his arm around my shoulder was more of a grip than a caress. This time his lovely rolling Ulster brogue took on a more sinister tone.

'Billy,' he said, 'you were absolutely shite against Liverpool.'

'Yes, Boss. Sorry, Boss.'

'I think we both know why?'

'Do we?'

'Yes, Billy, you've been doing too much relaxing and not enough training.'

'Well—'

He interrupted me, saving us both from having to endure the rubbish excuse that was forming itself in my mind.

'Don't worry; I have faith in you, Billy. I know that you are still young enough to turn it around. I know that you still care. You do still care, don't you, Billy?'

'Yes, Boss. Absolutely, Boss.'

'Good, you'll play against Middlesbrough on Saturday. I can't possibly imagine that you'll be as shite this week.'

We lost 1-0 against Middlesbrough. I *was* just as shite. Their right-back, John Craggs, took delight in kicking me all over the

211

park; he'd never been able to catch me before. I was slow and I couldn't understand why. I couldn't understand why my body was letting me down, failing to produce the power I needed to propel myself forward, away from the scything legs of the likes of Johnny Craggs. And, as my body let me down, I stopped trusting my instinct and I lost the bravery that I was known for; I lost the ability to see the ball before everyone else.

At half-time, I drank a hip-flask full of vodka.

After the final whistle, I lay on Brian the physio's bench drinking rum from a tin mug as he tried to massage the bruises away.

One of the club secretaries appeared at the door. 'Billy,' she said. 'There's a woman who wants to see you.'

I smiled. 'No surprise there.'

'She says she's your sister.'

I sat up at once.

I knew.

I stood up, still wearing only my towel, and left the physio's room. I walked down the spotless corridors, past fans and functionaries, oblivious to the looks I was getting, because I knew. I even knew exactly where I would find Carol, where she would be standing when she told me, as though everything had been preordained, a scene in a play that had been written and rehearsed.

And there she was. Just as I knew she would be, by the reception desk. I hadn't seen her in years. Broader than I thought she'd be. Older. Middle-aged, with cigarette-pull creases around her mouth and baggy eyes. Worn.

She looked at me. I knew what was coming next. I could feel my body racing, my heavy heart pounding.

'Hi, Billy.' She spoke quietly with a soft warm closed-mouth smile that hadn't spread to her eyes; her eyes showed only sadness.

'Hi Carol,' I said, trying to muster a smile for my big sister, because I might be wrong. But I wasn't.

212

'I'm sorry to come here, Billy,' she said, 'but I had no idea where else to find you.'

'That's alright,' I said.

And for a second we both stood there in silence. I noticed that her eyes were the same as mine: it was my last thought in the final few seconds before the confirmation.

'It's Mum,' she told me, and I nodded my head as a strange feeling of ecstasy swept through me, making me want to laugh. Don't get me wrong, I wasn't happy to hear that my mother was dead, Christ no – it was more as though happiness was evacuating my body and cleansing me of all other emotion as it did.

'They found her in her flat,' Carol continued, her eyes never leaving mine. 'If it wasn't for that dog she had—'

'Peppy.'

'Yeah, if it wasn't for Peppy, they wouldn't have found her for weeks.'

It had been two months, perhaps longer, since I had seen our mum. I'd meant to call round. Of course I had. I had told myself nearly every day that I should go and see my mother, but there had always been an excuse, there had always been another thing to stop me, another drink, another chance to drink.

I leaned my hands on the reception desk and bowed my head.

A day or so later, we went to clear out her flat: just me and Carol. It was cold. I could see traces of our mother: the indentation on the couch that marked where she'd sat; the worn spot on the arm where she'd rested a thousand glasses and mugs; an old copy of the *Daily Mirror* placed on her coffee table; the washing up still drying on the draining board, with a checked tea-towel folded neatly nearby.

Where was all her stuff?

We started to work methodically through her things, me and Carol, as though searching for something that had been lost to us, some kind of clue as to who we once were and who we had become. I became fixated with finding a red coat that I had bought her the previous Christmas: where was it? Why wasn't it in her wardrobe? I had been sure that she would have loved that coat. I convinced myself that if I found that red coat then it would mean that she had loved me. But she seemed to have nothing at all. Even fat Uncle Wilf's stolen relics from the Raj were missing.

'Where is everything?' I asked Carol. But she just shrugged her shoulders. 'I think she was selling stuff.'

'Selling stuff? Why?'

'Oh, Billy. For drink, of course.'

I sighed.

'But I would have given her money. Why didn't she just ask?'

Carol looked at me and I knew why. I didn't press it.

We went through her purses and handbags and drawers. I hoped to find maybe a few cuttings from the newspapers: *Parksy's Heroics Saves Hammers* or something, anything. But there was nothing.

I don't know what Carol was looking for.

All we found was a bundle of letters tied in pink ribbon from my father. We looked at them together, me and my big sister, sitting on our dead mother's bed.

Every letter started the same:

My Dearest Ruth

Every letter ended the same:

Until the day when I can come home and hold you and Carol in my arms once more,
All my love
Bill.

The bits in-between were a mixture of gossip from the war, details about where he was training, then where he was stationed, interspersed with random questions and comments about home.

The monsoon season has started here, you wouldn't believe it, one second it's very hot, then the next it's raining cats and dogs.

I was sorry to hear about your cousin Alan's house. Blooming Fritz, eh.

How's things down at the bus depot? Did they keep running the service out to Chingford?

You wouldn't believe how difficult it is trying to clean this Burmese mud out of the carburettor of an M3.

We chuckled at our father's stiff prose.

'She loved him,' said Carol, tears making their way down her face.

I nodded.

'You've got to understand, Billy, that when he came back, she was devastated; she was twenty-nine years old and she felt that her life was over. She couldn't understand why it wasn't enough for him that he was back with her.'

I wasn't sure I understood. It was hard for me to see my father as anything other than the man sitting in the kitchen who jumped into the canal. I had never thought deeply about the reasons that had taken him there, and I had never thought about the effect it had had on our mother.

'Why did *you* leave then?' It was a difficult question for both of us.

'I couldn't take her pain, Billy.'

I nodded gently; I understood this.

'Do you think she loved us?' I asked.

'I think so,' said Carol. 'But she lost the ability to show it, perhaps it was knocked out of her.'

I felt six years old again with my big sister. I wished we'd spoken like this before.

'I found a bottle of gin under the sink,' I said. 'You fancy a snifter?'

'Oh, go on then.'

We drank a glass of gin together, then her husband Ray came

215

and took her home. I carried on drinking. I never really stopped.

At the end of the season, Terry Neill left for Arsenal and Keith Burkinshaw stepped in. Super Manager was Keith, understated and clever. He tried to persevere with me. He called me into his room early on.

'What does football mean to you, Billy?' he asked.

'Everything,' I replied.

'OK,' he said. 'Then prove it to me. If you do, then we'll have a great few years here together.'

Fair play, he gave me a good run of games, he tried me in various positions, he talked to me and cajoled me and bollocked me, but I just couldn't get it back; I couldn't get back that ability to instinctively put yourself in the right spot, to have your body and your mind working in harmony on the football pitch. I kept telling myself that in a couple of games it would return, and, sporadically, it did, occasionally it felt right again. I scored a cracking goal up at Derby County and another one in front of the Stretford End after I'd given young Jimmy Nicholl the runaround, but it never came back for long. It never came back properly. It was never how it used to be.

And, in the summer of 1977, with Spurs relegated to Division Two, I went out to America to play with Bobby Moore, Harry Redknapp and Geoff Hurst for Seattle Sounders.

I was twenty-nine years old. I told myself that it was a brilliant move. I told myself that I could still do it. I told myself that it was the new start that me and Sandi and baby Rebecca needed. But the truth was that, at twenty-nine, just like my mum, the one thing I loved more than anything was dead to me. The rest of my life would be spent yearning for it, missing it, trying to block out what I saw as the meaninglessness of everything that I was left with.

Details: Match 13, 24 October 1975
Division One
Venue: White Hart Lane

Tottenham Hotspur 0 v. Liverpool 4
                    Keegan
                    Toshack
                    Neal
                    Cormack

Line Ups
Spurs: Jennings, Perryman, McAllister, Osgood, Naylor, Pratt, Conn, Coates, Parks, Chivers, Jones
Liverpool: Clemence, Neal, Smith, Thompson, Hughes, Cormack, Callaghan, Kennedy, Heighway, Keegan, Toshack

Attendance: 34,298

Details: Match 14, 2 November 1975
Division One
Venue: White Hart Lane
Tottenham Hotspur 0 v. Middlesbrough 1
                    Hickton

Line Ups
Spurs: Jennings, Kinnear, McAllister, Osgood, Naylor, Pratt, Perryman, Coates, Parks, Armstrong, Duncan
Middlesbrough: Platt, Craggs, Cooper, Maddren, Boam, Souness, Armstrong, Brine, Boersma, Hickton, Mills

Attendance: 29,997

22

I must have some kind of fever, or perhaps I am reacting to the tablets that Dr Aranthraman has given me: either way, I am lying on my couch, shivering, falling in and out of sleep, and dreaming multi-coloured dreams that are viciously real. I rouse myself and try to make a start on the jigsaw Maureen has given me, but I can't get beyond a few pieces; the colours and shapes just merge into one, as the pain in my stomach becomes unbearable, as though someone has replaced my insides with a collection of stones that grind together every time I move.

I know that drink would help. I know it. I bloody know it. A bottle of scotch would do the trick, end the dreams, chase away the ghosts, stop the pain, I know that and I want to scream, but instead I just lie down, sweating and panting and try to find a cold patch on my pillow. I have to get through the day. This day. Just one bloody day. Because tomorrow everything will be fine. Tomorrow everything will be alright. Tomorrow will be the greatest day: there will be no more pain after tomorrow, no more yearning for drink, no more regret. I'll start the process of making everything better. At ten o'clock, I'll see Rebecca. At twelve o'clock, I'll meet the Council of Football Immortals – it's all sorted. I just need to get through today. That's all.

I take a fistful of sleeping tablets and as many painkillers as I dare and sleep restlessly for a few hours, before I am awoken by a shudder of pain across my abdomen that causes me to wince and sit bolt upright. As I do, my eyes open with shock. Standing by my door is Johnny Smith. He is about twelve years old and carrying a brown leather football under his arm. His eyes are shining with the innocence of wanting nothing more than to kick his ball.

'Hey, Billy, when we're famous footballers, do you think we'll win the FA Cup?'

He bounces his ball and smiles his podgy beautiful smile at me, and I want to shout out: 'Do something else, Johnny, don't play football, do something that will make you happy.' But no sound comes out of my mouth, I struggle to find my voice, and instead, I hear my twelve-year-old self answering him: 'Course we will Johnny, and we'll meet the Queen, and then we'll play for England, and win the World Cup 'n'all.'

And I lie back and howl with fear and frustration and pain as Johnny and me skip off to play out our fantasies.

Sometime later, I don't know how much later, I awake again. This time I can see a light coming from the corner of my living room. I get up and walk towards it; I can see that my TV is on – something black and white – I walk towards it, then stop suddenly; there, sitting on the sofa, with her back to me, is my mother. I know it's her. The TV crackles and she turns around to me, staring up with maniacal eyes. 'There you are, Billy. Are you off out? You will come back to see me, won't you? You will, Billy, won't you? Don't forget now.'

I fall to my knees and bury my head in her lap. 'I will come round, Mum, I will come round to see you, I understand now and I'm going to make everything better.'

They all visit me that night, including my father, who stands silently, looking up at the bright sky that has formed itself in my consciousness.

'What are you looking for, Dad? What's up there?'

'Nothing, son. Just the sky. That's all.'

'Why are you looking up at the sky, Dad?'

'Because it's real, son. The sky's always there. It never changes. No matter where you are and how bad things are, the sky is always above you. Amazin' innit?'

I want to touch him, but I can't – you can't touch a dream or a ghost.

Then, when my dad has gone, I see Sandi, standing by the door of my kitchen. Standing next to her is Rebecca, she is about six years old and wearing a Mickey Mouse T-shirt and shorts. She is pure like untouched morning dew and looking bashfully at her toes. Sandi holds a suitcase in her hand, and without her saying anything, I find myself on my knees pleading: 'Please don't go, please don't go – I will change, this time, it will all be different, you'll see, this time, I'll stop drinking and everything, you'll see, just give me one more chance.'

'You said that everything would be alright once we got to America, Billy.'

'It will be. It will be.'

'It isn't, though, is it? Where've you been for three days? Where've you been?'

And she disappears. And Rebecca disappears. Just like they did all those years ago.

They all come to me that night – Bobby, Georgie, Barry Ross, lads I'd forgotten existed, lads I'd drunk with, girls I'd loved and smiled at. A steady procession of ghosts and dreams and God knows, until eventually they finally stop appearing, leaving me behind, shivering and wet with sweat, alone and scared. I open my tear-reddened eyes and check the room anxiously, waiting for someone else to appear.

But they don't.

I am awake now: my heart still pounding like a drill; my lungs and stomach churning; my breath pouring out of my body; and my eyes searching my room for more ghosts. But there are none.

Slowly I become calm. My body relaxes, my eyes focus and I am relieved to see it is morning; it is easier to control the need for drink in the daylight – the pain isn't quite so intense. I look at my clock: Maureen will be here soon to take me to see Rebecca. It is alright. I have made it. The ghosts have gone. The past has gone back to where it belongs.

I shower, the sting of the water rasping against my skin. It hurts to dry myself afterwards, but I do it because today I have to be Billy Parks – today, I need to be the man who could be a father and a grandfather and a scorer of goals.

I get out my best shirt, hand made by Chrissy Christalades of Mile End, the finest tailor in the whole of east London. I put it on, ignoring the stain on the collar and the fact that the chest swings empty on my skinny frame. Then I do up my West Ham United FC tie around my neck, ignoring the fact that it accentuates the scraggy baggy skin around my throat. I comb my hair – today, I am Billy Parks.

Maureen arrives and smiles at me.

'How do I look?' I asked her.

There is a pause before she answers, 'You look great, Billy.'

Why does she have sad eyes when she says it?

We make our way to Sidcup. I watch Maureen as she drives south through the mish-mash of life that is New Cross Road and Lewisham town centre, then out towards Chislehurst Road and Bromley, where it starts to become reassuringly better off. I am glad that my little girl is living out in the sticks. This is definitely a good thing.

Maureen stops at traffic lights. I look over at her – the act of concentration makes her pout. Perhaps when everything is settled again we could become more than friends, we could pick up where we'd started, years earlier. I could help her run a pub out in the countryside. Kent, perhaps. There could be pictures of me as a player on the walls.

'You know when all this is over and that, do you fancy coming out for a nice meal, just you and me, proper meal, you know, like a Chinese or an Italian up West, or something?'

'Are you asking me on a date, Billy?'

'Yes, I suppose I am. What's wrong with that?'

She pouts again and her eyes smile as she looks ahead at the road.

'We'll see how you get on.'

I suppose that is only right. I mean, she has seen me at some low points in the last few years.

She changes the subject, telling me that Rebecca wants to meet at a neutral venue, and that this is best for both of us – I agree. I am starting to get nervous now. I wonder whether Liam will be there as well. I try to picture him. I wonder how he will look – whether I will see myself in him. Whether I will meet him at all.

We drive to a park. Maureen pulls the car up by the kerb.

'What shall I say to her?'

Maureen turns to me. 'Just start with "sorry",' she says. 'Then let the rest take care of itself.'

I nod. That makes sense. Maureen is wise. I want to kiss her. I lean over.

'I think that must be her over on those benches,' she says, moving away from me.

I look over at some benches by a small park. On one of them, sitting on her own, turned slightly away from us is a woman. I nod at Maureen, thank her, then leave the car and walk tentatively towards the woman on the bench. I try not to limp. I walk across a grass verge and over a path and towards the bench: I can now make out the facial features of the woman. I scrunch up my eyes towards the figure on the bench and can see that she has moved her body so that it faces me.

It is Rebecca. Waiting for me. My daughter. My little girl, whose hand I had held, who I had let down and who I pray will give me a second chance, a chance to make everything right. She sits there, real and alone, and waiting for me. I feel tears start to well up in my eyes and the space in my throat clog up. I bite hard to prevent myself from crying, put my head down, and walk towards her. I give up trying to hide my limp.

She rises slightly as I approach her. 'Billy?' she says. Not Dad. Why not Dad? Why bloody not Dad?

'Becky?'

We stand and smile uncomfortably at each other, and I put my hands up on her arms. If she would let me I would hug her, but I know by her reaction that this isn't what she wants. I let go and look into her face: her eyes are unmistakably mine; her beautiful cheekbones are her mother's. Her hair is done nice, with some highlights that suit her. She looks as if she's doing alright. I stare at her and smile with a closed mouth. I am happy. I want to sing.

'How are you?' I ask.

'I'm fine,' she says. 'How are you?'

'Oh, I'm tremendous,' I tell her and she looks at me doubtfully. We sit down. I try to work out when I should say sorry.

'I didn't know you'd been ill. Maureen told me. If I'd have known I would have come to see you.'

'Don't worry; it's nothing, just a bit of stomach complaint. You know what doctors are like, they can't be too careful.'

'But you're feeling alright now?'

'Right as rain.'

She nods. Not far away I can hear children playing on some swings.

'Funny,' I say. 'I tried to find you a few weeks ago, back in your old flat down Beckenham way, and I got chased out of the park across the road by a load of women who thought I was a pervert.'

She smiles. 'You,' she says, 'that's about the one thing you aren't.'

I smile as well. I know she's joking.

'Maureen seems very nice.'

'Oh, yes, she is, a real diamond.'

'Are you and her …?'

224

'No, no, nothing like that, we're just friends.'

She nods, computing this information, painting a little picture of my life in her mind.

'How's Liam?' I ask.

'He's great.'

'Still at school?'

'Yes.'

I flounder; I want more than this, I want to be brought back into his life, I want her to place him on my grandfatherly knee.

'What's he like?' I ask. 'What does he do?'

She smiles to herself. 'He's changed a lot in the last seven years.'

Christ, I thought, is it really seven years since I saw them? Seven bloody years? Bloody hell.

'He's football mad,' she continues. And my heart leaps. This is fantastic. This means I had lived.

'Is he?' I say, my face breaking out into the biggest smile that has shone from me for ages. 'He must get that from his father's side of the family, eh?'

She laughs and we make more nice, happy, easy small talk about her bloke, Dean, and Liam's schooling and how he is doing well and hopes to do all his exams and I listen and nod and am genuinely, genuinely happy. But I still haven't said sorry, she still hasn't called me Dad, we still haven't gone beyond the superficial, the pleasantries. It is still a conversation that could be had by any two people. I still haven't had my second chance. Not yet. But I can tell that she wants to move the conversation forward as much as I do. For an awkward few seconds, we both listen to the children playing on the swing.

'Look,' she says. 'Billy—'

I interrupt her: 'Oh Rebecca, please, please don't call me Billy. I know it's been seven years, but I'm still your dad.'

'No,' she says forcefully, 'I'm sorry, I've thought about this a lot over the years: you have to earn the right to be my dad.'

I sigh, then nod. She is right. This is true.

'Alright,' I say, smiling gently at her. 'What do I have to do? How do I earn it?'

'I'm not sure,' she says, then she pauses and I know that she is composing herself to say things that she has prepared; things that she has probably wanted to say for years.

'I've got to be honest,' she says. 'I'd pretty much put you out of my thoughts. Then, when Maureen got in touch and told me you'd been ill, well, I had a decision to make, didn't I?'

I nod.

'And there's things I need to know.'

'What things?'

'Well,' she composes herself again. 'I need to know more about you and Mum.'

I shrug. 'What is there to know?' I know this sounds crass and stupid as soon as I've said it.

'Everything, for me,' she says. 'Before she died, she wouldn't talk about you. About what had happened between you. Christ, she even defended you, told me not to be too hard on you.'

Now it's my turn to compose myself. I look up at the sky, then let the air leave my mouth as pretty images form in my mind – images of the girl who I'd met at the West Ham Christmas Party forty-odd years ago, who had died of leukaemia in Canada at the age of forty-two, which is something I only learned about through her sister two weeks after the event. Two bloody weeks, because they couldn't find me. That still bloody hurts.

'She was lovely,' I say. 'We used to drive out to the country, Epping Forest, and lie in the grass and look up at the sunshine and make plans. Or, we'd go down to Margate or Southend and she'd laugh as people used to come up to me and ask for my autograph. I remember once, this old geezer walked up to me, and I thought he wanted me to sign a copy of the evening paper that he was waving around in his hand, so I'd taken the paper off him and the pen he had in the other hand, I'm about to sign it, when the old codger grabs it back and starts to tell me how crap

I was the previous Saturday. Your mother thought that was the funniest thing ever.'

I smile and let myself momentarily glide back to a place that felt safe and happy.

'The problem wasn't your mother,' I continue, knowing that I have to break away from the haven of warm benign memories. 'The problem was entirely mine. She deserved better. You both deserved better.'

'I thought you'd say that,' says Rebecca.

'What else *can* I say? It's the truth. Your mum was a beautiful sweet woman and I was this kid who couldn't say no to anything or anybody.'

'I don't think you should blame anyone else.'

'I'm not, I'm blaming myself – I had choices and I made the wrong ones.'

I pause as a man walks past us. His dog stops to have a piss on the bin opposite; it gives me a chance to collect my thoughts.

'I often think,' I continue, tentatively now, 'that when I was first with your mum, she used to be able to slow everything down for me, make me relaxed and contented, stop me from wanting to run around everywhere going barmy with the need to remind everyone who I was – it was wonderful. Then, when I wasn't with her, time would speed up again and sweep me away: I'd lose the ability to make the right decisions. So I just kept making the wrong ones – the hurtful ones. The bloody stupid ones.'

There is silence as she ponders this. I wonder if she might cry. And if she does, whether I will be allowed to hug her, tell her that it will all be alright, kiss her gently on her forehead, just like I must have done years ago when she was a little girl.

'What about me, though?' she says quietly. 'Couldn't *I* make time slow down?'

I feel my head drop. It's a good question. It goes to the heart of everything. It goes to the heart of me – why hadn't she been enough? My little girl?

'I don't know,' I say. Which isn't very helpful. 'I just want to put everything right now. I want to have a second chance. If I have a second chance, I'll make sure that I let you slow down time for me. I'll make everything alright.'

She doesn't like the words *second chance*, her eyes flash.

'You've had second chances before, remember, Billy: remember the time you came round, pissed, and argued with Dean and threatened him with a coat-hanger; remember the time you were supposed to take Liam out for a Saturday afternoon and you didn't show, he was only five years old; remember the time we invited you round for dinner and you arrived stinking of drink and slurring, two hours late. I'd spent all day cooking a beef bloody casserole. You've had a second chance and a third chance, and a fourth. You have had as many chances as you deserve.'

'I know, I know, I know all of that, but I'm different now, I've started going to AA and everything. My counsellor told me how I've got to learn to see the train carrying all my crap before it knocks me out of the way. I understand it all now. And my doctor tells me that if I carry on drinking,' I pause, 'well, I can't carry on drinking, can I? And Maureen, she's an angel, and she won't have anything to do with me if I treat you badly, she's told me.'

'This isn't about you, Billy, and your stupid train. This is about me. This is about me wanting to know as much as I can about my parents and about myself. That's why I agreed to meet you. I want answers to questions.'

'I understand that, Becks.' I want to tell her that I too had spent a lifetime pondering my parents, but I don't.

'What do you want to know? Ask me anything.'

'What happened in America?'

'America?'

'Yes, what happened in America?'

'Bloody hell, Rebecca, that was thirty-odd years ago.'

'It was when you and Mum split, wasn't it?'

'Yes.'

'Well, I want to know why.'

I puff out my cheeks.

A voice starts whispering in my head, dark whispers, telling me that a drink would take me away from this. It would be easy; I could get away from this uncomfortable space in no time. But I can't do that. I know it. I owe her more than that.

'We arrived,' I start, silencing the voice, 'after I'd left Spurs. Loads of footballers were going over there. I was given the chance to play for Sounders in Seattle – it was great, the money was great, the team was really good. Brilliant crowds. They put us up in a fantastic gaff, by this lake – it was wonderful. Do you remember it?'

She looks into the distance. 'A bit,' she says. 'I remember playing with the other kids from the club.'

'That's right, you would have been about five or six. Lovely it was. You used to play with Harry's boys.'

A beautiful image of me and all the old West Ham lads who were out there kicking a ball around by the lakeside and drinking beer and eating barbecued food jumps into my head – it *was* lovely, Sandi was gorgeous, all tanned and, for the first few weeks, very happy, and little Becky running around, chasing butterflies and Jamie Redknapp. It was an image I didn't want to leave.

'What happened then?' she asks me. 'What spoilt it?'

I compose my thoughts, prepare my confession.

'Drink,' I say. 'And –' I paused '– I had this thing with another woman.'

The words stumble out of my mouth like clowns in oversized shoes. She nods slowly, her eyes boring into the pavement underneath the bench.

'I didn't mean for it to happen.'

That sounds pathetic.

'Who was she?'

I sigh. 'Her name was Erica,' I say, and a brief period of my life comes whirring through my head like an old home movie – it features a slim, blonde woman with good teeth who worked at the football club as a secretary, and exciting sex in the club changing rooms, and drinks in the city's bars, and her apartment, where you could hear traffic all night, and me becoming more emboldened, and some of the lads telling me not to be so stupid and didn't I realise what a good thing I had? And I *did* know. I knew exactly what a good thing I had. And I knew that I had loved Sandi. And I knew that she would be the only woman who would ever come close to making me happy, but still, I couldn't stop myself, so I went back for more because I loved the rush of being Billy Parks more than anything else.

And that says everything.

'It lasted a couple of months,' I continue, 'and eventually your mum had had enough, and she took you and went back to England.'

'Was she worth it?' asks Rebecca; there is a lifetime's worth of venom in the question.

I pause. The correct answer is 'no'. The truthful answer is, well, maybe, after all, she contributed to the life of Billy Parks and I couldn't honestly say that it had been all worthless. But I try to say the right thing: 'No,' I say. 'I regret it every bloody day. And I'm sorry, Becky, sorry for everything.'

She sighs and I wonder if that is enough.

A cold silence grows around us, even the kids on the playground have stopped laughing and chattering and screaming. I want to put my arm around her. I have to say something:

'Becky, I'd really like to see Liam.'

'He'd like to see you too,' her voice is quiet and resigned; she is confused by the same gentle compassion that her mother had. I know that.

'Perhaps I could arrange to meet up with him or something, sometime; it will be good for me. It'll help me make things right, you know, help me be your dad again.'

'Well, if you want,' she looks at her watch. 'I'm just off to watch him play football now, you can come if you like. I know he'd like that.'

'Now?' I look at my own watch – it is already 10.45. This is tricky. If I go to watch Liam play football, I would miss my meeting with Gerry Higgs, I would miss my meeting with the Council, I would miss my chance. Gerry Higgs had said midday, be ready for midday. I couldn't miss this, my chance.

I prevaricate.

'If you've got something better …'

'No,' I say. 'No, there is nothing I'd like more than to watch the lad playing football. Nothing.'

And as the words leave my mouth I realise that I mean it and it feels good saying it. This is my second chance. This is my chance to see my grandson, this is my chance to put some things right. On another football pitch where my daughter's boy will be kicking a ball, may lie real, proper redemption. And, anyway perhaps it saves me the humiliation of being rejected by the Council of Football Immortals; after all, it is odds-on that they'll prefer Kevin Keegan, who am I trying to kid?

We walk towards Maureen's car. Maureen gets out and grins at us both, girlish in her enthusiasm for the reunion she has brought about; she gives us a lift to a football pitch nearby, where Liam is playing for his district under 15s against another team from Kent.

I stand on the side of the pitch with the other slavering dads and granddads and uncles. They had already kicked off. Liam is wearing a green shirt with the number 11 on the back. He has blonde hair that reaches his shoulders. He is taller than I had been at that age, sleeker, but as I watch him run, as I watch him call for the ball, position himself on the left-hand side, trap the ball neatly, turn nicely, tears cascade down my cheeks. Not because of his amazing skills, though he is a fine player, but because of the very fact of his existence.

Other parents shout and encourage, but I just watch with awe the amazing sight of this young lad moving, running, breathing, playing football. He is beautiful. After a few minutes, he gets the ball and advances towards the other team; he is quickly round the full-back and fizzing in a cross that the striker heads over the bar. People clap and I feel as proud as I have ever done about anything in my life.

His team wins 3-2. He played just fine.

Afterwards he comes towards us, still shining from the exertion. He spies me as he approaches.

'This is your granddad, Liam,' Becky says.

'Granddad?' says Liam. 'Granddad Billy?'

'Yes,' answers his mother.

'Hello Liam,' I say. 'Well played son, great cross for that second goal.'

'Thanks.'

The boy looks at me, then looks at his mother; he's heard stories, that's obvious, probably all kinds of stories from all kinds of sources and now he didn't know what to make of my sudden and unexpected arrival into his life after seven years of tall tales and absence.

'That full-back was a bit prickly, wasn't he?' I say.

And he grins shyly.

'In my day, we would have had a big hairy-arsed centre-half give him a sly dig.'

He smiles again, this time with less reticence.

We talk. I ask him questions that he answers timidly, usually looking down at the grass or up at his mother as he does.

He tells me that he loves his football and Crystal Palace and Charlton Athletic have been interested in him; he likes swimming as well, and hopes to get into the Kent team; school is OK; he doesn't know what he wants to do when he leaves; and, he tells me that he supports West Ham. That makes me happy. That is a pleasant surprise.

'Good lad,' I say. 'That was my father's team as well.'

An idea comes to me.

'Look,' I say, and I cast a glance towards Becky as I speak, 'West Ham are playing at home tomorrow night – would you like to come? I'll wangle some tickets. Probably get in to meet some of the players and what have you.'

He looks at his mother, a sparkle of excitement in his eyes. 'Yes, sure, is that alright, Mum?'

He is a good lad, asking his mother, I like that. He speaks nicely too. He is a credit to her.

Rebecca is unsure, but, as we both stand there smiling at her, two sets of twinkling blue eyes, she allows it.

I am overjoyed. This is brilliant.

'But, Billy,' she says gravely, 'if you don't take care of him, if you so much as touch a drop of alcohol, there will be no more chances.'

'I know.' I smile, a full open-mouthed Billy-Parks-Is-God smile. 'I know, you won't have to worry about a thing. Everything's going to be fine. Everything's going to be absolutely fine.'

We arrange to meet the following evening at Upton Park tube, then Maureen takes me home. I feel myself tiring now, as we head back into London and the painkillers and excitement start to wear off. My smile wanes and this strange pain in my cheekbones takes its place. Maureen drops me across the road from my flat. It is almost 2pm. I thank her and get out of the car.

'You will be alright, Billy, won't you?'

'Yes, of course,' I say, leaning into the open passenger door.

'You seem a bit quiet.'

'I'm a bit tired, love. It's been an emotional morning.'

She smiles at me; still with the sad eyes, though. Why is that? I don't understand that.

'You've got your second chance, haven't you?'

'Yes. All down to you. Fantastic.'

'You don't sound too sure.'

'I am. It's all going to be brilliant now and I'm still serious about that date.'

She smiles at me. 'And I still say that we'll see. I tell you what,

233

why don't you pop round later in the week, I'll make you some supper.'

'That'd be nice. Thanks.'

Later in the week. Not tonight. Later in the week. Sad eyes and later in the week.

Her car speeds off and I prepare to cross the road.

I am alone.

I will never know about the Council of Football Immortals. I will never know if they prefer me to Kevin Keegan and if I could score the goal against Poland and take England to the World Cup, and how things might have been different. I start to cross the road and a car sounds its horn at me. I turn to see a driver waving his fist, he winds down his window: 'What you playing at you old git.'

Wanker: can't he see that I'm struggling with a leg injury? Doesn't he know that my limp was caused by the effort of over 300 appearances in the First Division? Doesn't he know that I've been kicked to high heaven by the best of them? I bet he's never been chased by Ron 'Chopper' fucking Harris. Fuck off in your fucking Vauxhall car.

I continue to cross the road towards my flat.

I try to compose myself, control the sudden rush of anger and frustration: tomorrow I will take the boy to Upton Park, which is good. Then I will continue with the AA meetings; that is, well, that is good as well. I will do jigsaws and buy a laptop computer and in due course, when I am stronger, strong enough to control everything, I will start on the after-dinner circuit again, telling stories about Geoff Hurst and Bobby Moore and George Best. Good stories, good funny stories about football. And maybe I will get together with Maureen. We'll have family Christmases and holidays to a villa in Tenerife that I can get hold of. This is all good. Isn't it?

I walk past the newsagent's, next to the little alleyway that leads to my block of Housing Association flats. There is a heroin needle on the floor. A bloody heroin needle, just lying there outside the bloody newsagent's. Christ almighty.

I sigh. With every step I seem to be moving miles and miles away from the joy of seeing my grandson running down the football pitch, the joy of seeing my daughter again, the unbound pleasure of it all is starting to fade and time is speeding up; my body is starting to yearn. The idea of an afternoon, then a night, then another day, then a week, then a month, then for-bloody-ever in my flat, anonymous and glory-less, a stone's throw away from the junkies and pissheads and tarts, starts to hurt. I start to feel the scratchy frustration of being caged in, of being alone.

'Oi!'

I turn round to see Gerry Higgs following me unsteadily across the road.

Someone bibs him as well – and Gerry snarls and waves his fist at them.

He catches up with me.

'Where in the name of God have you been?'

'I'm sorry, Mr Higgs,' I say. 'I know I've let you down. I've been to see my grandson playing football. I didn't know when I spoke to you. It just sort of happened.'

'Never mind about that now,' he says. 'We've got to get to the Council.'

I look at my watch. 'Have we still got time? I mean it's nearly two o'clock.'

'Billy, these people are immortal, they've got all the time in the world.'

I hadn't really thought about that.

'But,' he growls, 'it doesn't look good, does it? It makes you look like a right muppet.'

'No, I suppose it doesn't look good. Sorry.'

'Come on, we'll have to get a cab.'

I hail a cab. 'Where to, Mr Higgs?'

'Wembley Stadium, of course.'

Of course.

In the cab I try to interest Gerry Higgs in Liam: 'You ought to go and have a look at him,' I say. 'He's got balance and speed, lovely left peg; Crystal Palace are mad for him.'

'The thing with young footballers nowadays, Billy,' Gerry says dismissively, 'is that they reach the age of about thirteen or fourteen and everyone tells them how brilliant they are, and they've all got their own agents and Italian bloody sports cars, and they believe it. They think they know it all, so they stop learning – that's why only a few of them ever actually become any good. It's why I've got no time for the modern game, Billy. No time at all.'

He pauses and looks at me, a sly smile curling around his mouth causes his moustache to twitch. 'Perhaps that's something that you can help stop, Billy.'

'Me?'

'Oh yes, Billy, think about it, if you score the goal, you can achieve so much after that. You can change everything. Nothing will be beyond your power, old son. You can make our beautiful game of football even better. Stop it from becoming the luxury toy of foreign nancy boys; keep it honest – a working man's game.'

I sit in silence in the cab and think about that; it's difficult, I can't comprehend such power; it's like imagining the size of the biggest possible number, or the distance to the stars. It is beyond the ability of my brain.

We get out by the massive new Wembley Stadium. I haven't been here before. In fact, I haven't been anywhere near Wembley since that fateful evening in October 1973. Funny that.

I look up at the new arch and the amazing roof and the glass walls. Gerry does the same.

'Amazing, isn't it?' I say.

'I don't like it,' he replies gruffly. 'No atmosphere and no history.'

We walk around the back, then up some steel stairs that lead to a door halfway up one of the stands. Gerry Higgs pushes it open and we emerge into a light beige corridor. We walk up the corridor. At the end of the corridor is a silver door with a bright-blue handle.

We walk towards it.

Me and Gerry Higgs.

Suddenly my heart starts to race, building up, faster and faster. I can feel sweat forming around the collar of my handmade shirt.

We get within a foot of the door, and Gerry Higgs reaches towards the door handle.

I put my hand out to stop him. 'Mr Higgs,' I say. 'I'm not sure. I'm not sure about any of this. I doesn't seem right to me.'

'Of course it's right, Billy. What isn't right about being given the chance of immortality?'

I sigh.

'But, say I'm selected?'

'If you're lucky enough, then you will have the privilege of making good the greatest footballing wrong in the history of the world: the failure of England to qualify for the 1974 World Cup Finals. Imagine the glory of that? That will be the greatest act of any modern Englishman.'

My mind races with the enormity of carrying out the greatest act of any modern Englishman.

'But what about now? What about my grandson, and Rebecca? What will become of them?'

'Billy, don't you see, if you score the goal you will be able to go back and make sure that they have everything that they want. You'll be able to put everything right, old son. This is the only true second chance you'll ever have. You will be a legend.'

'I don't know, Mr Higgs.'

Gerry Higgs puts his arm around my shoulder. 'Listen, you, my boy, were one of the greatest footballers of your generation. And now you've got a chance to go back to being twenty-five years old and live it all again – you weren't meant to do anything else, Billy. You were meant to kick a ball. You were meant to score goals.

You were meant to use your skills to divert grown men from the drudgery of their everyday existence. That was your role, Billy, and now you've got the chance to go back and do it again. Only this time, perhaps, you won't cock it up for yourself.'

I nod at him. He is right. This is my second chance.

I look at the bright-blue door handle. I take a huge breath from the stale strip-lit atmosphere of the corridor and watch as Gerry Higgs opens the door.

23

I stumble through the door and into a rather plain and uncomfortably well-lit room.

In front of me, in a line along a table, sit the Council of Football Immortals. In the centre is Sir Alf Ramsey, to his right, Sir Matt Busby, then next to him, Brian Clough; to Sir Alf's left, Don Revie, then Bill Shankly. They each have their names on pieces of card in front of them, like some kind of weird *University Challenge* team.

For a few uneasy seconds we stare at each other. Five pairs of immortal legendary eyes staring at me.

Sir Alf breaks the stand-off.

'Sit down, William,' he says, motioning towards a chair that is placed in front of the table.

'Thank you, Sir,' I say, and I kind of bow at him, which causes him to frown.

I sit down and look carefully at them. I'm not quite sure what I am looking for: signs of decay or trickery or plastic? Something to help me make sense of the fact that I am physically in the same room as these people, and that they are now looking straight at me, preparing to talk to me.

'Thank you for coming, William,' continues Sir Alf.

'No, the pleasure is all mine,' I mumble. 'I'm sorry that I was late.' I start to compose my excuse about watching my grandson playing football, but Bill Shankly cuts me short.

'It doesn't matter, you're here now.'

'Yes, thank you, sorry.'

'You see, time doesn't really matter that much to us, William,' continues Sir Alf.

'No. Of course it doesn't,' I add, as though I am fully conversant with the vagaries in the laws of physics that are making all this possible.

'Which is why we've been able to ask you to come and see us.'

'Yes.'

'You see, William,' continues Sir Alf, 'the Service has allowed us the chance to go back in time to replay the last ten minutes of the 1973 World Cup qualifier against Poland.'

'We're only allowed ten minutes, young man,' chips in Brian Clough.

'Not a minute more, and not a minute less,' adds Don Revie.

'I see. Yes, Mr Higgs did tell me a little bit about it.'

'Now, those ten minutes coincide with the time when Sir Alf took off Martin Chivers and brought on Kevin Hector,' says Sir Matt Busby.

I nod.

'Substitutions, with every respect, Alf, never were your strong point, were they?'

Sir Alf Ramsey ignores Brian Clough's jibe.

'You were on the bench,' says Don Revie.

'And so was Kevin Keegan,' adds Shankly. 'And now, Sir Alf has got the chance to bring one of you on instead of Kevin Hector: you or Kevin Keegan.'

I nod. 'Right, yes. That's clear.' I nod again, vigorously, athletically, hoping to convey the notion that I would be able to do the job just as well as Kevin Keegan.

'Do you understand, William?' asks Sir Alf.

'Oh yes.'

'It's a massive opportunity. You've got the chance to score the goal that Kevin Hector should have scored.'

'You've got a chance to carve a name for yourself in the annals of history, Billy,' says Sir Matt.

'I know.'

'So why the bloody hell should we let you?' bellows Brian Clough in his nasally up-and-down voice.

I am taken aback. Perhaps this was their plan – to suddenly and without warning unleash Brian Clough on me.

'I mean,' continues Clough, 'Kevin Hector was one of the best finishers in the business, not as good as me, but over 150 league goals for Derby County Football Club. Much more than you ever scored.'

'Yes,' I say. 'I remember Kevin, he was class.'

'He was just unlucky on that night, wasn't he?' Sir Matt adds quietly.

'Yes,' I say. 'I've watched it on a computer, he did everything right, it was just good defending by the Polish full-back on the line.'

'You were never really known for your heading, were you?' states Don Revie.

'No.'

'More for your diving,' he continues.

'Yes,' I say. 'Well, no, that was just one time, Mr Revie. I think I was better known for my dribbling.'

'I think you were better known for taking the mickey, lad,' says Bill Shankly, joining in what is becoming a savage assault on me.

'And your lack of ambition,' continues Brian Clough. 'Do you remember, young man, I offered you the chance to come and play football for the best club in the land, and what did you do?'

'I ran away, Mr Clough.'

'You ran away.'

'Aye, and you didn't manage to get yourself up to Manchester to play for me either, did you, Billy?'

'No, Mr Busby. I mean, Sir Busby. I mean, Sir Matt. But I had a good excuse for that.'

'You're the type of footballer who has excuses for everything,' says Don Revie. 'You're one of these people who will always say that it wasn't their fault.'

'No, I'm not, it was my fault, everything was my fault. Well, perhaps not everything.'

'Who will you blame if you miss the chance, Billy?' asks Bill Shankly.

I stutter an answer. 'I don't know. I won't blame anyone.'

'It's not looking good, is it, William?'

I sigh.

'No, Sir Alf, it isn't.'

I rearrange myself in my chair, as the five of them stare at me with cold eyes.

They exchange a series of thin-lipped looks with each other.

I knew I had to say something.

'The thing is …' I start talking, and as the words form in my head prior to being parachuted out of my mouth, I start to picture that grainy, greasy October evening in 1973; I start to see Tony Currie put the ball down and then float over the perfect corner, and Kevin Hector rise to head it as Jan 'the Clown' Tomaszewski floundered in his own six-yard box. As Hector rose, I rose with him. Powerful now. Twenty-five again.

'The thing is,' I repeat, 'that I won't have to blame anyone because despite all of these things, I am the only person who can score that goal that will change history. I am the only person who will put the ball in the back of the Polish net.'

They look at me.

'Why?' snaps Bill Shankly.

'Because, in the blink of an eye it took for Tony Currie's cross to come over, I am the only one who would have been able to change his body position and make sure that I connected with the ball well enough and with enough pace and direction to send it past the defender and into the back of the net.'

'Nonsense, that's just what Kevin Hector did,' says Revie.

'No,' I say, becoming increasingly confident now as the image of play is rerun again and again in my mind, just as I'd watched it on Will's laptop computer, only now, each time the corner comes over, it dawns on me what I would have done.

'What Kevin Hector did,' I continue, 'was perform a textbook header. Nothing wrong with that. But for moments of true genius, sometimes you need to go beyond the textbooks, don't you? What was it you said, Sir Matt, the unpredictability of genius? Machiavelli and all that.'

Sir Matt smiles at me.

Brian Clough scowls: 'So come on, young man, tell us how you'll do it?'

'Yes,' adds Don Revie, 'what will you do differently?'

'I don't know for certain,' I say, 'and even if I did know, I'm not sure I'd tell you.'

Sir Alf shakes his head disdainfully and turns to the others, muttering to them, 'See, I told you, no discipline, no team ethic – just a showboating pony, worse than that Rodney bloody Marsh chap.'

Only Sir Matt Busby seems interested in what I am saying.

'So, you're not going to tell us yet? You expect us to trust you with this monumental task?' he asks carefully.

I nod. 'Yes.'

'It's preposterous,' guffaws Don Revie, looking around the assembled Council for support. 'You're having a laugh with us.'

'I'm not,' I say. 'I'm telling the truth, that was how I played, that was how I lived. Right or wrong, I can't divorce one from the other can I? It was all natural with me, instinctive, everything just, well, just happened, and that is what you need to score a goal in a situation like that. A moment of inspiration. Unforgettable bloody inspiration.'

Now it is Bill Shankly's turn to look at me more closely, carefully considering what I have said.

'You do realise, son,' he says, 'that if you score this goal, millions of ordinary working men will wake up the next day happy, glorying in the gift you have given them.'

'More importantly,' adds Sir Alf, 'England will go to the World Cup and have the chance that was denied to us.'

'Yes,' I say. 'I understand all of that.'

'You do realise that you will change history,' continues Shankly.

'Yes.'

'You do realise that if England were to win the World Cup in 1974, everything might be different?' he carries on.

'Yes.'

'Governments may survive.'

'Or fall,' adds Sir Alf.

'The whole history of the British Isles could be different.'

'You understand all of that?' asks Sir Matt tenderly.

'Yes, I do.'

'And you still think you can change your body position and score the goal, because you will have a moment of inspiration?'

'I do.'

They ponder this for a few seconds. Glances are exchanged between them.

'And you can handle the failure if you miss?' he adds.

'Probably not,' I say. 'It's one of those moments in life, innit? The dark ones that haunt you in the middle of the night for as long as you live.'

'That doesn't bother you?'

'It means I lived, Mr Revie. That's all. One second in the millions that I had. Don't we live for even the chance to have a second like that? A second of glory.'

'Or tragedy,' adds Bill Shankly.

'Or tragedy,' I agree.

Sir Alf looks across the table at his fellow Council members. 'Anything else, gentlemen?' he asks them.

They shake their heads.

'Thank you very much, William,' he says.

'Is that it?'

'Yes, thank you, that's it.'

'Well, what happens now?' I look at each of them, my eyes skipping from one immortal to another. 'When will you let me know?'

'When the time is right, of course,' says Sir Alf, his face scrunching itself up into a forced smile.

I get up reticently and walk to the door. I put my hand on the blue handle, turn it and walk back out into the beige corridor.

Immediately, I feel a pain in my temple, followed by a massive surge of agony. Christ. For a second I can't see. I look around for Gerry Higgs but he isn't anywhere. I shout out for him, Gerry, but all I hear is a high-pitched whisper in my ear: *Service.* I'm sure that is what it says: *Service.* I put my hands against a wall, and wait for it to pass, which it does, and then I limp back down the staircase and into the car park towards the gates. I now feel incredibly tired, as though my whole body is shutting itself down and a big dark fug is enveloping my mind. I stop by the gates to get my bearings, collect my thoughts.

'You alright?'

I look up. A big Land Rover had stopped by me, the face in the driver's window is instantly familiar.

'Yes, thanks, mate, I'm fine, just a dizzy spell.'

'You take care,' says the driver, winding his window up and driving on. The hair, grey now, but still bouncing, the tan, the lovely infectious smile – unmistakable: Kevin Keegan.

He hadn't bloody recognised me.

24

I feel strange the next day, oddly clean and unburdened, as though the combination of the AA meeting and Rebecca and Liam and then the Council has somehow cleansed me. My head feels light; in fact, my whole body feels strangely light.

I wonder if I will hear from Gerry Higgs again, or from the Council of Football Immortals. Of course I do, but, somehow, it doesn't seem to matter as much. Somehow I have found contentment. Perhaps it was enough just to confront these men – take them on. I don't know.

True, I still feel a desire to go into a pub, but not to just get rollicking pissed. I feel a desire to sit with strangers and talk and ruminate and discuss the things I've learned; and not necessarily a pub either, perhaps I could go to a library or a café or a bus stop and just talk to people – tell them what I have learned, tell them about my newfound wisdom.

Maybe I've seen some kind of light. Perhaps that's it: maybe I've worked out the meaning of life. Live for the seconds and let the hours take care of themselves – yes, I like that, probably read it in a birthday card or in the *Daily Mail* or something.

Or perhaps quite simply, the fires of my discontentment have been extinguished by the sheer effort of unburdening myself to a group of strangers, my long-lost daughter and five immortal football managers in the space of about forty-eight hours.

I don't know. I don't know anything – well, I suppose I know that.

In any event, any temptation I might have had to go into the streets and prophesy about my newfound wisdom is dashed by the fact that I spend hours on the phone trying to get tickets for me and Liam to watch the West Ham–Chelsea game that night.

I phone the club, but they just politely put me on a waiting list. I try to track down long-lost friends, old players, but they no longer exist for me – I don't have many telephone numbers and the numbers I do have are old. I tell you, you don't know how embarrassing it is, trying to convince someone that you are genuinely attempting to make contact with Geoff Hurst.

In a moment of frustration, I call the club again and speak to a young girl:

'Hello, I'm sorry to trouble you again, my name's Billy Parks,' I tell her. 'I used to play for the football club, I'm trying to get some tickets for me and my grandson for this evening's match. I wouldn't trouble you, love, but I've never taken him to a match before.'

'Sorry, Mr Parkinson,' she says. 'Tonight's a sell-out, but I can put you on to a reserve list.'

'Yeah, you've told me that before, but I am Billy Parks, you won't remember me, but I'm pretty sure that someone at the club will.'

'I'm sorry, Mr Parkinson.'

'Parks.'

'I'm sorry, Mr Parks, but I'm afraid that's all I can do. Perhaps if you ring back later.'

I ring back later. No bloody joy.

I am getting desperate and the more desperate I get, the hotter I start to become, and soon the pain starts up again – a short darting pain that shoots from my abdomen up to my temple.

I have to do something. I can't let the lad down. That would

248

be disastrous: Rebecca would see it as another Billy Parks broken promise. I wrack my brain – could it be that bloody difficult? I mean, bloody hell, only twenty-four hours ago, I was talking to bloody Sir Alf Ramsey and Brian Clough, now I can't even get a ticket for a match at Upton Park.

As a last resort, I dial the number I have for Tommy McAleish, a mad, nicotine-stained Glaswegian from the *Sunday People*, and a former drinking buddy. As I dial his number, I realise that there is a good chance he's dead.

Amazingly, he answers.

'Tommy?'

'Who wants him?'

'Tommy, it's Billy Parks.'

'Parksy! Fucking hell. I'd heard that you were nearly dead.'

'Dead? Me, you must be joking, old son. I've never been more alive. I heard the same about you.'

'Nae dead man, just ever so slightly fucked. How are you anyway?'

'I'm super mate, absolutely first class.'

'I hope you've got a good story for me?'

'Well as it happens, I might have.'

'Oh aye? I'm all ears.'

'Where were you on the 17 October, 1973?'

'Christ, Billy, October 1973? You'll have to give me a clue, wee man, I canna remember where I was last Tuesday.'

'The Clown.'

'Oh yes.' He let out a deep throaty laugh. 'October 17 1973, everyone remembers that; you couldn't beat Poland – if you listen carefully you can still hear the sound of thousands of Scotsmen pissing themselves.'

'Well, what if I told you that there was a chance of replaying the match, only this time I come on instead of Kevin Hector?'

'I'd tell you that you were in the advanced stages of psychotic delusion. Now what do you really want?'

'I want two tickets for the big West Ham–Chelsea game tonight. I've promised to take my grandson – I can't let him down.'

'Can't you get them from the club?'

'No, Tommy, it's all corporate whatdoyoucallit these days.'

'Well, that's a fucking disgrace, Billy. In fact, that's a story in itself.'

'Well, feel free to quote me, old mate.'

'I'll tell you what I'll do – I'll make some enquiries and let you know.'

'Thanks.'

It feels better after talking to Tommy McAleish. Lovely fella, one of the old school. Christ, some of the things we got up to. I don't expect much from him, though.

I try a few more reporters – no joy. I try some more old players, and have a nice conversation with a bloke from Gravesend who, despite not being Ronnie Boyce, is able to remember him, and is even happier to indulge in a bit of a conversation about the Hammers.

Then, to my amazement, Tommy McAleish rings back.

'Good news, Parksy,' he says. 'I've found you two tickets.'

'Have you? Tommy: you beauty.'

'No problem, Billy, they're in the Bobby Moore Stand with all the headbangers, but beggars can't be choosers and all that.'

'No problem, mate, that's fantastic. How do I get them?'

'They'll be with a bloke I know; you won't know him, he was a friend of my son's. His name's Darren Wilson; fat bloke, receding hairline, about forty; bit of a twat, you can't miss him. One of those brought up in Buckinghamshire, but wants to be a proper Bow Bells East Ender.'

'It doesn't matter to me, Tommy. That's just brilliant – you've saved my life.'

'Nae problem. I've said you'll meet him in the Duke of Edinburgh at seven.'

The Duke of Edinburgh. The Duke of Edinburgh. At seven.

A proper boozer at seven. Part of my brain starts celebrating, while another part immediately sounds the alarm. The Duke of Edinburgh. The possibility. Christ, how many times have I been drunk in there?

I try to stop myself from thinking about it, thinking about drink. I'd got two tickets. I *am* going to take my grandson to a Hammers match. That is brilliant, but, bloody hell, not as brilliant as the idea of being in the Duke of Edinburgh at seven. Not as brilliant as walking up to a bar and ordering anything I bloody well want – anything at all. Just thinking about it makes the pain subside and the tiredness leave me. Suddenly, I feel light and excited. It is as though my body was already preparing itself for the wondrousness of alcohol.

At exactly 6.55pm I am standing outside the Duke of Edinburgh, carrying the Hammers shirt that I'd bought for Liam. It is busy. Fans are already drinking in the street and spilling out on to the pavement. Somewhere further up the street, I can make out the deep guttural chant of *Chelsea, Chelsea,* as the young invaders from the west mark their territory. There is a smell of fried onions and cigar smoke in the air and a feeling that violence isn't too far away.

The smell, sound and feeling of football.

I stand there and look at the pub – I know what will be inside, I know what walking through the doors would lead to, it would be so easy.

I take a deep breath.

I look at my watch. I will go in. I will get the tickets. I will leave and go and wait for Liam at the tube. I can do it.

I try to think of the locomotive train that is hurtling towards me, but it makes no difference. I am an alcoholic. *I am an alcoholic.* There, I've fucking said it.

I walk through the doors and start looking around. I am nervous. Why am I nervous going into a pub? I've never been nervous in a pub before?

251

I look across the sea of pint-glass-laden tables for a fat bloke with receding hair, about forty.

'Darren Wilson? No. Darren Wilson?' I meander around the tables.

'Anyone here called Darren Wilson?'

Eventually he finds me: 'Oi, oi, it's Billy Parks!'

'Darren Wilson?'

'Yes, mate.' Darren Wilson is squeezed on to a little bar stool with two or three of his mates sat around him – he is exactly as Tommy had described and sticks out a hand towards me.

'It's an honour to meet a legend, Sir,' he says and I smile, because I love it.

'No, the pleasure is mine,' I say. 'Tommy McAleish said you had a couple of tickets for me.'

He hands over the tickets in a rather embarrassingly theatrical way that makes me suddenly ashamed that I have had to stoop to getting them from this faux Cockney in a pub rather than from the club wrapped in a bow with thanks.

'Will you have a drink with us then, Billy?'

I pause. I pause for a second. Then I say: 'Oh, go on, just a lager, please.'

There. The words had come out of my mouth. Just like they had so often before. The weak alcoholic who can't say bloody no.

One of Darren Wilson's friends, Tony or Tiny or something, an exact replica of him albeit a little bit shorter, goes off to the bar and returns with a tray full of beers. He puts a pint of lager down in front of me: gold and perfect, with perfect little bubbles rising up the cold glass. Dr Aranthraman had said that one more drink could kill me – was this the one? How could it be? How could this most wonderful liquid, the liquid of the common ordinary man, kill me?

I take a sip from my glass. The lager surges down my throat and courses through my body – the first drink in almost a week, I feel every cell weep with joy.

'So who was the best player you played against, Billy?'

'That's easy, son, no doubt about it: Georgie Best. Quite simply a genius.'

'Did you ever go out with him?'

'Bloody hell, go out with him? Christ, I could tell you a few tales.'

I tell a few tales, then, thankfully, the clock strikes 7.30pm and Darren and his friends sup up their pints, shake my hand, and leave for the ground. They obviously have a routine. I am left alone – the queue at the bar means that I have only managed to have one pint in the time I've been with them. It is enough though. The locomotive has come down the track, chuffa-chuffa-chuffa, and bang, knocked me right on my arse.

I leave the pub and walk the short distance to the tube station – there is Liam with Rebecca. She eyes me suspiciously. I hope she won't notice the smell of lager on my breath or the slight bounce to my walk and speech that the single pint has given me.

She smiles as I get nearer. 'I thought I'd better come with him,' she says, 'just to make sure he was OK.'

'Shit, Becky, I haven't got enough tickets.'

'That's alright, I'm going to leave you both alone.'

We smile at each other, a small smile, a trusting smile. I turn to Liam and put my hand on his head and ruffle his hair.

'Alright then, just the fellas tonight, son?'

I hand him the plastic bag with the shirt in. 'I didn't know what size you'd be. And I guessed at number eleven; it was my number. I put Liam on the back – I hope that's alright.'

He smiles. 'Thanks Granddad, it's brilliant.'

He puts it on as Rebecca stands smiling. There are tears in her eyes.

'Are you alright?'

'Yes, Dad, I'm fine.'

Dad. She called me Dad. I beam at her. I want to hug her, but I realise that we aren't quite there yet, instead I just smile at her. She wipes a tear from her eyes.

'Right, hadn't you two better be off then?'

'Yes, come on, son,' I say. And I look at my daughter as she gives my grandson a kiss on the forehead and turns towards the tube station.

We walk to the turnstile. The Bobby Moore Stand. Poor Bobby. My Captain. The best of blokes. It crosses my mind that if I had managed to get selected by the Council of Football Immortals, I would have had the chance of getting Bobby to the World Cup in 1974 – now it would be up to Kevin Keegan.

We climb the stairs and emerge into the stand and gaze down at the pitch. Ah, I love that feeling, the feeling you get when suddenly you see the pitch in its verdant wondrousness and hear the noise of masculinity being unleashed from the four sides that surround it.

I turn to the boy. 'Marvellous, isn't it? You don't get anything like this anywhere else in the world.'

'Yeah.'

We sit down and talk about the game and his favourite players: some African striker I'd never heard of and that lad Parker who we sold to Tottenham. He asks me about Trevor Brooking and Frank Lampard's dad, and Harry Redknapp. I tell him that they were all great players. 'Especially Trevor,' I tell him, 'he was a lovely cultured footballer was Trevor.'

'Do you miss it?' he asks.

'Yes, son,' I tell him. 'I miss it every day. Every single day.'

I can't expect him to understand that. Not yet.

'So, does your dad still follow Charlton?'

'Yes,' he laughs, 'he tells me that if I don't do well in exams he'll buy me a season ticket.'

I laugh. We are conspirators. It is how it should be. God, he is a great boy and I am so very happy.

I haven't noticed the young lad standing behind me; he taps me on the shoulder – 'Excuse me,' he says, 'are you Billy Parks?'

'Yes, son, that's right.' I wink at Liam.

'My dad said you used to play for us.'

'Yes, that's right, a long time before you were even thought of.'

He hands me his programme and I sign it. I notice now that a couple of others have watched this happen. I can hear mutterings of 'That's Billy Parks', and a couple of fellas come over and ask me to sign their shirts. Suddenly, a chant goes up from behind us, a rhythmic chant I haven't heard in thirty-odd years:

(Clap, clap, clap-clap-clap, clap-clap clap-clap) *Parksy.*

It spreads around the old Bobby Moore Stand.

(Clap, clap, clap-clap-clap, clap-clap clap-clap) *Parksy.*

That is me. That is Billy Parks. I look down at Liam whose smile fills his beautiful face. That is me: I am Billy Parks.

'That's you, Granddad.'

I stand up and wave at the crowd behind me. They cheer. Then applaud. Applause – proper applause, a spontaneous type of clapping that says that you are being appreciated, that you are respected for what you did.

I sit down again.

For the next twenty minutes, I enjoy a wonderful feeling of contentedness. Time slows. I watch the movement of the young boy playing on the left-wing for West Ham; beautiful he is, lovely left foot, gliding, graceful style, defiant and confident in his own perfect talent.

I watch the faces of the crowd as they wait for him to get the ball: men set free from the shackles of their normal life. I listen to the noise they make and study the way they move; for those minutes during the course of a football match they are all liberated, all united in a common bond of emotion and understanding. It is everything. It is nothing. It does matter. Maybe.

I start to feel unwell. I think Chelsea are one up, now.

The pain in my temple suddenly increases as though someone has just flicked a switch and I experience a feeling of nausea coupled with a desperate desire for a shit.

'I'm just nipping to the toilet.'

'Are you alright, Granddad?'

'I'm fine, son. I'll be back in five minutes, let me know who scores.'

He smiles at me and I get to my feet. Christ, they are like gooey molten lead. I mutter apologies as I bump into everyone in my row, fearful now that I am about to vomit there and then. Thankfully, I don't; I couldn't have handled that, that would have been awful.

I stumble down the stairs, my hand clutching at the cold wall to keep my balance, and find the grey concrete toilets; I get there just in time, as my body hurls itself forward against my will and I throw up a horrible mixture of my last pint of lager, bought for me by a stranger, and whatever else was in my stomach. I stand there for a few seconds, panting – then, I spew again. This time it is worse, this time I taste blood in my mouth and feel a deep overwhelming pain that rumbles grotesquely around my abdomen. I stagger backwards towards the toilet door. I want to shout. But I can't. I want to do something to control the pain but I can't. I want to breathe. But breath is leaving me as I battle with the pain and a sudden tightening of my chest as though I am being squeezed by an invisible force.

I feel myself fall backwards towards the toilet wall and the pain changes, becoming duller, quieter, as though I am walking away from it, leaving it behind.

I hear a voice calling me.

'Billy, Billy, is that you?'

'Gerry, thank God, Gerry, I'm in here.'

The cubicle door opens and Gerry Higgs is standing there, looking down at me.

'Billy, there you are, old son.'

'Gerry, I think I'm ill, mate. I can't breathe, I can't move.'

'Nonsense – you're fine.' He spies me lying there, breathless, scared, still. 'Come on son, get up,' he says gently. 'You can't stay here in this khazi.'

'I don't know, Mr Higgs. You might have to get someone.'

He puts out a hand towards me and smiles. 'They picked you, Billy.'

'Eh?'

'The Council of Football Immortals: they rejected Kevin Keegan and picked you.'

'Me?'

'Yes, son, come on, we've got to go now. You've got a goal to score.'

I take hold of Gerry Higgs's hand and get to my feet.

'Come on,' he repeats.

'Back to 1973?'

'Yes.'

'I can't go now, Gerry, my grandson Liam's in the ground, watching the match.'

Gerry Higgs turns and looks me in the eye, he lets out a slight tender sigh and his eyes become soft.

'Don't worry about him, Billy, he's a smart boy, he'll know what to do.'

'But, he's on his own. His mother will go mental ...'

I stop, because suddenly I know what is happening.

I look down at the ground, then up at Gerry Higgs, silent tears are falling from my tired eyes.

'But I've still got so much to do, Gerry,' I say quietly.

'You've done it all, son,' he says. 'There's nothing left for you here now.'

I wipe my tears, because you get nothing for crying, and nod silently at him.

'Can I have one last look, Mr Higgs?'

'Of course you can, son.'

We walk back up the concrete steps and into the ground again. I can see Liam wearing the shirt I'd bought him, he is walking towards a steward who is standing at the end of his row. He *will* be alright, he is a great boy. His life will go on. He will remember.

I stand still for a few seconds and look out at the pitch and the twenty-two men moving around in their claret shirts and their blue shirts, kicking a football from one to another, trying to put it in between two sticks. I look at the swaying supporters and their faces, red with primal worry as they swear and shout and bay, and revel in the chase.

'Come on, Billy,' says Gerry Higgs.

And I turn my back away from the pitch and follow Gerry Higgs back up the stairs towards the exit, the way out, the end.

I stop. My heart beating. I am scared now. I turn away from Gerry and look again at the faces of the crowd: rage, glory, hope, love, excitement, humanity, all humanity.

They let out a roar and I know that a beautiful boy with slender hips and diamond glint in his eye has danced down the wing.

I close my eyes; that was me once, that *is* me – Billy Parks, West Ham and England. I am Billy Parks, footballer, West Ham and England. I am bloody Billy Parks.

The faces around me start to blur until I can no longer see anyone except Gerry, standing by the exit, waiting.

I close my eyes again and I feel my own rage, my own hope and excitement and fear, fall from me like curled petals dropping from a flower, their jobs done.

I take a step up towards Gerry, towards the exit. I hear the crowd roar again, then it dulls, becomes distant, dies.

Epilogue

17 October 1973
Wembley

They reckon that twenty-two million people watched the game between England and Poland on television that night. Twenty-two million people at home, and, of course, a hundred thousand packed in at Wembley.

It was a game England had to win. If they won, everything would be alright. If they won, there would be happiness, the rest of the English autumn would be mellow and misty, then the winter would be brilliant white with snow, and Christmas would be merry, then the spring would prosper giving rise to a World Cup in the summer in West Germany.

They just had to win. That's all. Against Poland. That's all.

Mr Clough had said their goalie was a clown. And Mr Clough was always right.

Sir Alf picked three strikers: Channon, Chivers and Clarke. They would score, because the Polish goalie was a clown.

And Billy Parks was on the bench.

Billy Parks: the best of all of them; the most natural, the most beautiful, the most easily distracted, as he carried the immense weight of his talent on his slender shoulders. Everyone knew that Sir Alf didn't really like Billy Parks: too fragile, he'd said, too inconsistent – somehow not English enough. We all knew that Sir Alf had only picked Billy for the bench because the newspapers and the fans had demanded it. But we loved him. Everyone loved him. We loved him *because* he was fragile and inconsistent and somehow not English.

The Polish Clown saved from Chivers.

The Polish Clown saved from Currie.

The Polish Clown saved from Clarke and Channon, then Channon again.

Then. Then. Then. Norman Hunter didn't tackle Lato, the Polish midfielder. Norman Hunter, who normally took bites out of human legs, who never let anyone past him, missed the tackle and Lato played it through to Domarski who sent it tamely past Shilton. They weren't winning. They were losing.

Attack.

The Polish Clown saved from Chivers and Channon and Clarke and Hunter and Bell.

Then Clarke scored a penalty. But that wouldn't be enough. They had to win.

And Billy Parks sat on the bench. In between Kevin Keegan and Bobby Moore. His knees drawn into him against the cold, his mind wandering to the two hundred and fifty quid he'd bet on an England win.

A win that would make everything alright. A win would bring colour to the grey beige of the seventies. A win would change everything.

But the Clown saved every shot that came his way.

So Sir Alf looked to his bench. Destiny called for someone. Sir Alf looked at his bench and thought about which valiant hero would bring forth triumph. Who would forge their name in the fires of destiny. Score a bloody goal.

Billy Parks sat, cold, he avoided Sir Alf's gaze. His mind on the barmaid from the Golden Swan who he would pick up later in his inferno-red TR6.

Eventually, because he knew he had to, he looked up. Five minutes to go. He looked towards Sir Alf and Sir Alf looked at him, desperately, directly, into his soul; he knew that his was a destiny that was slipping away. He knew that something special was called for. He looked at his watch and sighed.

'OK, Parks,' he said, 'warm up, I'm bringing you on.'

Parksy didn't jump up, instead he eased himself forward, a look of ashen fear suddenly covering his face.

Sir Alf looked at his watch: 'Come on, quickly, William, we haven't much time left.'

Bobby Moore leaned over to him. 'Enjoy yourself, son,' he whispered, 'use your instinct, do what you do best. Get us a goal. Do it for every good honest Englishman.'

Billy nodded, his face brightened, he winked at his West Ham captain and stripped off his tracksuit.

The crowd roared their approval at Sir Alf Ramsey's substitution – the last throw of the dice, the final deep breath of desperation.

In the gloom, England got a corner. Billy Parks took his place on the edge of the six-yard box by the near post. He looked at the Polish defender on the line and the Polish goalkeeper, who was clapping encouragement to his teammates. He breathed easily, contentedly, he could hear nothing of the fervid rumbling crowd, he could hear nothing of the nation sucking up the air as it sat on the edge of its seats. Somewhere in the back of his mind, the image of his father looking up at the east London sky had formed and Billy looked up at it too – he was calm, he was ready.

Tony Currie put up his hand then swung the ball in. The ball soared through the night, through time; for once, the Clown was nowhere, he was beaten by the flight of the ball. He had positioned himself too far out. Billy Parks watched without thinking, he made one step to his right towards the flailing goalkeeper, then acrobatically he leaped, like a gymnast, like an antelope, like the most beautiful of dancers into the air, his left foot thrust out towards the incoming ball, six, maybe seven, feet off the ground. The crowd stared, their hearts stopped as every eye watched the flight of the ball. The twenty-two million people at home stopped breathing. There was no life as the ball glided towards Parksy's left foot. There was no noise as the ball collided with his boot.

Then.

There was only joy.

(*Taken, in part, from the little known, but highly acclaimed, 1977 biography of Billy Parks*, Parksy: The Last Genius of Upton Park, *by veteran* Sunday Times *football journalist, Philip Clarence.*)

Acknowledgements

Marcella Edwards and Mark 'Stan' Stanton, for believing in and encouraging this story at various times.

David Ridings at MBA Lit, for his quiet wisdom and patience.

Scott Pack, for his enthusiasm and support.

Rachel Faulkner, for making sense of my tortured prose.

And Jo and Alan at LightBrigade, for their wonderful ideas about how to bring Billy Parks to the masses.

To all those involved in the 'beautiful game' and in particular anyone lovingly referred to in this book.

To my wife Ines, who listened and knew when to criticise.